P9-DTA-172

THROUGH THE GRAPEVINE

THROUGH THE
GRAPEVINE

David Hudson

Palmetto Publishing Group
Charleston, SC

Through the Grapevine
Copyright © 2018 by David Hudson
All rights reserved

No portion of this book may be reproduced, stored in a retrieval system, or
transmitted in any form by any means–electronic, mechanical, photocopy,
recording, or other–except for brief quotations in printed reviews, without
prior permission of the author.

First Edition
Printed in the United States

ISBN-13: 978-1-64111-171-3
ISBN-10: 1-64111-171-2

ACKNOWLEDGMENTS

Grateful acknowledgments are made, first, to my teacher Christine Desmet for her invaluable instruction and constant support, to Palmetto Publishing Group for their skillful editing and design work, to my friend Carole Herman for her enthusiastic encouragement, and to my wife Katharine Rodgers Hudson for being a model of compassionate, courageous womanhood and helping me see the world through a woman's eyes.

CHAPTER 1
THE FUGITIVE

Lynn Peterson pulled the covers up against the chill of an early August morning on the ridgetop, a thousand feet above the valley floor. She squinted toward the window. A rooster crowed. She closed her eyes, scrunched into the mattress for one last decadent moment, and swung her feet to the floor. She reached for her clothes on the chair beside the bed and watched the sky lighten as she pulled on worn jeans, her favorite chamois shirt, soft against her skin, and a nondescript gray sweatshirt.

She crossed the hall to the kitchen, filled an insulated mug from a programmable coffee maker, and stepped out onto the porch that spanned the front of the house, into the new morning. A faint breeze stirred the wind chime hanging from the metal roof. She sipped her steaming coffee and breathed long and slow, inhaling the moist fragrance of earth and grass and evergreens. Waking birds welcomed her from the trees across the road that glowed where golden light poured down on them like syrup. On the western horizon, a thin blue line brightened—the vast Pacific Ocean.

Lynn walked behind the house toward the barn. Stopping short, she tilted her ear toward the pasture below it and beyond, to a mechanical hum, just discernible. A car approaching from the south, a half mile or more down the road, surprised her, grew louder. *Who could be coming up here this early?* she wondered. *And why so fast?*

Chickens clucked when she opened the door of the old barn, which had stood since the ranch's earliest days in the 1890s, its rough, unpainted siding a rich, weathered gray, its metal roof—once a glittery silver—now rusty red. The interior was cool and dark, suffused with rich aromas of hay and manure, barnyard animals, and ancient unfinished wood. She smiled and stroked the door frame beside her as if to absorb the earthiness, authenticity, and unapologetic simplicity of the place. Then she flipped on the light and began her rounds, swinging open the big east-facing doors, letting the bright, young daylight in and the chickens out.

The hum had become a roar. Drawn by it, she stepped outside. The car crested the rise just beyond the big metal equipment barn, too fast, she thought. *Where's it going in such a hurry? What?* Instead of speeding on by, it slowed at the big oak and turned into the drive, dust washing over it as it came to a stop in front of the house.

She walked toward it. The driver stepped out of the car. There was no mistaking her friend Karen Boyd, the nurse. She was Native American, Dakota Sioux, sixtyish, of average height and build, bearing the weight gain of age. Her brown skin glowed. Long silver hair flowed over her shoulders. High on her left cheekbone, beside and just below the eye, she bore a small tattoo, a light, faded blue, of a bird in flight.

Karen walked around the car and opened the door for her passenger, who lay slumped in her seat, head down, staring at the floor. The woman eased out of the car and stood expressionless, blank-faced. She was a youthful-looking, middle-aged Latina with a pretty face—strong jaw, high cheekbones, petite nose—long dark hair.

"Lynn," Karen said, "I'm sorry it's so early, but this is important."

Her tone brought Lynn to full attention.

Holding her passenger by the arm, she said, "This is Teresa, a friend of mine. She's had a rough time of it. She was attacked last night at work, raped. It's a mess. We need help."

Lynn grimaced, jarred out of the reverie of her easy, comfortable early morning routine.

"What about the police?" she asked.

"They can't help us. We're on our own."

"To do what?"

"To hide her from the guy who attacked her—her supervisor."

"Her supervisor? What?" Lynn gasped. She knew well about sexual harassment in the workplace, but she couldn't imagine a workplace where a woman could be raped.

"The vineyards can be tough places to work for a woman. The bosses are men. And the picking happens at night, when the air is cool. It's easier on the grapes."

"And why can't the police help?"

"She's undocumented. And she's not safe. He knows that she knows he's stealing from the winery."

"I'm so sorry." *She's right; it is a mess. And she wants me to . . . what? Harbor an undocumented worker from the feds—ICE? I want to help, but this could go badly in any number of horrible ways.*

Finally, not knowing why, responding from some ingrained sense of duty and obligation, Lynn said, "I can't promise you how long, but she can stay here for now, until you figure out something better."

Karen spread her arms wide, hugging Lynn in a tight embrace. "You're a lifesaver, honey. I know what you must be wondering. We'll go over it all when I get off work. I'll be back then." She hugged Teresa and reassured her. "You'll be safe here. Trust me." And with that, Karen climbed in her car and started back down the road toward Cazadero and Guerneville.

Teresa and Lynn stood facing each other. Trauma showed in Teresa's deep-brown eyes and her disheveled hair. Oversized clothes hung awkwardly from her shoulders and hips; Karen's clothes, Lynn imagined. Without knowing any of the details of Teresa's ordeal, Lynn eased out of neutral, taking the first step of her sudden new mission.

With an outstretched arm, she showed Teresa through the back door and into the house, where the gurgling of the coffeemaker and the sizzle of bacon greeted them. Her husband, Hank, stood to their left at the stove, fixing a country breakfast. *Just what we need.*

"This is Teresa," Lynn said, pouring two cups of coffee and offering her guest a chair at the kitchen table. "She's had a rough night. I told Karen we could put her up for the time being. That was her who just left. She'll be back tonight."

Hank turned and offered Teresa his hand. "It's nice to meet you. Are you hungry?"

She shook her head and muttered, "Thank you, but no, I'm not."

Hank looked at Lynn.

"Are you sure?" Lynn asked. "Food would be good for you."

"I don't know."

"That's okay," Lynn said, "but please sit. I know you're tired."

Lynn pulled out a chair. Teresa sat, and Lynn followed.

Hank reached into the fridge. "I'll make a little more in case you change your mind," he said over his shoulder. "You'll like these eggs. They're from right here on the ranch, and so's the bacon."

Teresa's eyes moistened. "Like back home—in Mexico."

"Mexico?" Lynn asked.

"Michoacán."

"You speak good English. How long have you been here?"

"Many years. I came when I was twenty," she said softly, her face dark with sadness.

"Would you like some clothes that fit you?" Lynn asked.

Teresa nodded.

"Okay then, let's get them." She stood, and motioning for Teresa to follow her, led her across the back hall to the bedroom, where she dug a pair of jeans and a blue work shirt from her dresser. "We're about the same size. Try these on." She left the room and closed the door behind her.

"What's going on?" Hank asked when Lynn walked back into the kitchen.

She sighed, exhaling the tension of the previous half hour, and told him what little she had learned from Karen. "Hopefully we'll learn more today."

In a few minutes, Teresa appeared in the doorway, looking less like a waif.

Lynn smiled.

Teresa struggled to return it.

"That's more like it," Lynn said.

Hank seconded her opinion, waved them to the table, and served Lynn and himself his breakfast of scrambled eggs, bacon, and skillet potatoes. "Are you sure you don't want any?" he asked Teresa.

"Okay, maybe a little."

Hank took another plate from the table and served her.

"I'm Hank," he said as he took his seat. "Welcome to Bella Vista. You're safe here."

"Gracias. You're very kind."

"Eggs aren't very good when they get cold. Please don't stand on ceremony."

They didn't. Within minutes the plates were empty, even Teresa's.

"Thank you. I guess I needed that," Teresa said.

"You're welcome," Hank replied. "It's no trouble."

The ritual of the morning meal could not erase the fact of Teresa's crisis. She was sitting right there with them, and questions were begging to be asked. But this was not the place to ask them.

"I didn't finish my chores in the barn," Lynn announced. "Would you like to go with me?" she asked Teresa.

"Okay."

Lynn cleared their plates, took a pail from a cupboard beneath the counter, and led Teresa out the back door. The sky was a cloudless brilliant blue, typical for late August in Sonoma County, California. High on a ridge, twenty-five miles north of the Russian River Valley and its vineyards, this was more cattle than wine country. There were a few vineyards, to be sure, but most of the ridgetops were pastures, cleared of redwood, fir, and oak long ago and fenced for fancy cattle now bound for Whole Foods and the steak houses of the West. "The top of the world," Lynn liked to say. Ridges stretched away to the east as far as she could see, all the way to the Sierras on the clearest of days, she imagined. This was such a day. It demanded that she pause to take it in.

"This is a beautiful place," Teresa said. "You are lucky."

"Yes, I am," Lynn replied. "That's what I remind the owners every time I see them, which isn't very often."

Teresa's puzzled expression posed the obvious question.

"This isn't our place. Hank and I are just the caretakers. The owners live in San Francisco. We keep an eye on the place for them; mow the grass, take care of the animals, keep it looking nice."

As they walked toward the barn, she went on to explain that she had discovered the ranch on a site called the Caretaker's Gazette. "Until last spring I'd never heard of this kind of work. I like it. It's peaceful and quiet up here." Lynn cringed as the words left her mouth; it struck Lynn how different Teresa's work life must be from hers—anything but peaceful.

Lynn led her into the barn. She took a basket from a shelf by the door and handed it to Teresa.

"Would you like to gather the eggs?" she asked, pointing to the coop on their right.

"Yes, of course," Teresa replied.

Lynn opened the door to a stall on her left. A white goat looked at her expectantly, bleated, and flicked its tail like a handkerchief. Lynn pulled up a stool, sat, and milked her. Finished, she placed the pail on a shelf by the door and led the goat out into the pasture behind the barn. When she returned, she scooped soiled hay from the stall with a pitchfork and replaced it with fresh hay from the loft above. *That should keep her happy.*

Teresa handed her the basket, now heaped with eggs, when Lynn emerged from the stall. Lynn took it and sat on a bench beside the stall. With her hand on the seat beside her, she invited Teresa to join her.

"How are you doing?" she asked.

"Not so good," Teresa replied.

"Do you want to talk about it?" She shifted on her seat, apprehensive, uncertain. "I get it if you don't."

"No, it's okay."

"Really, you don't have to."

"No, it's okay."

And Teresa began her story. At the age of twenty, she'd crossed the border from Tijuana with her boyfriend. They stayed in Southern California together for a few years, then she left him and came north to work in the fields as a *campesina*, a female farmworker, picking vegetables in the San Joaquin and Sacramento Valleys for twenty years. A few years ago, she'd taken a job at the vineyard in the Russian River Valley, which was where she'd been working just a few hours earlier. She liked the place, and they liked her. She was a good worker, good enough that they began to teach her pruning and planting when she expressed an interest.

"The only problem with the vineyard is Juan Carlos," she said.

Juan Carlos Hernandez was her supervisor, a legal Mexican immigrant, hired because he was a big, strong guy who spoke Spanish.

Teresa caught his eye, and he began making advances soon after she arrived at the vineyard.

"He asked me out. I didn't really want to, but I was afraid, so I went out with him—once. But I didn't like him. When he asked me again, I said no. And then he got mean. He made rude comments, and he touched me all the time. He would laugh and threaten to report me to ICE. Then last night, he found me alone on the back side of the vineyard. The picking was over, and I had gone back to find something that had fallen out of my pocket. He grabbed me and tried to kiss me. 'You really want me, don't you?' he said. I struggled."

It had been the perfect place for an assault: remote, hidden by grape trellises thick with leaves and fruit.

"It was awful." Tears came. She slumped on her seat, covered her face with hands, sobbed. It wasn't okay.

Lynn cringed through Teresa's graphic retelling of the horrible ordeal, feeling the hard grape bin, the attacker's rough hands, the pain, the humiliation.

"He kept telling me he would send me back to Mexico if I screamed. When he was finished and fastening his belt, I ran."

Terrified, she'd fled through long lines of trellises, desperate to elude the predator she imagined was just a step behind her. She stumbled into the workers parking lot, reached her car, and glancing over her shoulder, saw he hadn't followed her.

"But he was still there, still a monster. Why didn't he chase me? Because he knows there's nothing I can do. Nothing, nothing." She sobbed again.

"I drove away from there fast, as fast as I could," she blurted. "I called Karen. She told me to meet her at the clinic in Guerneville. I did, and then she brought me here." Teresa's chest rose and fell, her breathing laboring against the weight of her ordeal.

Lynn put a hand on her shoulder. "I'm so sorry." She winced, imagining herself in the same awful place, wondering what she would have done in those circumstances, whether she would have struggled and screamed as she'd been taught, or whether the dreaded prospect of deportation might have overtaken her, too. It didn't matter. Teresa's fear seeped into her across the bench, the fear that is never far from the surface in any woman.

"Are you still afraid?" she asked. "Do you think he's coming after you?"

"I know he is. He's crazy. He knows I know his secret, and he wants to shut me up before I can turn him in."

"Shut you up?" Lynn asked.

"Yeah, kill me if he has to. He doesn't want to go to jail." She rocked back and forth, holding the bench below her in a death grip that whitened her knuckles. "He's a bad dude."

"You're safe here," Lynn said, not knowing that Teresa was. But what else could she say? Certainly she was safe for now, in this moment. But for how long? How resourceful was this guy, Juan Carlos? How crazy?

She studied Teresa's pretty face, now tarnished with exhaustion. Lynn led her back to the house and up an open staircase by the front door to a loft just large enough for a narrow mattress, a bedside table, and a small lamp.

"Try to get some sleep," Lynn said. "You'll be safe here," she added for reassurance, for her own as much as Teresa's. "I'll be downstairs."

CHAPTER 2

THE RESCUER

ALL AFTERNOON, LYNN WATCHED AND LISTENED FOR CARS through the open windows. What would she do if this crazy Juan Carlos showed up? How likely was it, ten miles north of Cazadero on a narrow, winding road through the redwoods, twenty-five miles north of Guerneville? How could he track her here? Surely, Teresa was safe. Surely, they were all safe.

Safety had not been her concern when she and Hank had moved there just three months earlier from the suburbs of Atlanta when they'd retired. She had been a first grade teacher in the local elementary school, and he had been a manager with Home Depot. As much as she loved young children, teaching was a difficult job for her, an introvert. She could play the role of extrovert. But doing so—getting herself up for the job every morning—required conscious effort. And that daily effort, year after year, was tiring. So, after thirty years in the classroom, she longed for a change of pace—and a change of scenery.

There was nothing holding her in Atlanta. Lauren, their daughter, had married an Australian and moved down under, half a world away.

Neither she nor Hank were ready for full-time rest and relaxation. Rather, they wanted the activity and income of some kind of low-stress work. Caretaking, in a new, exotic place like California, seemed to fit the bill. Hank was handy around the house, comfortable and competent with tools. Lynn enjoyed gardening and working in the yard. Both were responsible, hard-working people. They easily met the qualifications of the position, and they accepted the post as soon as it was offered. It was everything they had imagined. The ranch and its setting were dramatic, beautiful. The work was challenging and difficult at times, but on the whole, life there was unhurried, even peaceful, tranquil.

It felt anything but tranquil now. While Teresa slept upstairs Lynn worried about Juan Carlos. Her mind manufactured horrible scenarios, racing to the most extreme ends, as it had as long as she could remember. Calming Teresa—feeding her, seeing to her needs—had calmed *her*. But that effect was absent while Teresa slept out of sight.

What would Lynn do if Juan Carlos came here when Hank wasn't around? Like now, when he was running an errand in town? How long would Karen want her to keep Teresa? Why couldn't Karen hide her at her own place down in Cazadero? Lynn couldn't keep her here forever. Teresa would have to go somewhere, sometime.

Lynn sympathized with Teresa's plight. It was awful. She wanted to help her, but she couldn't see how she could provide anything but the most temporary aid. And there were the ranch owners, the Tillsons. Certainly they wouldn't want a fugitive on their property.

Footsteps sounded on the front porch, followed by the rap of knuckles on the door. Lynn stiffened as every muscle fiber in her body contracted. *So this is it.*

If this was Juan Carlos, she would lock the door, bar it with a chair if she had to, and call Hank, or George, the ranch foreman.

"Who is it?" she called from the kitchen table.

"It's me, George. Can I come in?"

"Sure, George. It's open."

Her tension ebbed as George lowered his head to come through the doorway. He was a tall man, well over six feet. She had never been so happy to see his weathered cowboy visage—his bushy Fu Manchu mustache and pale-blue eyes barely visible under the brow of a straw hat bent down like the spout of an old-fashioned water pitcher. He looked the part of ranch foreman. Frayed jeans sagged over his dusty black cowboy boots. The sleeves of his tan work shirt, with the words "Seaview Ranch" embroidered over the left pocket, were rolled up above his elbows.

George Nicholson owned the adjoining ranch, a mile to the south on Mountaintop Road. He'd been born there, like his father and his grandfather before him. His ancestors had been among the first Anglo settlers of the area, clearing the ridgetops of trees in the 1890s to make way for their cattle. Ranching was in his blood. While Lynn and Hank cared for the Tillson's house and grounds, the gardens, and the barnyard animals, George managed the ranch itself; the cattle, the heavy equipment, the pastures, the fencing. The ranch could not run without him.

"What can I do for you?"

"I was over by the equipment shed when Karen drove in with that Latina this morning."

"And?" Lynn replied.

"And I saw she left without her." He folded his arms across his chest and settled back on his right hip. "She's a troublemaker, you know. We can't have any of that up here. If that woman's still here, you need to think about getting her out of here."

Lynn was not a good liar, but she tried. "There's no problem. She's just a friend of ours, an artist from the valley who needs a place to stay for a few days."

"She didn't look like no artist. She looked like a Mexican." He took a deep breath. "ICE is on the warpath. I don't want to mess with them, and neither do you." He turned to go.

"There's no need for them to mess with us," she said.

"We'll see," he said. "You're a smart woman. Be smart." He bent his head again, ducked, and closed the door behind him.

Lynn closed her eyes and sighed under the weight of her new dilemma. The ceiling above her creaked. She looked up to see Teresa's face peering over the edge of the loft.

"Is he gone?" she asked.

"Yes, you can come down."

At the bottom of the stairs, Teresa stopped and looked out the window by the front door. George had left. She turned toward Lynn. Sleep seemed not to have restored her. She looked exhausted, worn out, still terrified.

"I can go," she said in a voice little more than a whisper. "I can find another place to stay."

Something in Lynn begged her to accept Teresa's offer, but another voice spoke over it.

"Where will you go?"

"I have friends."

"Are you sure you'd be safe?"

Teresa shrugged her shoulders. "I don't know."

Lynn knew Karen would not have brought Teresa to the ranch if she had a better option. The farmworker community in the valley was large, but it was also tight. Juan Carlos would find her there. No, she was probably safer here. Karen would know.

A forty-five-year-old image flashed in her mind like an ugly neon sign: military policemen escorting a young man away from his supposed safe house; his girlfriend railing through her tears—at her, Lynn—over and over, "You said you'd help me get him across the border. How could you let us down? I'll never trust you again." The memory passed, leaving its residue of pain. *I can't let that happen again.*

"Then you're staying here, at least for now. Let's see what Karen has to say when she gets back." Again, Teresa's presence—with its obvious, crying need—stiffened Lynn's backbone, drew out her courage and resolve. She would wait for Karen. In the meantime, she would try to lift Teresa's spirits.

"I'm going to have a cup of tea. Would you like some?"

Teresa nodded. "Yes."

Lynn put the kettle on and offered Teresa a seat at the table. She retrieved mugs and tea bags from a cupboard beside the sink, and while the water boiled, she began to make the first preparations for dinner, breading chicken pieces with corn meal. *Yes, Karen will know what to do,* she thought.

STANDING AT THE KITCHEN COUNTER, LYNN RECALLED how she'd met her friend Karen. Their first Sunday on the ranch, Lynn and Hank had taken a drive down the Coast Highway to Bodega Head, the massive, treeless bluff guarding the only protected harbor on the Sonoma Coast. George Nicholson had described it as spectacular, and it was indeed.

A brisk afternoon sea breeze was blowing the tops off the waves, turning the ocean to foam. Ravens soared on the wind rising up the cliff face, croaking in delight, floating back and forth along the bluff without so much as the flick of a wing feather, maneuvering with only their clever wedge-shaped tails. She and Hank sat on a cushion of soft grass, watching the lines of ocean swells moving toward them endlessly from beyond the horizon, unimaginably far, listening to the waves crashing on the rocks hundreds of feet below, savoring the brush of wind against their faces and the whispers of meadow grass behind them.

On their return they had stopped at the Cazadero General Store to buy coffee and the Sunday paper. The rustic sign on the building simply read Cazadero, as if *it* were the town. The building had been there as long as the town, built in the 1880s. Long and low, its dark, unfinished siding spoke of the durability of redwood, and of the logging of the big trees. Rust stains on the metal roof spoke of fog and mist and Pacific storms. Tables and chairs on the broad front porch invited guests. Inside, it was clear the store was a gathering place, a center of life; as such, it *was* the town.

No longer a general store in the strict sense of the term, it sold groceries and sandwiches, beer and wine, coffee, souvenirs of the town—T-shirts and mugs—fishing tackle. Its low ceiling darkened the space, creating a kind of comfortable intimacy, as did the dark wooden floor that showed the wear of more than a hundred years.

Waiting in line at the counter, Lynn glanced at the local paper, the *Santa Rosa Press Democrat*. A headline read "ICE Denies Rumors of Immigration Raids in Sonoma County." "Look at this, Hank," she said quietly, "ICE is going crazy here, too. What a disaster!"

When they reached the counter, the friendly teenage cashier addressed them as though they were old friends. She had heard Lynn's comment, and gesturing toward the four short grocery aisles, said, "You should talk to Karen over there. She's all over this immigration stuff." Raising her voice, she projected it across the room. "Aren't you, Karen?"

Karen looked up and laughed. Lynn noticed the little tattoo high on her cheekbone. Karen exchanged smiles with her. Lynn paid the bill, and she and Hank left the store.

But outside, Lynn hesitated at the car. She had no interest in remaining as anonymous as she had been in the suburbs. This small place invited participation and engagement. She intended to pursue it, and she intended to pursue it then and there with this interesting woman, Karen. So she asked Hank to wait there with her.

When Karen emerged, Lynn took a step toward her and introduced herself. "Pardon me if I'm being too forward," she said, "but that was an interesting exchange in there. I'm not used to cashiers knowing their customers. Obviously they do here."

"Yes," Karen replied, smiling. "It's both a blessing and a curse. Everyone knows everyone else's business. I'm Karen Boyd, by the way. I rent a little house on the Cazadero Highway, south of here in the redwoods. It's nice to meet you." She reached out her hand to Lynn and then to Hank, her deep, chestnut-colored eyes radiating kindness. "They know I'm sympathetic with the immigrant cause. I'm an outsider, too; Lakota, born on the reservation in South Dakota. It's ironic, isn't it, that we're the outsiders? Anyway, I'm sympathetic with other outsiders, which means the non-Anglos in this state." She smiled again and pulled a card from her purse. "Call me if you want to talk about this some more; we can use all the help we can get."

And Lynn did; she invited Karen to dinner at the ranch a few days later, and she came up late the following Sunday afternoon. Lynn showed her the little house, two rooms down and the sleeping loft above supported by exposed ceiling beams. It was a ranch house in the original sense of the word—low, simple, open, functional—a house built by ranchers. White walls brightened the space; cracks here and there suggested the plaster was original.

The back door was open, pulling a pleasant breeze through the house. Wisps of smoke drifted past the door. Lynn opened it and introduced Karen to Hank, who was lighting a fire in an old Weber grill. They returned to the front porch, where they sat side by side in two country rockers and shared their stories.

"My mother was unfit to raise me," Karen said. "My father divorced her and moved to Sacramento, where I grew up. He remarried, and my new mom inspired me to become a nurse. And they both made sure I knew where I came from. I'm a member of my tribe in South Dakota. I'm a grandmother elder. And I'm a shaman. My daughters don't understand that—they think it's silly—but hopefully they will someday."

Lynn was fascinated by this woman, who was growing in her estimation as they sat there on the porch, soaking up the warmth of the late afternoon sun. What might this sage think about the immigration crisis that seemed to have reached this part of California? Lynn reminded Karen what the young cashier in the general store had said about Karen, that Karen was "all over this immigration stuff."

"I'm not an expert," Karen said, "but I know a lot about what's going on." And she told Lynn how she regularly encountered farmworkers, many of them women, in the Guerneville health clinic, and heard their stories of long hours, low pay, physically demanding work, sexual harassment, and for the undocumented, the fear of deportation.

It was a sad story that Lynn had imagined, but had never heard in such detail. It had moved her.

———————

BOTH LYNN AND TERESA STARTED AT THE ROLLING crunch of tires on gravel. A car door slammed. Once again, Lynn's muscles tightened, but just as quickly, they loosened. It was only Karen.

She came through the front door without knocking, smiling broadly, her eyes glistening with kindness and warmth. Karen was irrepressible. Granted, it had not been her misfortune the previous night, but the nurse in her could not help but radiate good cheer. Teresa warmed to it and rose to greet her friend. Karen embraced her, rocking her like an infant, tenderly. Tears ran down Teresa's cheeks and disappeared into Karen's sweater. She lifted her head and wiped her eyes on her sleeve. Neither spoke.

"I hope you'll stay for dinner," Lynn said.

"Of course," Karen replied. "I wouldn't miss it." She raised her eyebrows, looked straight at Lynn, and added, "We have a lot to talk about."

When Hank returned from his day-long errand in Oakland, Lynn served her dinner of ranch-style chicken cooked on the stovetop in red wine and broth, seasoned with nutmeg, coriander, cumin, and chili powder. Then, while Hank cleared the table, the women refilled their wine glasses and retired to the front porch to assess Teresa's situation.

They sipped their wine and rocked in the ever-present breeze. Lynn spoke first.

"Have you thought about a U-visa?" she asked. "Aren't they for undocumented crime victims?"

"They are," Karen responded, "but there's a quota, and there are way more applications than visas. Remember, this new administration isn't exactly friendly to immigrants. I don't think it's worth the risk."

Karen and Lynn looked at Teresa.

"You're right, but it doesn't matter. I can't apply for one anyway."

"Why not?" Lynn asked.

"I can't tell you. Believe me."

Karen and Lynn glanced at each other in sudden recognition that Teresa's problem was deeper than they thought. They would have to proceed without knowing this thing that Teresa could not reveal.

"Okay, what then?" Karen asked of Teresa.

"I don't know. I—" She hesitated. "I don't know where to begin. I feel trapped, like there's no way out." There was pain and desperation in her voice. "How am I going to find work where he can't find me? I can't go back to that vineyard. And I can't go back to my apartment. He knows where I live. Where will I go?" Her face sagged with fatigue and resignation. Fear shone in her tired eyes like the flickering of dying embers.

"First things first," Karen said. "We need to find you a place to stay."

As Lynn had known all along this was that place. It couldn't be Karen's. Juan Carlos had seen her at the winery distributing flyers for Lideres Campesinas, the female farmworkers organization. He didn't know her, but he knew of her. Karen was unmistakable. With a little sleuthing, and some pressure applied to other workers at the winery, he would find out where she lived and worked. If Teresa were living with her, he would find her.

"You can stay here, Teresa, until we can find another place," Lynn said.

"Are you sure?" Karen asked.

"Yes, I am." Lynn had already done the calculus and reconciled herself to her decision.

Next, came the problem of finding a job—a good job. It had taken Teresa two decades in the fields of California to find a good place to work. That meant a vineyard, not the vegetable fields. It meant a vineyard with other female workers, and it meant a vineyard that would allow her to do more than picking. She liked working in the vineyards—*la uva*, as the campesinas called them—and she wanted to stay if she could find another good place.

Karen volunteered to go to the vineyard the next day to talk to the manager.

"Please, don't," Teresa pleaded.

"I won't tell her what happened," Karen promised. "I'll just say that you liked working for her but you had to leave for personal reasons. And I'll ask her if she can recommend some other good vineyards. I've met her. I think she will."

"It can't get back to Juan Carlos. Please, please."

"Don't worry. It won't."

Karen's reassurance did little to calm Teresa's concern, but she agreed. They decided that Lynn should take Teresa to her apartment in Santa Rosa the next morning to pick up clothes and personal things and then drop her at the clinic to pick up her car. Teresa would follow Lynn back to the ranch.

Twilight had faded to a thin blue glow on the horizon when the evening chill chased the women back into the house. Karen hugged her friends, thanked Lynn for the meal, and retreated back down the mountain to Cazadero.

The day had caught up with Teresa. "I'm tired, senõra. I should sleep."

"Of course." Lynn fetched a pair of pajamas, a towel, and a toothbrush, and went out to close up the barn while Teresa washed and changed for bed.

In the barn, the chickens had settled onto their roosts, while outside, the goat bleated her impatience by the big back doors. Lynn led her into her stall and then stood for a moment absorbing the calm peacefulness of the place, as she had early that morning. She then turned off the lights, closed the door, and walked back through the blackness to the house.

Hank was waiting for her in the kitchen. He stood back against the counter, legs crossed, hands in his pockets. His gray hair swept back over his ears and collar. He'd grown a full beard that was more trimmed than not. His plaid shirt was frayed at the cuffs and collar. Dirt smudges showed on his khaki work pants where he'd wiped his hands. His well-worn boots had formed to his feet. Ranch life had grown on him, too.

"What's the plan?" he asked.

CHAPTER 3

TENSION IN THE VINEYARD

A GAUZY WHITE MIST WAS STILL RISING FROM THE CREEK the next morning when Lynn and Teresa descended the steep forested ridge to the valley floor. Voices of the natural world poured through the open windows of the car—the melodies of songbirds that changed with every bend in the road; soft to loud, sweet to raucous, simple and short to long and complex. Small farms appeared; here and there along the stream, a pasture, a garden plot, an orchard; tall firs and, beneath them, spreading oak and orange-barked madrone.

Mountaintop Road joined Cazadero Highway just north of the village and its handful of simple structures—the general store, a post office, an auto repair shop, a small junk yard shielded by a tall metal fence, a few houses, and two small, classic nineteenth-century churches. Below the village, the road tunneled into towering redwoods that blocked all but the cleverest rays of the sun. Small houses—weekend retreats, fishermen's camps—stood where the creek veered briefly away from the road.

At one such place, Lynn slowed the car where an indistinct dirt driveway led down through the trees to a tiny shed-roofed structure painted a whimsical lime green. It sat at the edge of the sunlit creek, a perfect retreat or sanctuary, she thought. This was Karen's place. For a moment she tried to convince herself that Teresa would be safe there. It would be so much simpler for everyone. But Karen's reasoning came back to her, and she let the thought go.

"That's Karen's place," she said. "It's probably good for you to know where she lives."

Teresa nodded. "Thank you."

A few miles south, where Austin Creek emptied into the Russian River, they turned left toward Guerneville, the commercial and civic hub of the valley. Restaurants, taverns, mom-and-pop grocery stores, several banks, and gas stations lined the three blocks of the main street. Most were simple, one-story frame structures, well-maintained, freshly painted. From the look of it the town was healthy and thriving.

A sign pointed south down a side street, past a liquor store and a real estate office, to the "beach," a strip of sand on the river usable only in the dry summer season. To the north, a road led past the fire station and the Catholic church to a small stand of virgin redwoods preserved as a state park.

East of the town, forest-covered hills crowded the river. Vineyards covered the flats where flood waters had deposited sand and loam. At the town of Mirabel Park, the river turned north, the terrain leveled off, and the vineyards multiplied. Teresa pointed toward the river.

"It's up there," she said.

"What's up there?"

"The winery."

Lynn pulled onto the shoulder, checked for cars, and turned around. This was not part of the plan she had described to Hank the previous evening, when she had doubted she could help Karen and Teresa in any meaningful way. Hank had protested, encouraging her as he always did, suggesting that she had more to offer than she thought. "Stick with it. They need you," he'd said. She had dismissed his support, as she often did, but here she was, unconsciously acting in a way he had imagined.

"What are you doing?" Teresa asked, wide-eyed.

"I'd like to see the place." Lynn was curious about this place at the center of Teresa's drama, but beyond that, she wasn't sure why. She just had a feeling that it might be important.

"Do we have to?"

"Don't worry. No one will see you. You can duck down in the seat, if you want. Just point it out to me."

"Okay. It's a couple of miles, Valley Run Wines."

Lynn tried to reassure her, but Teresa remained pensive. At a ninety-degree bend in the road, Teresa shrunk down in her seat.

"Is this it?"

"Yes."

They approached a cluster of artfully designed, professionally landscaped buildings; several old metal-roofed barns, weathered to a deep chestnut brown; a visitors center of stone and wood; a tasteful stone-walled entrance with the name Valley Run on a bronze plaque above a bed of yellow poppies. Oaks hung over the road. Tall redwoods and firs stood between and around the buildings of the compound, providing color and contrast to the lines of trellises that swept to the river on one side of the road and to the hills on the other. It was a substantial, prosperous place.

Teresa craned her neck up just enough to peer out the window and quickly ducked back down.

"What?" Lynn asked.

"That's him." Teresa shrunk lower in her seat.

A swarthy, muscular man with a worn straw hat—more sombrero than Stetson—stood in the doorway of a barn that faced the small visitors parking lot, his back to them.

"He didn't see you. Don't worry."

Lynn sped up and followed the road up the west side of the river to Healdsburg, where she turned south on US 101, the Redwood Highway, toward Santa Rosa. It would have been quicker to turn around and get back on her original route, but Lynn chose not to alarm Teresa further.

Seeing Juan Carlos had terrified Teresa, and it had frightened Lynn, too. The disconnected name had taken on living form for her. The threat was real. The predator breathed and walked, and they had come much too close to him.

Two miles south of the center of Santa Rosa, the county seat, Lynn exited the freeway at Hearn Avenue. Teresa guided her through Roseland, a one-mile square section of the city that had served for years as an entry point for immigrants from Mexico, Central America, Asia, and the Polynesia. Teresa was not a minority there. More than half of the population was Mexican.

They drove past blocks of small, neat family homes with well-maintained yards to a nondescript, no-frills two-story apartment building on the north end of the district. At the entrance, a few scrawny shrubs grew below a pair of tall California palms. Lonely sprigs of grass struggled for life on an otherwise barren lawn. A torn screen sagged in a second-story window.

Lynn parked, and Teresa led her up a wooden staircase to a dark breezeway littered with disintegrating pizza-shop flyers and newspaper circulars. She stopped in front of a door marked 2B, dug the key from her pocket, and entered. The apartment was clean, orderly, and tiny—kitchen, living room, and one bedroom, which Teresa shared with two other single women. In the bedroom, she knelt beside a narrow twin bed and pulled out a long, shallow cardboard box—her dresser. She stuffed a duffel with clothes, her toiletries, her bed linens, personal items from a shelf over the bed—pictures, a tattered Isabel Allende novel, a crucifix—and two jackets hanging behind the bedroom door. She checked the other rooms, found nothing, and they left, having spent all of fifteen minutes in the place.

"I'll never see that apartment again," Teresa said as Lynn started the car.

Lynn couldn't argue with that. She backed out of her parking space and pointed the car toward Guerneville. She would take Routes 12 and 116, avoiding Valley Run. There had been enough excitement for the day.

She found the Guerneville Health Center, Karen's clinic, just off the main drag behind a Subway and a nail salon. Teresa's car was still there.

"I'll follow you," Lynn said, wanting to be sure not to lose her. "Just look for Cazadero Highway. I'll flash my lights when we get close. It's six or seven miles."

Teresa got in her car and turned right on River Road toward Jenner.

Accelerating to stay behind her, Lynn settled back into her seat and felt the tension drain from her neck and shoulders.

———

A FEW MINUTES BEFORE NOON, KAREN STUCK HER HEAD through the open door of the winery manager's office. It was just inside the barn, where a few hours earlier, Teresa and Lynn had seen Juan Carlos. She had called ahead, and the manager, Kelly Ahearn, had agreed to see her.

"May I come in?"

Karen's eyes sparkled, and her face wore a radiant, disarming smile. Kelly rose to meet her. She was a handsome woman in her late thirties, with short, wavy dark hair. She wore a khaki shirt and the ubiquitous blue jeans.

"Please do. What can I do for you, Karen?"

"It's about one of your employees, Teresa Alvarez."

"Oh?"

Karen wanted to tell her exactly what had happened two nights before, but she resisted the temptation and stuck to her promise. "Teresa didn't come to work because of a personal problem related to the winery. She likes working here, but she just can't."

"And you can't tell me what this problem is?"

"No, I wish I could, but I really can't."

"I can't solve it if I don't know what it is."

"I know. I know."

"So, why are you here?"

Karen explained that Teresa liked Valley Run. There were other women; she had the opportunity to learn new skills and work year round; management was fair. She hoped to find another such winery, just not in the valley.

"Not in the valley?"

"Yeah, Napa maybe, or the Anderson Valley."

"Wow. So there's someone here she has such a big problem with that she can't be within twenty miles."

"I can't say that."

"Okay."

Karen respected Kelly. She was fair. She was also tough. She had to be to supervise staff and workers. But would she go out of her way to help a woman who could no longer work for her, and couldn't tell her why? Karen hoped she would.

"I'll give it some thought. There might be a couple of places."

"That's all we ask. You're kind to do it."

Karen took a business card from her pocket and gave it to Kelly.

"If you can think of some places that might be good for Teresa, please send me an email."

She rose and extended her hand.

"I will."

They shook hands. Karen thanked her and turned to leave.

"I'm terribly sorry to lose her," Kelly said. "She's a good worker and a good person. I can't imagine what problem she might have here, but I won't ask again."

Late in the afternoon, Kelly walked out into the barn to check on pinot noir grapes cold soaking in big, circular stainless-steel fermenters more than a dozen feet wide. The grapes had been picked in the cool fifty degrees of the previous evening, de-stemmed, and crushed. She grabbed the handle of a wooden paddle leaning in one of the vats and stirred the soup of crushed grapes and their juice—the "must"—as she would twice a day, for several days, until it warmed up enough for native yeasts from the skins to start the fermentation process.

A new heavy-duty Ford pickup, white and shining, pulled into the yard behind the barn. The driver climbed out and walked toward the open door of the barn with a dinner pail and thermos, arriving for the evening harvest.

"Juan Carlos," she said as he crossed the threshold.

He looked up.

"You didn't tell me that Teresa quit. What's that all about?"

"I don't know," he said, trying to look surprised. "I didn't know she quit. Did she tell you?"

"No, Karen Boyd did this afternoon."

"Who's she?"

"The nurse who works with the Latina farmworkers group, Lideres Campesinas. You've seen her."

Her eyes locked onto his. "Is there something going on I don't know about?"

"What do you mean?" His eyes bounced this way and that under her gaze.

"She won't come back here, like she's afraid."

27

"I don't know what that's about. All I know is she didn't show up last night. I thought she was sick."

"There's something going on. Dig into it." She tightened her grip on the paddle and gave the must a healthy stir.

"Do you have enough pickers for tonight?"

"Yes, ma'am."

She pulled on a faded Giants cap and walked out into the rows of trellises behind the barn to examine the bulging clusters of purple grapes hanging expectantly from the vines.

As Juan Carlos watched her disappear into the vineyard a thin, knowing smile spread across his face.

Later, at midnight, four tractors growled quietly as they crept through the vineyard. Two held powerful lights aloft. Two others pulled half-ton grape bins on low trailers. Pickers walked along behind them, snipping bunches of ripe grapes into smaller plastic bins called lugs and dumping them in the trailer bins as they filled them. They appreciated working in the cool of the evening, and the winemaker appreciated working with the cool, firm fruit picked at night.

Juan Carlos pulled one of the trailers, looking back from side to side as he drove to observe the pickers behind him.

"Jessica!" he called as a woman emptied a full forty-pound lug into the bin on his trailer. He motioned for her to approach. "Do you know the nurse who works with the campesinas?"

"Karen?"

"Yeah, her."

"Yes, I do."

"Do you know where she works? I need to talk with her."

"No, I don't," Jessica lied. "Sorry."

"That's okay. I'll find it."

She returned to her picking, and Juan Carlos drove on, calculating his next move.

CHAPTER 4

HOPE GROWS

THE TASTING ROOM WAS DARK AT SIX THIRTY THE NEXT morning when Juan Carlos drove around behind it and eased his truck up to the loading dock. He quickly unlocked the door, took eight cases of wine from the storeroom, and slid them onto the truck. He pulled a tight-fitting tarp over the bed, locked the door, and left the winery by the workers' entrance.

He had done this once a week for years, supplementing his salary enough to allow him the luxuries of a new truck and a comfortable, up-scale apartment. It had taken him a while to devise a system that would avoid detection, but it had proved to be uncomplicated. He enlisted the aid of the young woman responsible for stocking the tasting room. His plan was simply for her to deliver fewer cases of wine to the tasting room than she signed out. He took the balance the next morning, sold it, and gave her a piece of the proceeds.

That morning, as with every such load, Juan Carlos pulled into the driveway of a small bungalow on a quiet street in Roseland. Two young men—one stocky, one skinny; both, heavily-tattooed—emerged from the front door and swaggered across the lawn toward him.

"Right on time, compadre," the stocky one said, shaking his right hand and slapping him on the back with his left.

Juan Carlos pulled back the tarp. The men unloaded the wine, opened the boxes, and checked the labels of the bottles.

"Okay," the spokesman said. He reached into his pocket and pulled out a wad of bills. He took five hundreds off the top and handed them to Juan Carlos. "Same time next week?"

"Yeah," Juan Carlos replied. He backed his truck out of the driveway and drove across town to his apartment. He didn't know where the wine went or what they'd gotten for it. He didn't want to know. They were gang members—*Sureños*. The profit they made from the wine he sold them was protection money, a contribution to his safety. His immigration papers, too, were suspect, and they knew it. The wine he had sold them was worth $4,000 retail. But he wasn't complaining. He had no reason or right to complain. He was lucky they gave him anything.

———————

At noon, Karen's phone rang. *Kelly Ahearn*, read the caller ID. She answered.

"This will be quick, Karen. Harvest time is crazy. But I thought of a place that might be good for Teresa. It's in the Anderson Valley—Philo, near Boonville. My friends have a winery there called Mendo Wines; Jack and Amy Henderson. You'll like them. Go see them. Gotta run."

After work, Karen took Kelly's suggestion straight to the ranch. She found Lynn and Teresa tilling and weeding in the vegetable garden.

"We have a lead!" she shouted from across the yard, waving her arms over her head in a kind of celebratory dance.

Lynn and Teresa stopped their work and stood up. Karen lowered her voice as she drew closer.

"We have a lead for Teresa—a good one, I think—up in Mendocino County, the Anderson Valley."

Excitedly, she told them she really hadn't expected Kelly to get back to her, as busy as she was. Sure, Kelly liked Teresa, but she couldn't have been too high on Kelly's list. Karen speculated about Kelly's motive. Was she just being kind? Or was it Teresa's not wanting to go back to the winery, a fear of the place?

"Mendocino County would be good," Lynn said. "A couple of hours north of here."

"Yeah, on the edge of wine country. Safer. Do you want to go up there tomorrow? Teresa, what do *you* think?"

"I like it."

"Sure, I'm happy to go," Lynn said. Although she knew not to count her chickens before they hatched, she felt a sense of relief. It had been only a couple of days since Teresa's attack, but Lynn already was growing uneasy, impatient. *We're just marking time. We have to find a place for Teresa—and soon. She can't stay here.* The litany of reasons played in her head: *It's not our place. George doesn't approve. Juan Carlos is too close—what if he comes when we're here by ourselves? What if he sends ICE?*

A long trip to the Anderson Valley was a perfect antidote to Lynn's mood: it represented forward motion; it would take her mind off her anxiety; and it just might solve Teresa's problem—her problem. She looked forward to it.

———

THE FASTEST WAY TO PHILO FROM THE RANCH WAS ALSO the prettiest, Lynn thought. So after breakfast, she and Teresa drove north on Mountaintop Road for seven miles along the open ridge, turned right at an old tin barn in a broad pasture, and dropped down through dense evergreen forest to the Coast Highway at Stewart's Point.

Here, the road followed a narrow grassy plateau—a coastal prairie—several hundred feet above the ocean. Where the road arced sharply around a cove, or more gradually around a long bay, they could see waves crashing on the rocks at the base of the bluffs. Huge columns of black rock—sea stacks, products of eons of erosion—stood just offshore, breaking up the waves and sending spray skyward. In places, it seemed that one could see twenty or thirty miles of coastline. The scene lifted Lynn's spirits; the golden-brown of the summer grasses, the blue of the sky, the deeper blue of the ocean, the frothing white at the water's edge, the greens of the forest. *Jaw-droppingly beautiful. If I needed a reason to be here, this would be enough.*

They passed through Sea Ranch, with its stables, horse trails, and weathered gray houses that blended tastefully into the landscape, and beyond, the contrasting little beach town of Gualala, at the Mendocino County line, where old and new, pedestrian and sophisticated, peacefully co-existed in their own colors and styles—a historic hotel, a gas station, condos, a little supermarket.

At the tiny hamlet of Point Arena, whose famous lighthouse was the closest point to Honolulu in the Lower Forty-Eight, they turned east and wound up and over the wooded coast range to the Anderson Valley. There, settlers had cleared the forests for sheep and cattle, as in much of northern California, but little of that old economy remained. After the Second World War, winemakers began planting the alluvial terraces along Anderson Creek and other tributaries of the Navarro River with vines, and their craft became the mainstay of the area. More remote than Napa and Sonoma—and smaller—there were fewer people here, less attention. Lynn was encouraged by what she saw. She could imagine Teresa absorbing into life and work here, hiding in a way that would be more difficult closer to the city. In Boonville, where their route turned northwest on Highway 128, she saw signs of the presence of Hispanics—*carnicería, mercado, lavandería*. Teresa's people were here, working the vineyards.

This might be the place. Her hopes rose.

They passed through the center of Philo—a few houses, a market, an inn, a Methodist church, an old lumber mill—and turned off the road at a split-rail fence planted with red and yellow roses and a carved wooden sign that read Mendo Wines. A small parking lot flanked with black-eyed Susans in full bloom stood before a small rustic tasting room that had just opened for the day. She and Teresa were the first to arrive.

Inside, a cheerful young woman greeted them, and Lynn introduced herself.

"A friend of ours from Healdsburg sent us. I'm Lynn Peterson, and this is Teresa Alvarez. We're looking for Mrs. Henderson, or her husband."

"Yes, she said you might be coming. She's back at the winery. Follow the drive. I'll call and tell her you're here."

At the end of the drive, a short woman in soiled work clothes and a broad-brimmed straw hat stood beside an open Jeep. Lynn pulled up beside her and parked.

"Hi, I'm Amy," the woman said. "Care to go for a ride? You just caught me on my way to the back vineyard to collect some samples."

Lynn smiled, introduced herself and Teresa again, and eagerly accepted. She waved Teresa into the front seat, climbed in the back, and they set off through rows of leafy trellises undulating toward the golden-brown hills on the far side of the valley.

"Kelly said you're a good worker. She's sorry to see you leave," Amy said, glancing over at Teresa.

Teresa met her gaze. "I'm sorry to leave her, too. She's a good boss."

"Why do you say that?"

"She's fair, and she let me learn new skills so I could work for her year round—planting, pruning, building trellises, working with the must. I hope I can find another boss like her."

"You will," Amy said as she stopped the Jeep. "Walk with me a little."

Amy led Teresa and Lynn up one row and back the next, stopping to examine grapes, checking for ripeness, snipping off a bunch here and there and putting it in a metal pail.

"So, you like la uva," she said.

"I do," Teresa replied. "It's so much better than picking vegetables."

Amy stopped and turned to Teresa. "Well, you're the kind of person I like to hire."

Lynn felt a rush of hope. *Tell us this is it*, she prayed.

"There's a good chance I'll have an opening soon. One of my best workers is in line for a manager's job at another vineyard, but I'm not going to know for a couple of weeks. If it happens, you'll be the first person I call."

Teresa smiled politely. They returned to the Jeep, and headed back through the vineyard to the barn. Alone in the back seat, Lynn felt her spirit ebb. In a silent internal dialogue, she struggled to reverse the tide of her emotions.

No, this isn't the end of the world. It's just one opportunity lost. There's still a chance here. And if this doesn't work out, something else will. Her skeptic pushed back. *This is going to be harder than we thought, take longer than we thought. I've got a life to live. I can't spend it all doing this.*

Amy pulled up beside their car.

"I'd ask you to lunch, but I can't today. I'm straight out. Got grapes to harvest, wine to make, and nature won't wait for us."

Lynn rose to the occasion, feigning equanimity. "We understand completely. Thank you for taking the time you did. You're very kind."

"Thank *you* for coming all the way up here. It's in my interest to spend time with good prospects like you, Teresa. I'll be in touch."

They shook hands and parted company.

————————

LYNN TURNED LEFT ONTO THE MAIN ROAD TOWARD Philo. Neither woman spoke, each processing in her own way the meeting with Amy, clinging to hope, trying to stay optimistic.

"Are you hungry?" Lynn asked Teresa as they approached the little cluster of buildings.

"I guess."

Lynn stopped at the Philo Market. Like the Cazadero General Store, it sold the basic necessities of daily life—just enough to hold body and soul together; ice, beer, wine, groceries, fresh produce, sandwiches. They bought drinks and fresh sandwiches and ate their lunch at a table on the store's front porch. As they rose to leave, Lynn hesitated. She had planned to go directly back to the ranch the way they had come, but now that didn't seem like the right course. What would they do there but dwell on the uncertainty of Teresa's future? They had come a long way to meet with Amy. There were other wineries in the valley. It seemed silly to head home now just because they had hit a minor speed bump. In fact, that little setback suggested their mission wasn't over.

Lynn was not moved by optimism like Hank was. His cheerfulness in the face of much worse than this bit of uncertainty was just so much Pollyanna to her. She was moved by practicality, diligence, and responsibility. She had signed up for this excursion with Teresa, and there was still light in the sky.

"How 'bout going back a different way? See the rest of the valley while we're here. What do you think?" she asked her companion.

"That's okay," Teresa replied. "If you want."

"All right then, we'll do it. I'll be right back." Lynn went into the store and came back with a map of Anderson Valley Wineries. She spread it out on the table. "We're right here," she said, pointing to Philo. "Let's follow the highway all the way to the coast. It looks like there are ten or twelve more wineries along the way. You can make notes on the map if you see something you want to remember."

Back in the car, Lynn turned around and headed back the way they had just come. They passed the Henderson winery. The valley widened, even as they approached its northern end. Twice they turned off the highway onto unpaved side roads, following signs to wineries. Lynn was encouraged. *There are plenty of opportunities here. We just need a connection.*

Five miles northwest of Philo, the hillsides steepened, the vineyards disappeared, and the forest closed in. The road turned west along the Navarro River through second-growth redwoods, bending with it for ten miles until it emerged on an open flood plain and ended at State Route 1, the Coast Highway.

Lynn turned left, crossed the river, and where the highway began a steep climb out of the valley, she pulled right onto a narrow, barely paved road that ran down into a stand of trees beside the river. She stopped. A sign read Navarro River Estuary State Marine Conservation Area.

"Let's try this," she said.

Teresa nodded, and Lynn continued into the woods and out to a sandy parking area at the mouth of the river, just a few hundred yards from the highway. To the right, the river pooled in a broad lagoon behind a high dune that now, at the height of the dry season, blocked its access to the ocean. Only when winter rains renewed its flow would it break through again, allowing young fish to venture out to sea and mature salmon to continue the long journey upstream to their spawning grounds.

Lynn stepped out of the car. Teresa followed, and together they started up over the dunes toward the roar of surf. They took off their shoes and walked to the water's edge, letting the waves wash up over their ankles and back, in the endless rhythm of the sea. At the end of the short beach, they sat at the top of the dune and watched the waves rise, crest, curl, and crash in hypnotizing regularity. The roaring, tumbling surges washed away Lynn's anxiety. For the moment, there was only the fabulous blue-green foaming water and the cries of gulls. The place soothed her. She hoped it soothed Teresa.

"How are you feeling?" Lynn asked.

"I liked that woman. I'm hoping the job comes through."

"I hope so, too." Lynn wasn't very hopeful, but she tried not to betray her pessimism.

"I like the beach," Teresa said. "Thank you for bringing me. It reminds me of Michoacán. The sand is different. It's whiter and softer there, and the water's warmer, but it's the same color, and it sounds the same."

Lynn smiled. "I'm glad." But as pleasant as the scene was, she couldn't help returning to the task at hand—finding a safe place for Teresa to live and work. "It might be hard to find what you're looking for in the Anderson Valley, or even in Napa," she probed.

"I know. I worry about that."

"Would you consider picking vegetables again?"

Teresa's eyes remained fixed on the waves as she answered. "I can't go back to that. I'd go back to Mexico first."

"Really?"

"Really. It's what the new immigrants do, because nobody else wants to do it. It's back-breaking. There's no joy in it. And there's no future."

"Have you thought about moving farther away, even to a different part of the country? You'd be safer in Florida or Wisconsin."

Teresa turned toward Lynn. "I can't do that either. It's impossible."

"We could help you."

"I know you would, but you don't understand. There's something I haven't told you." She turned back to the water.

Lynn waited. There wasn't anything to say. Teresa would speak when she was ready. The waves ran up the beach with a drawn-out whoosh, and receded with a playful sizzle.

With her gaze still on the water, Teresa said, "I have two children in California, in the Central Valley, and grandchildren. I can't leave them."

Lynn wasn't surprised. Teresa was a pretty woman. She had been in California long enough to have adult children. It was just that in the four days they had been together, she hadn't mentioned it. *Why? Do they know what happened to their mother? Where she is?*

"What about them? Could they help you?"

"No." Teresa shook her head. "They know nothing about it, and I want to keep it that way."

"But—"

Teresa interrupted her. "They have enough to worry about. I don't want to worry them more. And on top of that, he knows who they are and where they live. It's out of the question."

"I understand," Lynn said, taking Teresa's hand. "I understand." Now she understood the boundaries of the problem, and she understood that it wouldn't be easy.

The long tongues of the waves crept closer as the tide rose. When the water reached their toes, the women stood and walked back across the dunes to the car and returned to the Coast Highway.

———

THE ROAD CLIMBED UP TO THE COASTAL PLATEAU AND curved around a deep cove guarded by mammoth sea stacks. The beauty of the scene caught Lynn's breath, competing with the road for her attention. They passed a handful of turn-of-the-century cottages on the ocean side of the road, and slowed as they entered the village of Elk, a quaint place that looked little touched by the twentieth century, let alone the twenty-first.

"Can you stop here?" Teresa asked as they approached a small white church with two short towers flanking the front door and a simple cross on the peak of the roof above it. It was a Catholic church, an old one. A small plaque above the door read 1896. "I'd like to go in."

Lynn stopped, and Teresa got out of the car. She walked up to the heavy, varnished wooden door, tried it, and found it locked. She looked at Lynn, standing beside the car in the shade of a large cypress, as if to ask for direction, then turned back to the door and pushed a small button on the door frame.

A side door opened in a small single-story brick house beside the church—the rectory, it seemed—and a short elderly man with thin white hair stepped out. He wore khaki pants and a long-sleeved black tunic with a white clerical collar.

"May I help you, miss?" he asked when he reached the steps of the church.

"I'd like to pray," she answered quietly.

"Very well. That's what churches are for. Please come in," he said with a flourish. He unlocked the door, opened it, and with his hand on her elbow, ushered her in. "I'm Father Angelo."

"Thank you very much, Father. I saw the church as we drove by, and I realized I needed to pray."

"The spirit moves in mysterious ways," he said. "I'm glad you stopped." He turned and waved to Lynn, beckoning her. "Don't be shy!" he called.

Not wanting to be rude, Lynn accepted his offer and joined them. It had been many years since she'd last been in a Catholic church, for the wedding of a college friend. And she had forgotten how different they were from the austere Protestant churches of her youth. It wasn't the space itself. This one was simple—white walls, dark, worn wooden floor, wooden benches. It was the iconography—the statues of the Virgin Mary and Saint Joseph that flanked a fancy traditional altar hung with an embroidered linen cloth, and just outside of, and to either side of the chancel facing the congregation, the statues of Jesus and the patron saint of the parish, Saint Anthony of Padua. It took Lynn a moment to adjust.

Father Angelo led Teresa up the red-carpeted aisle to the front of the church, and withdrew to the side while Lynn watched from the doorway. Teresa slipped into the second row of benches and knelt, resting her head on her hands, folded and placed on the back of the bench in front of her.

Lynn was struck by a strange sensation. She had never prayed, at least not since childhood, when she had said bedtime prayers at her mother's behest. For her, there had been no point, no one to hear or respond. Prayer to her was a futile gesture, an exercise in magic.

But now something moved her, compelled her, to walk forward, kneel in the row behind Teresa, and say silently, *If you're listening out there—up there, anywhere—send guidance. We need help.*

CHAPTER 5

NEW EYES

At six o'clock the next morning when her nighttime shift had ended, Jessica walked across the workers parking lot to her car.

Juan Carlos intercepted her. "Let me ask you again," he said. "Where does Karen work?"

"I told you I don't know."

"I think you do. And I think you're gonna tell me."

"Really?"

"Yeah, really." Juan Carlos had a trump card, and he played it here. "I know about your parents. They're illegal. I'll report them in a nanosecond if you don't tell me what I need to know."

Jessica liked Karen and wanted to protect her, but the welfare of her parents was more important, so reluctantly, she gave Juan Carlos what he wanted. "She works at the Guerneville Clinic."

"Good," he said, placing a hand on her bottom.

Jessica pulled away and glared at him. She climbed in her car and sped from the parking lot. Juan Carlos was not impressed. Inappropriate use of power and sexual harassment were the tools of his trade in the vineyard. He used them whenever and wherever they suited his ends. This was just another of those times.

———————

BEFORE SHE REACHED HOME, JESSICA CALLED KAREN.

"Karen, I'm so sorry. I told Juan Carlos where you work. I had to. I'm afraid."

"That's okay, honey. We'll deal with it. I'm not afraid of him."

"Are you sure?"

"I am. Don't worry. Take care of yourself."

Karen was not without concern, but neither was she frozen with worry. She had dealt with bullies before, and she knew her own strength. She was not easily intimidated. Juan Carlos knew how to find her, and she knew he would. Her job now was to remain strong and keep him from Teresa.

During her lunch break, she called Lynn.

"We've had a setback," she said. "Juan Carlos found out where I work. He'll be coming—soon."

———————

THE WORDS "OH NO" SLIPPED FROM LYNN'S MOUTH, AND she went silent. They all had known—Teresa, Karen, and Lynn—that Juan Carlos would pursue them, but until now, it had been only an idea, a possibility. Now this news tapped like footsteps in her ears, the footsteps of a predator. What might be, had become. Karen had been wise not to harbor Teresa at her place in Cazadero. But how long would it be before Juan Carlos followed the trail up the mountain to Bella Vista? Lynn felt powerless to protect her new friend. And should she continue to hide Teresa at the ranch, she felt powerless to protect herself.

"Let's talk about it tonight," Karen continued. "I'll come up right after work."

"Okay, see you then." Lynn hung up, wearing the face of distress.

"Who was that?" Hank asked. He and Teresa were both at the kitchen table with her, eating their lunch.

She relayed what Karen had told her. "I'm worried," she said. "He'll find us, for sure. Then what?"

"Let's not jump to conclusions," Hank said. "We don't know he will. Karen isn't gonna tell him, and if he does find us, we'll deal with it. We just need to be smart and keep looking for a place for Teresa. Who knows, that job in Philo just might come through."

Teresa rested her elbows on the table and lowered her face into her hands. "I'm sorry for this," she said. "I can find another place. I should do that."

Teresa's plaintive tone and mournful expression pulled Lynn from her anxiety, for she was nothing if not loyal. She hadn't invited Teresa to the ranch. It had been Karen's idea, but now that Teresa was here, Lynn felt committed to doing right by her. Right was right.

"No," Lynn said again, "don't worry. We'll protect you."

Again, she didn't know how, but she would accept Hank's optimistic view that they would find a way. It occurred to her that it might not be a good idea to keep George in the dark. On the one hand, he hadn't been sympathetic, but on the other, she imagined that he could become so. He didn't seem to be without compassion. His eyes—and his muscles—might be useful, should Juan Carlos find the ranch.

"Maybe we should tell George what's going on," she said. "We might need him."

"I think you're right. I'll tell him this afternoon."

In an earlier stage of their marriage Lynn would have been happy to accept Hank's offer. "Yes, please do," she might have said. But this was her struggle, not his, and it was as much a struggle with herself as with Juan Carlos and all he represented. It was a struggle for her agency. And *that*, she could not relinquish for the sake of convenience and comfort.

"No, I'll do it," she said with a voice of authority that surprised her. "I started this conversation with George. I need to finish it."

————————

IT HAD BEEN HER IDEA, BUT LYNN WAS NOT LOOKING FORward to speaking with George. He was a rough, died-in-the-wool cowboy, and he intimidated her. She knew what he would say. He'd already said it: ICE would make trouble for them. He didn't want trouble, and neither did she. If she were smart, she would send Teresa on her way and be done with the whole mess; Teresa could take care of herself.

George's resistance, such as she imagined it, had the odd effect of steeling her resolve. Hank's support and encouragement were important to her, but resistance curiously added extra incentive. So, when she saw George's beat-up ranch truck by the equipment barn, she went to see him. She found him on his back, changing the oil on a tractor.

"You were right about my friend," she said.

"I know," he said, tightening the drain plug with a wrench. "She don't look like no artist, and she's still here." He pushed himself out from under the tractor, stood up, and wiped his hands on a rag hanging from his pocket.

"I want to talk to you about her. Her name's Teresa, and she's undocumented."

"I figured as much."

"How?"

"You're sneaking around. She's keepin' her head down, not goin' anywhere," he said, grinning.

"That's because there's somebody after her."

"The feds?"

"No, her boss in the vineyard. He's a bastard. He raped her."

"What? When?" George's spontaneous expression of shock and surprise startled Lynn.

"A few hours before she showed up here."

"And she can't report him because she's illegal."

"Right."

"So why is he after her?"

"Because she knows he's stealing from the winery."

George stood with his feet spread wide and his arms folded across his chest. He tilted his head back and then lowered it slowly, peering directly into her eyes.

"And you want to suck me into this little drama."

"It's not so little, George," she said, nodding her head for emphasis. "This guy's coming after Teresa. And he's nasty."

"I told you I didn't want no trouble."

He had, clearly. Lynn realized they were now at the crucial point in the conversation, when she would either push him away, or draw him closer with her words and her bearing. So she dug deep to remind herself why she had come to speak with him. She smiled.

"I know. But I figured you should know what's going on."

"I appreciate that," he said, "but I can't be a part of your plan, whatever it is."

"That's not what I'm asking. But I'd like you to keep your eyes open for this guy."

He took a deep breath. Lynn wouldn't have bet on his response, but she had a good feeling about their conversation. He hadn't shut her down. To the contrary, he had listened. He hadn't joined the conspiracy, but she hadn't expected him to.

"I can do that much," he said, nodding.

She thanked him, turned, and left the barn, inwardly breathing a sigh of relief. Their meeting had gone as well as she could have expected. And she felt good about it. George was on their side, something she would not have predicted when Teresa arrived.

————————

LATE IN THE AFTERNOON, KAREN PARKED HER SUBARU wagon in the shade of the old live oak in front of the caretaker's cottage. She knocked at the front door and then called through the open screen door. When there was no answer, she walked back to the barn, and then to the big house next door. There she found Lynn and Teresa working in Becky Tillson's flower gardens, weeding and watering.

"Hello, friends!" she called from across the yard in her usual cheerful tone.

They stood up and brushed off their hands.

"Good timing, Karen," Lynn said. "We're through here. We'll put our tools away and meet you at the house."

She and Teresa washed their tools with the hose and hung them up in the barn. Then they joined Karen on the front porch of the cottage, where she had already found a rocker. Lynn went into the kitchen and returned with a pitcher of iced tea and three glasses.

"So what now?" she asked as she poured the tea.

"It's not the end of the world," Karen said. "He was going to track me down at some point. It just happened sooner than I expected."

"But what do you do when he does find you?" Lynn asked.

"I'm not worried. I'll just tell him she ran, left the state. Why wouldn't she?"

Why wouldn't she, indeed. Given what he had done to Teresa, Lynn was surprised that Karen wasn't more afraid of him.

"We have some leverage," Karen said. "Maybe we should threaten to use it, put him on the defensive." The old wooden floor creaked beneath her as her chair rocked back and forth, as regular as a metronome.

"His stealing?" Teresa asked. "The problem is we don't have any proof."

"Then we need to get some."

"How?" Lynn asked.

"We need to find someone at the winery, maybe Jessica."

As they talked about her, what she might know, and how she might uncover more, Lynn's anxiety returned. When she'd overcome her initial reluctance, she had committed herself to protecting Teresa. But snooping around the winery, spying on Juan Carlos, represented a level of involvement—and risk—that she was not sure she was prepared to take.

CHAPTER 6

SKIES DARKEN

THE DEW LAY HEAVY ON THE WINDSHIELD OF HIS TRUCK like a blanket of glowing bubbles, giving Juan Carlos the feeling of being suffocated as he climbed into the driver's seat. He started the engine and turned on the wipers. Straight ahead, the sun hovered above rows of vines, saturating them with new, life-giving light. He lowered the shade, took a pair of aviator sunglasses from his front pocket, and pulled them on. He backed away from the winery barn, drove out to the road, and turned left toward Guerneville.

Where's the girl, man? The gravelly voice of Rico, the stocky Roseland gangbanger, filled Juan Carlos's head, covering the chatter of drive-time radio jocks. Thin veils of fog drifted over the river bank here and there, slowing him down. Rico had called him late the previous evening.

Juan Carlos had tried to remain calm. "I'm looking for her right now," he had said after Rico had reached him, sitting on his tractor, supervising the end of the nighttime harvest in the Valley Run vineyard. "I've got a good lead."

"You better find her, compadre. She knows too much."

"I know."

"And you know we'll fuck you up, man, if you don't."

"I know. Don't worry."

"Remember, we know where you live."

Juan Carlos knew that Rico meant business. Just a few months earlier he and Jorge, Rico's sidekick, had caught up with a Roseland friend, Hector Sanchez, outside a strip mall in Healdsburg and stabbed him three times. He'd been lucky to survive. Everyone knew who'd done it, but Rico had escaped prosecution because Hector was unwilling to testify against him.

We know where you live. There was no escaping these guys. How had Juan Carlos let himself slip into this mess? It had seemed so simple, selling a few cases of wine to guys who could move it easily. He cringed, imagining himself impaled on a sharp blade, bleeding to death in the bushes by the side of the river. Or worse, his wife assaulted, or his kids. *We know where you live.*

His hands gripped the wheel as though it were a life ring. His breathing was rapid and shallow. Perspiration saturated his under arms, despite the cool air.

He slowed as he entered the town, just beyond the Route 116 bridge. It was seven o'clock in the morning. The clinic wouldn't open until nine. Karen would arrive at least fifteen minutes before that, he guessed. He would need to station himself by the back door at eight thirty to be sure not to miss her. In the meantime, he could eat breakfast.

In the next block, the door of the Sawmill Grill stood open beneath its faded, once-black awning. It was perfect—just around the corner from the clinic. He passed it, found a place to park, and walked back on the empty sidewalk. A few cars headed east on Main Street toward the city. The gas station was open, a few other restaurants, but otherwise the town was still waking.

In the Grill, early risers—a pair of policemen, shop owners, retirees—sat beneath black-and-white photographs of lumberjacks posing like conquerors on the stumps and fallen carcasses of old-growth redwoods. Those alone, thumbed their smartphone screens. A few diehards held newspapers. Tables of twos and threes chattered over the background drone of CNN. The cook flipped hash browns and bacon on the grill, nursed omelets in their pans. A busboy cleared tables and wiped them hurriedly with a wet cloth. A waitress moved from table to table topping off coffee mugs.

Juan Carlos took a seat by the window on the outer edge of the hubbub, where he could ready himself for his confrontation with Karen. He didn't know this woman, but he knew her reputation as a tough, no-nonsense defender of the campesinas—a do-gooder. *She's a pain in the ass. I'm going to set her straight.* He closed his eyes and tried to slow his breathing.

While he sipped coffee and ate his breakfast tacos, scenes of the unpleasant news of the day rolled across the television screen in the corner. The attorney general read a statement at a podium. Border agents led bedraggled immigrants to a van beside a border fence. Protesters mouthed the words, "Build the wall! Build the wall!"

He paid his bill, left the restaurant, and returned to his truck. The clinic was a block north and a block west. In less than a minute, he was in a parking space across the street from it, waiting. It was 8:20 a.m. His cellphone in hand, he watched for cars entering the parking lot, glancing down occasionally to check his email and Facebook page.

At 8:35 a.m., a green Subaru plastered with left-wing protest stickers turned into the parking lot beside the clinic. He climbed out of his truck and hustled across the lot in time to be standing beside her car when Karen opened the door and stepped out.

She looked up at him with eyes wide, and gasped.

"I know you've got Teresa," he said. "And I'm going to make your life miserable if you don't tell me where she is."

"She's long gone. Left the state." Karen tried to move past him.

He stepped in her way. "Where?"

She pushed against his chest.

He leaned into her hands and stood his ground.

"She didn't tell me. But if I knew, I wouldn't tell you." She pushed against him again. "Now let me go to work, you bully."

He glared down at her, as rigid as a statue. "You're lying."

"I'm not, but I'll scream if you don't let me by." She glared back at him.

A small convertible sports car, its top down, eased into the spot next to them. "Good morning, Dr. Andruzzi," Karen said cheerily.

"And a good morning to you, Karen."

Juan Carlos stepped back and let her pass. She strutted toward the back door of the clinic. He called after her, "We'll talk later!"

She showed not the slightest hint of acknowledging him and kept walking.

Damn! What I am I going to do? He trudged back to his truck, smothered in a fear that intensified the weariness of a long night. *I could sleep right now, here.* But he would wait until she reemerged, as crazy as that seemed. *I know she knows where Teresa is.*

———————

LYNN ARRIVED AT THE COMMON GROUNDS COFFEE SHOP at three o'clock that afternoon, as Karen had requested when she'd texted her just before nine that morning. *It's important*, the text read. A dark-skinned Latina with pronounced indigenous features sat at a table in the back corner of the room, watching Lynn as she ordered at the counter. Lynn engaged with the glance. She paid for her coffee and walked back to the table.

"You wouldn't be Jessica, Teresa's friend from Valley Run Wines?" she asked, knowing that Karen had texted her too.

"I am. And you must be Lynn."

"Yes. Have you been waiting long?"

"No, ten minutes."

"I forget how long it takes me to get down here from the ranch." Lynn sat and surveyed the room, saturated with the rich aroma of fresh coffee, tapping her foot to the exotic melodies and rhythms of world music. The place was small but cheerful, painted in bright, bold turquoise and crimson. The work of local artists hung on the walls—oils, pen-and-ink drawings, watercolors—scenes of the rugged Sonoma coast, the Russian River winding through steep forested hillsides, redwood groves. *No wonder Karen likes this place.* And it was convenient for her, just a few doors down from the clinic.

The door opened. Jessica looked up and watched a customer enter. "Not Karen," she said. "Do you know why she texted us?"

"Not exactly, but I'm sure it has something to do with Juan Carlos. We're trying to figure out how he's covering up his stealing, and we thought you might be able to help."

Jessica's face tightened. "I don't know, ma'am. I don't like him either, but he scares me. I don't know . . . " she said, her voice trailing off.

Lynn understood. He was a mean, nasty guy. "Maybe you can help without actually getting involved," she said, trying to relieve Jessica's fear. "We just thought you might know how he's doing it."

"I really don't know. I've just heard rumors. You should talk to Teresa."

"What do you mean?"

"Talk to Teresa."

"So, she knows something?"

"Yes."

Karen needs to be here. Lynn took out her phone and texted her.

While they waited, Lynn felt the absence of Karen's confidence and strength. She sat like a soldier lost without orders, an apprentice without a firm guiding hand. When after five minutes Karen had not replied, Lynn rose. "Do you want to take a walk? Let's go down to the clinic."

"Sure."

It was a short walk, the length of the block. At the front desk Lynn asked for Karen.

"Do you have an appointment?" the receptionist asked, her tone flat and her face long and expressionless.

"No, we're just friends. She asked us to meet her at the coffee shop at three, and she didn't answer my text."

The receptionist's long face grew longer. "Ooh, I'm so sorry." She searched for words. "She's had a heart attack. This morning, just after we opened. They rushed her to the hospital, Santa Rosa Memorial."

Lynn's hands flew up to her own chest. "Oh my God. Oh my God." And then, "How is she? Do you know?"

"She's in ICU. They say she'll be okay, but she's had a tough time."

"Thank you so much!"

Lynn and Jessica returned to their cars and headed east the twenty miles to Santa Rosa.

Out of habit Lynn took River Road, through Rio Nido, Korbel, and Hilton, five miles to Hacienda, where she crossed the river. Her eyes were on the road, but her mind was on her friend and her mysterious early morning message. *Why did she want us to meet this afternoon? What prompted that? What was the urgency?*

Lynn kept Jessica's car in her rearview mirror, but she needn't have worried. The route was simple—River Road, California 101, then twelve blocks on College Avenue to the modern, multi-story hospital befitting a city with a population pushing two hundred thousand.

The receptionist directed them across a welcoming, light-filled lobby to an elevator that took them up two floors to the intensive care unit. Signs led them down a wide, properly institutional corridor, to the ICU. Lynn had forgotten how well such units were set up to monitor their charges. "Intensively" was the operative word. Single rooms opened inward on a nerve center, where vital signs paraded across computer screens in reds and greens and blues, computers hummed, and monitors beeped.

Lynn approached the main desk. "We're here to see Karen Boyd."

A young nurse in blue scrubs, with a long blond ponytail, pointed across the room. "She's in room five, but she's asleep right now. If you like, you can wait in the visitors' area right behind you." Two people sat in a nook large enough for eight or ten. "They're here to see Karen, too."

One, a priest, stood to greet them, his white clerical collar shining like a beacon of hope against the black of his traditional garb. Wavy silver hair flowed over the tops of his ears. "I couldn't help but hear that you're here to see Karen. I'm Father Mike, from Guerneville." He extended his hand.

"I'm Lynn, a friend, and this is Jessica. It's nice to meet you." She took his hand. It was comforting, reassuring. "How is she?"

The other fellow rose, a youngish man with close-cropped dark hair. "I'm Ted, one of the doctors at the clinic. She's had a rough go, but she'll recover. She was lucky."

"How so?"

Ted continued. "Distance, time, expertise, systems. This isn't a large hospital, but it's got one of the best cardiac units in the country. When Karen complained of chest pains a few minutes after we opened, we called the EMTs. They arrived in a flash, ran an EKG on the spot, transmitted it here, and a cardiologist diagnosed a heart attack. Thirty minutes later, a team was wheeling her into the ER, and in no time they had the catheter in her vein. With heart attacks it's all about time. Not too many years ago she would have been dead."

Lynn exhaled a pent-up breath, overcome by all that had happened in so little time, a modern miracle. "Recovery, you said? How long?"

"A while, at her age. She'll need to take it real easy for at least six weeks."

"I think she has a pretty good support system," Mike said.

"She does," Lynn replied. "She has lots of friends. She's that kind of person." She looked toward Karen's bed. "Can we see her?"

"Sure," Mike said. "She may not wake up, but there's no harm in standing next to her."

The four of them moved to her beside. She lay with a drip tube in one arm, an air tube in her nostrils, and even in sleep, the sign of a faint smile on her face. Lynn rested her hands on the side of the bed near her friend, and studied Karen's face. *You are such a fighter! Of course you're going to recover. I'm so grateful! But what am I going to do without you? I'm not you. I'm unprepared. I'm not strong enough. I'm scared. And I need your help. Oh my God, imagine that, asking for your help now!*

Lynn stood motionless for several minutes, finding an odd comfort in the white sterility of the room. Healing was happening here. Her own worries ebbed, and her thoughts returned to Karen and her well-being. Then she turned to leave the room. "I'll come back later," she said, and walked back to the visitors' nook. The others followed. "Father Mike, may I speak to you in private?"

"Of course." He led her out into the hallway. "What's on your mind?"

Lynn took a deep breath and steadied herself. "I may need sanctuary."

His kind face absorbed her message with no hint of judgment or surprise, putting her at ease. "For yourself?"

"No, no, for an undocumented Latina Karen knows from her work with the farmworkers organization."

"Yes, I know them—and her work—well."

She told him about Teresa and their commitments to keep her safe and help her find a decent job in the vineyards. "She can't stay in the valley as long as this guy's still here, but until we can find work for her in Mendocino or Napa, we may need some kind of sanctuary, like a church."

"I would take her in," he said.

Lynn was touched. "Thank you, but no, it's too close. What about Mendocino County?"

"Let me see," he said, his eyes wandering off down the hall. "There's Saint Mary of the Angels in Ukiah; Saint Anthony's in Mendocino; Blessed Sacrament in Elk."

Elk, of course! Lynn lit up at the mention of the village and its quaint little church, a hundred miles up the coast. "Tell me about that one, in Elk."

"That's Father Angelo. He's a good man. He'd probably take her in, but it's a tiny place."

Lynn took both of his hands in hers. "I have to tell you, Father, how uncanny this is. We were there, in Elk, just a few days ago, driving back from Philo. Teresa saw the church and asked me to stop. Father Angelo let us in so she could pray—*we*, I should say. I have a good feeling about the place. Can you talk to him for us, just in case?"

For as long as she could remember, Lynn had been a rationalist. But something else moved her now—feelings and intuition. *Yes, this is out of character, listening to my gut and my heart more than my head. But is that a bad thing? It feels right to me.* It was strange new territory, and she rather enjoyed it.

Father Mike's eyes smiled back at her. "I would be happy to speak to Father Angelo for you."

She squeezed his hands. "Oh, thank you so much. I'm so glad I met you."

"So am I." He squeezed her hands in return. "Here's my card. Call me anytime, or come and see me. I'm very interested." He opened the door, and they returned to the waiting area.

Lynn and Jessica said their goodbyes, and left.

––––––––––––

AFTER DINNER THAT EVENING WHILE HANK CLEANED UP the kitchen, Lynn and Teresa went back to the barn to close up for the night. Lynn fetched the goat from the pasture, and Teresa shooed the chickens in from the barnyard. After they closed the stall and the coop, Lynn led Teresa up the stairs to the loft, where she swung open its big west-facing door and sat cross-legged on the floor, looking out at the sun hanging just above the horizon.

"Sit down," she said, patting the floor beside her.

Teresa did, and together they watched the massive, shimmering orange sphere sink into the ocean. The open doorway pulled in cool sea air to mix with the pungent fragrance of hay. As the light faded, the birds grew quiet, and crickets filled the void, chirping; first one, then more, in their primordial courtship ritual.

"What will we do without Karen?" Teresa asked.

Lynn was wondering exactly the same thing. *I'm a schoolteacher. What do I know about hiding people from bad guys? How did I get into this?* "I don't know. Regroup, I guess." She leaned back on her arms, the breeze playing through her hair. "Jessica said I should ask you how Juan Carlos is covering up his wine stealing."

"I don't know."

"You don't know? Why did Jessica say that?"

"I guess I mean that I don't know how to tell you."

"It's okay, you can tell me."

In a voice barely audible, Teresa said, "I know how he's been doing it because I've been helping him."

Lynn sat bolt upright. "What? Why didn't you tell us? All this time!"

Teresa hung her head. "I was afraid."

"Did he make you do it?"

"Yes."

"What did he make you do?"

"I was the lookout."

"How does he do it?"

"It's simple. The tasting room takes less from the storeroom than they sign out. And he takes the difference."

"What does he do with it?"

"He sells it to a gang in Roseland, the Sureños, not far from my old apartment. They have him under their thumb. He does what they tell him to do."

Lynn's picture of Teresa's life grew darker. *A few cases of wine, a few hundred dollars a week. Why is he so desperate to capture her? There must be something more.* "Does he make you do anything else?"

Teresa said nothing. In the deepening dusk it was impossible to read her face, but Lynn sensed that Teresa was wrestling with something.

"Teresa?"

She began to cry. "He makes me collect money from the workers without papers every week, and he gives it to the Sureños."

Oh my God! I get it! "Are the Sureños smuggling these workers from Mexico?"

"They are, and these are not guys to mess with."

"How bad are they?"

"People disappear. They end up in the river. No one knows who they are. And no one talks, because they're afraid." She told Lynn the story of Hector Sanchez. "That's why I'm so afraid. Juan Carlos is looking for me because they told him to."

"How do you know that?"

"I don't, for sure. But trust me. That's the way they work."

An arc of robin's-egg blue still lit the western horizon. It brought Lynn little comfort. *I can't believe this! What the hell? Stabbings in broad*

59

daylight? Bodies dumped in the river? I didn't sign up for this. It's crazy. This is too much.

――――――――

HANK WAS READING BY THE FIREPLACE WHEN THE WOMEN returned to the house. Teresa excused herself, and started for the stairs. Lynn reached out and hugged her, offering a balm, all too insufficient for her troubles, which had taken on a new order of magnitude in the last hour. Teresa trudged up the stairs and disappeared into the sleeping loft.

"Would you join me on the porch?" she asked Hank, motioning toward the front door with her head.

"Sure."

She opened the door for him and closed it behind them.

"It's been a long day," he said, standing on the edge of the porch.

"Yeah, it has. Fortunately Karen's going to be okay, but you wouldn't believe what Teresa just told me. This mess is a lot deeper than we thought."

"What do you mean?"

"There's a gang involved—immigrant smugglers, bad characters." She explained how they were extorting money from the undocumented workers and coercing Teresa into collecting it for them. "They're after her because of what she knows. And they've sent Juan Carlos to find her."

"Whoa!" He ran his hands through his hair. "You need to get out of this now. This is way too dangerous."

"What do we do with Teresa?"

"I don't know. Maybe you've done enough by finding the sanctuary in Elk. They'll take care of her, and we can go back to our lives here." Hank stepped off the porch. The sky was black now. Stars had emerged. The crickets were in full chorus. The air was refreshingly chilly. "Do you want to take a little walk?"

Lynn followed him out the driveway to the road, where they turned right—north. "What have I gotten myself into, Hank?" she asked as they started up the hill.

"It seemed simple a few days ago, didn't it?"

"Yeah, it sure did."

They stopped at the top of the rise and sat on a grassy bluff above the road. Moonlight exposed the outlines of ridges and valleys, and threw shadows of fence posts on the pasture. A faint strip of yellow light rested on the horizon, the last remnant of day.

"Thanks for suggesting this," she said. "It's so peaceful." *It was nothing but peaceful up here a week ago.* As much as Lynn longed for that peacefulness, something in her gut told her that peacefulness was not enough. The voice was not clear, but she knew that it demanded something else—something that felt like strength and purpose.

———————

LYNN LAY AWAKE FOR HOURS, WORRYING. SHE WORRIED about Teresa and her tormenters. She worried about her own strength and resolve. And she worried about whether taking on this challenge was the right thing to do. *How many of my friends back in Atlanta would take on a gang? It would be easy to walk away. How would I feel if I did that? I promised Karen.*

The quandary still circled in her mind when she stepped out into the morning, and it failed to slow at the friendly clucking of the chickens. Soon Hank's voice began to play over them in a loop: *This is dangerous. This is dangerous. This is dangerous.*

Her chores finished, Lynn stood in the barn door wondering how to tell Teresa to find another protector.

CHAPTER 7

ALL IN

THE AROMA OF SIZZLING MEAT MET LYNN WHEN SHE stepped through the back door into the kitchen. Sunlight filled the room. Hank and Teresa were at the stove, focused on a pair of black, well-seasoned cast-iron frying pans. He held a spatula; she, a wooden spoon. A mug of steaming coffee sat on the counter by each of them.

Lynn felt her resolve melting. The woman in front of her was not an anonymous immigrant. She was a real person with a real name—Teresa—with children and grandchildren, with real problems and real fears. *I'm not ready to cut her loose. There has to be something I can do. But I'm scared to death of Juan Carlos and the gang.*

With some effort, she set aside those thoughts and brought herself back to the room. "What's cooking?" she asked as she put a basket of eggs on the table.

"Something Mexican, of course. Breakfast tacos," Teresa said. "It's my turn to do some cooking."

"You have everything you need?"

"No, but we're making do. They'll be good. Trust me!"

Lynn looked over Teresa's shoulder into the pan.

"It's the chorizo you bought—the most important ingredient." Teresa said.

"I thought you might like it. Is there anything I can do?"

Hank scooped a tortilla out of his pan and placed it on a stack of others keeping warm under a towel. "You can beat up some of those eggs."

Lynn cracked and beat eggs in a glass bowl and set them beside Teresa. She poured coffee for herself and took a seat at the table. While she watched Teresa and Hank at their work, Juan Carlos and the gang reinvaded her consciousness. *I need to know how unsafe we are up here.* "Teresa, is there anyone besides Karen who knows you're up here?"

"I don't think so. Jessica knows I'm with you, but I don't think she knows where we are. Why?"

"The gangbangers scare me. Juan Carlos scares me, but they scare me more."

"They should."

"The guy who was stabbed—Hector—is he still around?" Lynn gripped her cup as if to strangle it, and focused on Teresa.

"No, he left, went to Fresno. He wouldn't talk to you, anyway. He's too scared."

"What are you getting at, Lynn?" Hank asked.

"I'd like to know what we're dealing with."

Hank stiffened at Lynn's detective-like response. "We shouldn't be dealing with them at all! We need to stay out of this!"

"I know," Lynn said. He made sense. She put the remaining eggs back in the refrigerator. *He's right.*

"Do you know these guys, Teresa?" Hank asked.

"Not really. I know who they are. I've met them. But I never deal with them. Juan Carlos does that."

Lynn closed the refrigerator door and announced that she would be going into Santa Rosa in the early afternoon to see Karen.

HANK FOLLOWED LYNN OUT TO HER CAR PARKED IN THE shade of the big oak in front of the house. "I thought you were reconsidering this mission, Lynn," he said through her open window.

"I am, but I can't just abandon her. I need to know more. I'm hoping Karen will have some advice."

"Me, too, but in the meantime we need to get prepared. These guys are going to find us eventually."

"I know. What are you thinking?"

"I'm thinking Teresa shouldn't be left alone in the house—like today, when you're away and I'm out fixing fences. I'm going to ask George if we can move her to his place."

"Good idea."

"One more thing—I'm going to make sure that shotgun in the pantry is loaded, and I'm going to start carrying my handgun up here."

He reached through the window and kissed her. "I'm proud of you, honey, but I don't want you getting killed for your principles. Be safe."

"I will." Lynn put the car in gear and eased forward.

Hank hollered after her, "I'll be looking for another caretaking assignment while you're gone!"

"Go ahead, but I'm not ready to leave yet!" she hollered back.

AS SHE DESCENDED THE NARROW, WINDING ROADS through redwoods and fir to Cazadero and the river, Lynn wanted to feel safer. *The ranch is so remote and hard to reach.* But she knew that sooner or later, Juan Carlos *would* find them. He'd ask around. He'd follow someone. He'd get to Karen or Jessica. And the Sureños still frightened her. Shielding Teresa from *them* felt overwhelming. She had to make a decision, and she wanted Karen's input before she did. *Karen will know what to do.*

An hour and a half after leaving the ranch, she arrived at the hospital. The nurse at the ICU desk recognized her. "You're in luck. She's awake. Go on in."

Lynn waved across the unit's nerve center, and Karen waved back. She was alone, propped up in bed. The morning sun brightened the otherwise antiseptic institutional setting.

"Karen, what have you done to yourself?" Lynn said when she reached her friend's bedside.

Karen smiled broadly. "The ancestors tried to call me back home, but I wasn't ready to go."

"I can see that."

"This modern medicine is pretty strong stuff."

"Almost a miracle."

"No, it *is* a miracle," Karen replied, turning serious. "I'm very lucky—and very grateful."

"How are you feeling?"

"Sore, but it could be worse. I'm glad they don't have to carve you open anymore."

Lynn related what she had learned from Teresa in the previous twenty-four hours—the gang involvement, the smuggling and extortion of workers, the coercion of Teresa. "I'm in way over my head, Karen. I'm scared. I feel inadequate."

Karen took Lynn's hand. "You're not, dear. I wouldn't have brought Teresa to you in the first place if I thought you were."

"I appreciate that, but seriously, what can I do against a gang of thugs?"

"You don't have to go up against the gang. Let the cops do that—a gang unit. You could just point them in their direction, if you were up for it. Let's think about it."

Lynn took Karen's outstretched hand in both of hers. "Karen, I love you, but you're trying to talk me into something I really don't want to do."

"No, I'm not."

"What do you mean?"

"I mean that deep inside, I think you do."

Do I? Lynn suspected she might. That was the problem. She wished she could just be done with it, as Hank had counseled. She pulled up a chair beside the bed and sat. "What would that look like? We have Teresa's evidence, but we can't use it."

"Maybe it's time to go to Kelly at the winery, tell her what we know, ask her not to approach Juan Carlos yet, but watch him and gather her own evidence."

"What about the extortion and smuggling?"

"That's bigger. We need to get that to the police."

"You mean me?"

"Are you worried about it?"

"Of course I am. It's a big deal."

"You can do it, honey. It's not that hard. I'm sure there's some kind of gang hotline or tip line."

Lynn struggled with the direction of their conversation and its obvious endpoint—a commitment to engage the police.

"Okay, I will." *I will. Will I? Of course I will. I have to.* She didn't want anything to do with the gang, but Karen was right. *It's a tall order.* "But what about Teresa? And the other undocumented workers at the vineyard? We don't want them caught up in a police raid."

"Well, Teresa is safe with you, and we can warn the other workers. I'll talk to Lideres Campesinas. They'll know what to do."

"Are you up for that?"

"Of course I am. I still have a voice." Karen reached for a glass of water on her bedside table.

"I should go. I don't want to tire you out."

"Okay, honey, I'd love you to stay, but that's probably wise." She took another sip of water. "One more thing," she said. "See what you can learn about that stabbing."

"Teresa said the victim left, went to Fresno."

"It probably made the paper. You could talk to the reporter. Check it out."

"I will." Lynn leaned forward and kissed her friend on the cheek. "Be well. Do what the doctors tell you!"

———————

Lynn found a seat in the hospital lobby and took out her phone. She googled "man stabbed three times in Healdsburg." Up came an article in the *Press Democrat* from April, written by a Nicki Simpson. "Man stabbed in the neck, back, and arm in broad daylight in a Healdsburg shopping center. Investigation stalled because the victim would not cooperate. Police declined to identify the victim. Officers are hoping to hear from witnesses to the assault. Call Sergeant Rodriquez."

I told her I'd call. Here goes! She called the paper and asked for Ms. Simpson.

"Hello, this is Nicki."

"Hi, Nicki. My name's Lynn Peterson. I'm working with someone with an interest in your story last spring about a man stabbed in Healdsburg. Could you discuss it with me?"

"That depends. Who are you? Who is this someone? What's this for?"

"Can you keep it confidential?

"Of course."

"The someone is an undocumented vineyard worker in the valley who was raped by her supervisor. She fled to a friend of mine, a nurse at the Guerneville Clinic. The nurse brought her to me to hide her from him. It turns out the guy is connected to a sureño gang in Santa Rosa, stealing wine from the winery and extorting money from other undocumented workers."

"And how do you know that?"

"He was forcing her to collect the money, which he handed over to the gang."

"And what's the connection to my story?"

"She knows the guy who was stabbed."

"How can I corroborate your story?"

"You can talk to my friend, Karen Boyd. She's over at Santa Rosa Memorial. I'm calling from the lobby."

"What happened to her?"

"She had a heart attack the other day—probably brought on by this mess."

"I'll call her. Wait a few minutes, and I'll call you back."

Lynn put her phone down and leaned back in her chair. *Wow, Karen was right. That wasn't so hard. Maybe she'll actually be able to help us.*

Ten minutes later, Nicki called back. She suggested meeting at a Starbucks near the paper's downtown office, just a few blocks from the hospital.

"Now?" Lynn asked.

"Why not? You're here. I've got time. It's on D Street. You can't miss it. Look for the big green awning. I'm short, shoulder-length black hair, blue blouse. I'll see you in a few minutes."

Lynn found the store easily, a nook in the front corner of a Barnes and Noble bookstore in what appeared to be an old department store, spacious, with a high ceiling supported by hefty columns. Despite the uniqueness of the space, the Starbucks felt like all others in its vibe. She preferred funkier independent shops, but this would be fine. The coffee would be good.

A woman fitting Nicki's description sat with an iPad at a table by the big floor-to-ceiling front windows.

Lynn ordered and introduced herself. "Thanks for meeting with me."

"No problem. It's my job. Do you mind if I take notes?" She took a legal pad from her bag.

"No."

"And record the conversation?"

"Okay, but it's confidential for now?"

Nicki put a recorder the size of a flip phone on the table and turned it on. "Yes. Now, the worker you're protecting knows the guy who was stabbed at the strip mall in Healdsburg?"

"Yes. His name is Hector Sanchez."

"What's her name?"

"Teresa Alvarez."

"And where does she work?"

"At Valley Run Winery, just north of Mirabel Park."

"What do they know?"

"Just that she left the winery because of a personal problem there."

"Does Teresa know the gang members?"

"Yes, two guys, Rico Guerrero and Jorge Rodriguez."

"And she thinks these guys stabbed Hector Sanchez?"

"That's what she heard."

"That's the problem. The victim is an undocumented immigrant, indebted to the gang in some way, which he wouldn't reveal to the cops. The cops have a pretty good idea of who stabbed him, but they can't pin it on him. The victim was too scared to talk. I think he left the area."

"He did. And you're right. He *is* indebted to the gang, like Teresa. The gang isn't just extorting money from undocumented workers. They're bringing them up to Sonoma and then extorting them. It's barbaric, and it goes on right under the noses of the cops."

"They get away with it because no one will talk. Someone, some day, needs to talk."

Is that someone Teresa? Lynn couldn't imagine her ever doing that. She nodded.

Nicki turned off her recorder. "This is good stuff. We know about these guys, but this helps fill in the picture. You need to talk to the police gang unit. Are you up for that?"

"I don't know. It scares the hell out of me."

"I get that. So let me ask you. Why are you on this crusade?"

The memory flashed again: Her friend screaming, "It's your fault!" The decades-old accusation assaulted her, rolling and echoing in her brain like a shout in a canyon. "He'd still be alive if it weren't for you. I hope you burn in hell." *That's why. That can never happen again.*

"It's complicated. It goes way back, and I'd rather not get into it. Let's just say I couldn't live with myself if I didn't."

"Okay, then. I hear you. So, do you want to talk to the police?"

There it is again. There's no escaping it. I'm committed. "I know I do, but it's tricky. I also want to protect Teresa. How do I do that?"

"There's a Maria Sandoval in the gang unit; call her. Here's her number." Nicki pulled up Maria's number on her phone and showed it to Lynn. "She's a good cop. She'll help you. I'll let her know you'll be calling her."

"I'd appreciate that."

"At some point they'll probably want to talk to Teresa. Would she do that?"

"I don't know. I've wondered. It might be a stretch. She would need to know she'd be protected from deportation."

"I can't speak for the authorities, but they might be willing to work that out. It depends on what they have to gain. In the meantime, don't worry. Your names are safe with me."

"Thank you."

"Stay in touch, please, and let me know as soon as you learn anything else about these guys. It's a shame they're getting away with murder, to use an unfortunate expression. Could you meet me here next week, same time, say, just to touch base?"

"I can. I will." *I will. There it is again. When am I going to stop saying that?*

"Good. You've been very helpful. I'm glad you called."

———

Lynn had every intention of driving straight back to the ranch, but when she reached the intersection in Mirabel Park where the road went north to the winery, she turned right. *Why wouldn't I talk to Kelly? She needs to know what's going on, and we need her help. Why wait?* She drove the five miles through vineyards and wooded hills, across Mark West Creek and the Russian River on narrow steel bridges, to the elegantly repurposed farm that was now Valley Run Wines.

A sign in the visitor's lot directed her to the manager's office in the big barn, where she found the door open and the handsome woman with the short, wavy dark hair, Kelly.

"May I help you?" Kelly asked.

"I hope so. Do you have a minute?"

"What's on your mind?" she asked, motioning to a chair beside her desk.

Lynn sat down. "I'm a friend of Karen Boyd's."

"How is Karen?"

"Not well, but improving." Lynn told Kelly of Karen's heart attack and explained that she had just come from the hospital. "We have something we need to tell you."

"About Teresa?"

"Yes, partly, and it's delicate. We're hoping you'll work with us."

"That depends."

"Teresa is undocumented, and someone here has been taking advantage of that."

Kelly's eyebrows lifted. "Oh?"

Lynn screwed up her courage. *Here we go. I'm going out on a limb here. Please, God, convince her not to saw it off.* "This is where I hope you'll work with us. Teresa left here because one of your supervisors, Juan Carlos, raped her."

"That bastard. I had a feeling. How is she?"

"She's recovering, but she's scared, like me."

"And she didn't report him because she's undocumented."

"Right."

"And how do you want me to work with you?"

"You need to know he's stealing wine from the tasting room and selling it to a gang in Roseland."

"That son of a bitch."

"He's been forcing Teresa to help him. Now he's trying to find her. We want to get him to back off by threatening to out him, hopefully convince him to leave the area. But we know the minute we report him, he'll report her to ICE."

"Where's Teresa now?"

"She's staying with me. We haven't found her a job yet, but think we've found sanctuary. We're hoping you can hold off on approaching him until we're ready to move."

"I can't promise you that. You've just told me I have a thief and a rapist here. I need to investigate this, and as soon as I can prove it, I'm going after him."

"I understand."

"How's he doing this?"

Lynn explained his method: signing out a certain amount of wine from the warehouse and delivering less to the tasting room.

"Sloppy bookkeeping. I'm not too worried about the wine. He's not going to break us, but I sure don't like hearing the word 'gang' in the same sentence as 'Valley Run.' The sooner he's out of here, the better."

Should I tell her about the extortion? Rico has his fingers in her business. I have to. "About the gang—they're extorting money from the undocumented workers in your vineyard."

"What? What do you mean?"

"Juan Carlos was forcing Teresa to collect protection money from them. Then he passed it along to the gang."

"Teresa told you this?"

"Yes."

"Well, that ends the day I fire him. All the more reason to get him out of here."

"I understand. Will you let me know when you confront him? We need to know when they're coming after us."

"Yes, I can do that. What's your number?"

Lynn dialed Kelly's number, and each added the other to her contact list. "Thank you so much, Kelly."

At the other end of the barn by the fermentation vats, Juan Carlos watched Lynn emerge from Kelly's office. He had seen her arrive in her black Prius, the woman who'd left the coffee shop with Jessica the day before. He *had* been willing to wait in his truck all day—not for Karen; he had seen her wheeled into the ambulance early in the morning. No, he had waited to see this woman who was hiding Teresa from him, for, when Karen texted Lynn and Jessica, asking them to meet her at the coffee shop, Jessica had called him.

He hurried to his truck, reaching it in time to see her turning left at the winery entrance, toward Mirabel Park. He followed.

———————

A HALF MILE BEYOND MIRABEL PARK, LYNN TURNED OFF River Road at the entrance to Steelhead Beach Regional Park. She parked, and followed a path to the river. Juan Carlos found an inconspicuous spot to park, and waited in his truck.

The river was low, as it always is at the end of the summer. The beach was a sandbar on the inside of a sharp bend in the river, where water didn't move fast enough to hold its sediment.

She took off her shoes and scrunched through the sand to the water's edge. Pant legs rolled up, she waded into the warm green water. She closed her eyes. The current pulled her worries from her, and its quiet rippling and moist fragrance soothed her.

What have I done today? Have I gone crazy? Gone past the point of no return? It doesn't feel that way. I told Hank I wanted Karen's advice. I got it. It was good. I talked to a reporter. No harm done. I talked to Kelly. Had to do that. I did what I needed to do. I'm okay with all of it.

Hank may well have looked for a new caretaking gig while she was gone, but Lynn still wasn't ready to leave. She had moved forward, and it felt good. For just a moment she let herself think she was capable and strong, after all.

From the parking lot she texted Hank, *Picking up Mexican take-out. No need to cook.*

———————

THE SUN HAD SET BY THE TIME LYNN REACHED RIO BRAVO, the Mexican restaurant on the west side of town, across the road from the river. The place was in full swing. Why wouldn't it be? This was a popular spot. It was Saturday night. And it was happy hour. The tables were filled, inside and out. Thirsty customers stood two deep at the bar.

She and Hank had become regulars. They were comfortable here. Lynn knew the take-out routine. She walked to the near end of the bar, placed her order—three carnitas tacos, three fish tacos, chicken enchiladas, and three margaritas—and leaned against the bar, letting the atmosphere relieve her tension. Mariachi music and raucous laughter reverberated off the dark pine-paneled walls. The logos of Mexican cervezas glowed red, blue, and yellow behind the bar. Steak and chicken, peppers and onions, sizzled on the trays of passing waiters, filling the air with the appetite-teasing aroma of fajitas.

From where she stood, she could see the front door. It opened, and through it walked a muscular young Latino. He looked her way and started toward her. It was Juan Carlos, her adversary, the rapist. *Oh my God. It's him. What's he doing here? He can't hurt me here. I know he can't hurt me here.* But nonetheless, her heart raced, her breath shortened, her focus drifted. She struggled to retrieve her anxious thoughts. *What do I do?*

She had not seen him since that day when she'd driven Teresa by the winery on their way to Roseland—and that was at a distance. But this man was clearly him. He strutted, his chest out, head held high.

"We need to talk," he said when he reached her.

"I don't know you. You must be mistaken." She hoped he was mistaken. If he wasn't, maybe she could convince him he was.

"No, I'm not. You know who I am. Come with me, and don't make a scene. I can make your life miserable."

He clamped a big hand on her waist and squeezed. She looked around in panic for a witness, someone who could confirm her distress. He glared at her.

Yes, he can make my life miserable. "Okay, where?"

"The other end of the bar, where those people are getting up from that table. Don't make a scene."

Lynn squeezed through the bar crowd to the table, with Juan Carlos right behind her. "What do you want?" she asked.

Beneath his show of bravado, he looked nervous, uncomfortable. Perspiration beaded on his temples. His eyes darted around the room. "You know. I want Teresa, and I know she's with you. You can make this easy, or you can make this hard."

A waitress came by, smiled at Lynn, and asked if they wanted drinks.

"Not yet," he said politely.

"I can come back in a few minutes."

"That would be good."

He moved incessantly, shifting in his seat, looking left and right, over his shoulder, as though sensing a threat—the police, an enemy—and searching for a way out. "Hand her over to me and this will all be over for you. You can go back to your life. Just tell me where. Here, anywhere."

Without turning her head, Lynn snuck a peek toward the bar. The bartender had seen them move. She made eye contact. Then Lynn summoned her innermost strength. When she felt it rising in her, she said, "I know your little winery scheme. I've got witnesses, and I've got proof, and I'll turn you in so fast you won't know what hit you if you don't back off and leave Teresa alone."

Her words shook him. He struggled to gather himself.

The waitress came by again. "Can I get you anything?" she asked.

Flustered, he stammered, "No, I, I don't think so. I'm, uh, not staying."

Lynn wasn't surprised when he said to her, "You do that, and I'll call ICE. You know I will."

She remained strong, knowing she had the upper hand now. Adrenaline surged through her veins. She was fully alive, every nerve ending tuned to the task of the present moment. She was on high alert. "Your game is over," she said. "All you have to do is agree to leave her alone."

He leaned back in his chair and put his grape-stained hands on the table. "I'll think about it."

Lynn's confidence was growing. "One more thing," she said. "Quietly resign from the winery and agree to leave Teresa alone, and this whole thing will go away. But keep it up, and you're finished."

Juan Carlos stood up to leave. "I'll think about it."

She stood, facing him squarely across the table, pushing back at the angry brown eyes boring into her. "You'd better," she said.

As Juan Carlos disappeared through the door, Lynn slid through the crowd to a window at the front of the restaurant. She watched as his white truck backed out onto River Road and headed east toward the center of town and Santa Rosa. Relieved, she wound her way back to the bar and slumped against it, exhaling as she had never exhaled before, a long, slow, release of tension and fear. She had stood up to the bastard in a way she had never imagined. But the ordeal had exhausted her.

"Are you okay?" the bartender asked when he'd worked his way down to her.

"I think so."

"That guy was giving you a hard time? He looked like a creep."

"Yeah, and he is a creep—worse."

"Just let me know next time. You don't have to put up with that shit in here."

"I will."

He mixed a margarita and put it in front of her. "Here, this is on me. You look like you could use it."

"I could. Thanks." There was an empty stool next to her. She settled onto it and tasted the margarita. It was perfect. *Yes, I needed this, and I couldn't leave now if I wanted to. I need to get my feet back under me.*

The bartender brought her take-out order. Lynn worked on her drink and continued to breathe, bringing herself back to earth.

A𝐬 𝐬𝐨𝐨𝐧 𝐚𝐬 𝐡𝐞'𝐝 𝐠𝐨𝐭𝐭𝐞𝐧 𝐨𝐮𝐭 𝐨𝐟 𝐬𝐢𝐠𝐡𝐭, J𝐮𝐚𝐧 C𝐚𝐫𝐥𝐨𝐬 turned around and returned to the restaurant, parking across River Road, far enough away to avoid detection, but close enough to see the front door. Lynn had thrown him off balance with her bold move, but he wasn't about to back off. His prey was dangling in front of him. He had to be smart now to pull it within reach. *That woman is crazy. What is she thinking? She can't report me. They know I'll turn Teresa in. They must think I'll actually go away. Maybe they'll let down their guard. I've gotta think.* He called Jessica.

"Juan Carlos?"

"I just found the bitch."

"Who?"

"Who do you think? Your friend Lynn. She thinks I'm going to back off. Where does she live?"

Jessica said nothing.

"Jessica, don't mess with me."

"I don't know."

"You'd better know. You must know something."

"I really don't."

"I'll turn you in so fast, Jessica. It's not going to help you to hold out on me."

Again, Jessica said nothing.

"Jessica, this is not going to end well."

"Please, Juan Carlos. She never told me where she lives."

"She must have told you something, some little thing. Think! I don't have much time."

The line was silent.

"Jessica!"

Finally she began to speak, in a voice weak and soft.

"Jessica, speak up!"

"Yesterday at the coffee shop she said that she always forgets how long it takes to get down to Guerneville from the ranch."

"That's it?"

"Yes, I'm sorry."

"You'll have to do better."

"I can't."

"Ask your friend."

"She'll ask me why."

"Make something up."

"Maybe you should just forget it, Juan Carlos. You know she'll turn you in."

"That's the least of my worries right now. I've got my reasons." He pulled his phone down from his ear, then raised it back. "Call me tomorrow with some better information."

He hung up and leaned back in his seat. Rico's menacing voice reminded him that he didn't have much time. It didn't matter that Lynn might turn him in. Worse, was his fate at Rico's hands. The wash of river water against its bank below him raised the horrifying image of a body floating face down in it—his. *I have to figure this out—now.*

While he'd been talking, the sun had set behind the ridge to the west. The valley darkness grew. He would exercise the only option he had left: to follow her when she left the restaurant. Juan Carlos sat in his car, his eyes on the restaurant door, prepared to wait as long as it took. *The longer she takes, the darker it will be. Take your time.*

It wasn't long before the door opened and Lynn appeared under the entrance light. She climbed in her car and headed west on River Road toward Jenner. Juan Carlos eased out onto the road and followed, close enough not to lose her, but far enough behind to avoid suspicion. He lost sight of her briefly on the tighter turns along the river, but managed not to lose total contact. Ten minutes later, he had the Prius in sight when Lynn turned right on Cazadero Highway. He slowed and followed.

Another ten minutes brought them to Cazadero. Lynn slowed at the general store, and Juan Carlos dropped further back, but not so far as to miss her turning right on Mountaintop Road at the far end of the village.

This stretch would be trickier for him, as it offered more diverging options. Numerous roads branched off, up a steep grade or into a narrow valley. Several times he was sure he had lost her. But at an intersection five miles north of the village, where a road went off to the right along the creek, he saw the Prius slowing around a tight hairpin turn on Mountaintop Road above him. He had no doubt it was Lynn.

She forgets how long it takes to get down to Guerneville from the ranch. So it's up there! That's all I need to know. He stopped, turned around, and returned to Santa Rosa.

———————

HANK AND TERESA WERE ON THE FRONT PORCH WHEN Lynn arrived at the ranch. There was still light out over the ocean, but overhead, the sky had turned to indigo. "What took you?" Hank asked as she got out of the car.

"You're not going to believe this: Juan Carlos ambushed me at the restaurant."

"Oh my God," Teresa whispered. "Where is he now?"

"I told him we'd turn him in if he didn't back off."

"You didn't. You know he'll turn me in."

"Yeah, he will, but he was going to do it anyway. We just have to get you to Elk as soon as we can."

"You're damn right," Hank said. "We're going to lock the doors and windows in this place. I'm carrying a pistol, and that shotgun is going to be loaded." He walked into the house and came back with the shotgun. "You know how to use this thing, Lynn?"

"No, but it can't be that hard—aim and fire."

"That's right. Squeeze the trigger—and be ready for a kick."

Lynn opened the door. "Put that thing back, Hank. Let's go in and heat up this food. I'm hungry."

She walked back into the kitchen and the others followed. While she heated the food in the microwave, Teresa set the table and Hank polished the stock of the shotgun with his sleeve.

Lynn poured the margaritas into glasses, put the food on plates, and they sat down to eat.

"That just blew me away," Lynn said. "I *never* saw it coming. It was like a nightmare."

"Did he threaten you?" Teresa asked.

"Yeah, he threatened me. He grabbed me, and I saw you, Teresa, in the vineyard. And I saw myself there, too."

"So he just left?" Hank asked.

"Yeah, I guess he figured he couldn't do anything to me there."

"Where'd he go?"

"I don't know. I watched him drive back through town toward Santa Rosa."

"How did he find you?"

"I don't know. He must have followed me from the winery. He came in right behind me."

"From the winery? I thought you went to the hospital."

"I did, and I also went to the winery. And I met a newspaper reporter at Starbucks. And I had a major confrontation with Juan Carlos. It was a long day. I've never had one like it."

When they finished, Lynn cleared the table and put the dishes in the sink.

"What about the rest of your day?" Hank asked. "What did you learn?"

"I learned that Karen's going to be okay. She's tired, of course, but she's already on the mend. She's one tough cookie."

"And what was that about stopping at the winery?"

"We decided to tell Kelly about Juan Carlos," Lynn said, looking at Teresa.

"You didn't!" Teresa blurted, her face awash in horror. "He'll report me for sure."

"You're right, but we had to tell her what's going on in her winery."

"And the reporter?"

"Her name's Nicki Simpson. She wrote the article about Hector Sanchez. She thinks I should talk to the gang unit about Rico Guerrero."

"Oh my God," Teresa moaned. "Oh my God. You can't do that. They'll kill you. They'll kill me. Please don't do that. You didn't do that, did you?"

"No, I didn't, but I might. She gave me the name of a detective."

"This was Karen's idea?" Hank asked.

"It was, and it was good advice."

"It doesn't sound like you're backing off."

"No, it doesn't."

Hank made the rounds of the little house, locking windows and doors. Then he opened the pantry door and put the shotgun behind it. "Do you see where I'm putting the shotgun, honey?"

"I do."

"Good. Just remember it's loaded."

ON ANY OTHER NIGHT, THE BREEZE PLAYING IN THE branches above the house would have lulled Lynn to sleep. The curtains fluttered at the open window. She pulled the blanket up to her chin and pulled it close. Questions begged her for answers. *Where is this leading? Do I want to go there?* Scenarios formed in her brain and played themselves out long into the night: What if this? What if that? This was her way. Sleep waited while her mind worked.

Hank lay unconscious beside her, breathing in the slow, rhythmic pattern of one deep in sleep.

She loved him now more than ever. He was her loving rock, her steadfast supporter and defender, her champion. *Could I do this without him?* Now he counseled caution. She respected that, but something was stirring deep inside her, calling her, demanding, almost, that she claim her own strength and agency. That image flashed again: a desperate young man, waiting in vain for her to pick him up and drive him across the border into Ontario. And then again, it was gone.

She slid from beneath the covers, stepped into her slippers, and walked out the back door into the night.

A dome of light to the southeast marked the location of Santa Rosa, but in every other direction, the sky was black and the stars brilliant. *How quiet.* There was no sound but that of wind in the trees. The world slept. She stood in awe of this cathedral of the night. She marveled that this awe never diminished. *I love how this never gets old.*

Cosmic power streaming through the unfathomable vastness of space filled her. The energy of the wind and stars around and above bolstered the strength and resolve growing within her. The confidence she had felt on the beach that afternoon returned. She knew what she had to do. She felt anointed by the night.

CHAPTER 8

JUAN CARLOS MAKES HIS MOVE

HANK LAY ON HIS SIDE, ADMIRING HIS WIFE IN THE PRE-
dawn twilight. After thirty-five years of sharing a bed, he still delighted in her sleeping visage; her delicate eyebrows, the perfect slope of her nose, her silky, ungroomed hair seeking its own course on the pillow. She stirred. *Funny how she seems to know I'm looking at her, even in her sleep.* "You awake?"

"Mmm." She rolled toward him and cracked open an eye.

"You awake?"

"Yeah."

"I'm going down to Guerneville this morning."

"Why?"

"I need to talk with Father Mike."

"Why can't you call him?"

"It's Sunday. He'll be busy with mass."

"Then why go?"

"Because I know he'll be there. I'll talk to him when it's over."

"Oh, okay."

"And I need ammo."

"Ammo?"

"Yeah, bullets for the pistol. Not much good without them."

"You're serious."

"Yeah, I am. This *is* serious."

"When are you leaving?"

"Now." Hank climbed out of bed and pulled on jeans and his blue work shirt. He flipped on the light in the bathroom, splashed water on his face, and brushed his teeth.

"I'll be back as soon as I can!" he called from the front door.

"Good, it won't be soon enough." Lynn closed her eyes, surrendering to a lingering weariness.

TERESA WAS AT THE KITCHEN COUNTER, WATCHING THE road, when Lynn emerged from the bedroom.

"Worried about him?" she asked.

"Juan Carlos? Yeah, and ICE," Teresa replied without turning away from the window.

"Me, too, but you'll be long gone by the time anyone gets here."

"I hope so." Teresa wiped her eyes.

Has she been crying? "What is it?"

"It's everything." Tears came. Her shoulders rose and fell. "It's that night. I feel helpless, used, like a rag, something you throw out because it's dirty and useless. I used to be happy. But he stole my happiness. And he's still out there, chasing me."

Lynn hugged Teresa and pulled her close. "I won't let him hurt you. Believe me."

"I know."

Lynn poured coffee for the two of them and set the pot back on the counter. She wet a sponge and wiped down the range. Sunlight streaming through the window above the sink warmed her face. She closed her eyes, savoring its touch, then turned to face Teresa. "Hank will be talking with Father Mike this morning. Hopefully he'll have good news for us. We should get you packed and ready to go."

Lynn's confrontation with Juan Carlos had escalated the urgency. What before had been only a possibility, was now an imminent reality. Someone would be coming for Teresa. The ranch simply was no longer safe.

"I think we should look for work again in Philo and Boonville—once we get you to Elk."

"I do, too."

Gravel crunched on the driveway. *That must be George.* His coming to the house was a little odd. When he came to Bella Vista he usually went straight to the equipment barn.

Feet clomped on the front porch. The front door swung open. Teresa screamed and bolted for the back door. Her chair clattered to the floor. A man raced through the main room—Juan Carlos. He leaped over the chair.

Instinctively, Lynn stepped into his path. He plowed into her, knocking her off her feet. She fell backwards, and crashed head first into the counter. *Ahhhh!* She got to her feet, reached behind the pantry door, and grabbed the double-barreled shotgun leaning in the corner. She'd been skeptical of the need for it, but hadn't pushed back when Hank insisted she keep it there, loaded.

From the back door she saw Juan Carlos tug at the barn door, rip it out of Teresa's hands, and step through. She called George. There was no answer. As she ran toward the barn, the sounds of terror grew louder—the screams of a woman, the bleating of a goat, the squawking of chickens.

Reaching the open door, Lynn peered into the cool, cave-like darkness to see two figures at the far end of the barn, like shadows, Juan

Carlos stalking Teresa, backing her into a corner. Teresa held something in front of her. *A pitchfork! Good!*

Lynn crept closer. Teresa jabbed the pitchfork toward Juan Carlos. He lunged for it. She stabbed his arm.

"Damn you, bitch," he growled. "You're coming with me. That's for sure."

"Like hell I will." Teresa screamed, "Lynnnnnn!"

"That's not gonna help you."

Teresa jabbed at him and screamed again.

"Goddamn you." He tore the fork out of her hand and grabbed her arm.

She pulled away.

He threw an arm around her and slammed her against the wall.

Lynn was close enough to see the fear on Teresa's face. The barn reeked of it. Aggression and fear had overwhelmed the rich, earthy aromas of hay and chicken manure and old wood.

Lynn raised the shotgun to her shoulder. "That's enough. Let her go." She tried to sound in control. The shotgun was such an alien object to her; it offered little comfort. But for the time being, it did offer her control.

Teresa's eyes grew wide.

Juan Carlos wheeled around, holding Teresa against the wall with one arm.

"I'll shoot."

"Sure you will," he snarled, mocking her.

She did. Aiming above his head, she squeezed the trigger. A blast erupted from the shotgun, a sound she never had heard. Birdshot splattered against the wall with an emphatic thwack.

Juan Carlos let go of Teresa, who remained glued to the wall. He took a step toward Lynn.

Oh my God, I have to shoot him.

Another step.

I don't want to shoot him. I can't shoot him. Her heart accelerated, running out of control. She struggled for air.

"You can't shoot me." His words sounded distant and disconnected. *He's right, I can't.*

He leapt at her legs like a linebacker tackling a breakaway runner. Upended, she pulled the trigger, and the shotgun roared again, peppering the roof. The gun flew from her hands. Juan Carlos scrambled to his feet in time to stop Teresa as she tried to run by him. He dragged her toward the door.

Lynn lay bruised on the hard barn floor in despair and defeat. Karen and Teresa had trusted her. Again, she saw the young sanctuary-seeking soldier being hauled away by military police. *Not again! I swore I would never let this happen again.*

A deep male voice bellowed from the front of the barn. "Stop. Right. There. You'll wish you left before I showed up, you son of a bitch."

Lynn rolled onto her knees and looked toward the voice. Juan Carlos had frozen. The silhouette of a tall man loomed in the doorway against the bright light of morning and stepped into the barn. It was George, holding a shotgun.

Juan Carlos dropped Teresa's arm. She shrank away.

George took two steps toward Juan Carlos, and with the shotgun still in his hands, smashed the butt of the gun against his jaw.

Juan Carlos slumped to the floor. In the dim light of the barn, Lynn saw blood trickling from between his lips. He groaned. George stood over him and pulled back the butt of the shotgun again. Juan Carlos pleaded for mercy with his eyes.

"Don't, George!" Lynn cried. "You'll kill him."

George stood up.

"He deserves it, but we'll get him in other ways," she said, rising to her feet. "We've got the goods on him."

She followed as George shoved Juan Carlos toward the door and kept the shotgun trained on him as he stumbled across the barnyard toward his truck, his hair disheveled, straw clinging to the back of his shirt, trails of blood dripping down his arm where Teresa had stabbed him with the pitchfork.

When the roar of his engine faded down the ridge, Lynn became aware of another sound behind them in the barn, a human sound, a plaintive sob.

Inside, Teresa sat slumped against the wall of the goat stall, her head hanging from her shoulders, shaking with the rhythm of her tears. Lynn slid down beside her, wrapped an arm around her shoulders, and squeezed with a mother's tenderness. "He's gone. Don't worry. He won't be back."

"I know," Teresa muttered through her sobs. "But ICE will."

Lynn lifted Teresa to her feet and led her to the door.

George followed. As they stepped out into the sun, he placed a hand on Lynn's shoulder. "You okay?"

She turned to acknowledge him. "Yeah, I think so. Just feeling like an idiot."

"Don't. You never had to train a gun on nobody before."

"I know."

"Well, that son of a bitch sure won't be coming around here again."

"Yeah." *But Teresa is right. Now ICE will come.*

Lynn wanted to feel good about the way the morning had turned out, about Juan Carlos getting what he deserved. But she knew they were in for more, for worse, and she had no idea how to deal with it. *Oh, I wish Karen were here now.* Even the azure sky and the dry, cool air of a late summer Sonoma morning could not raise her spirits. Absentmindedly, she brushed herself off. Her chamois shirt, the one that had become perfect in its old age, the one that caressed her skin like a kid glove, her favorite chamois shirt, was smudged and torn. The morning breeze snuck through a large rip on the left elbow. A white-crowned sparrow sang from a bush by the back corner of the house. Even it could not cheer her. She felt the way the shirt looked—bruised and beaten. And she could see no way ahead.

———————

GEORGE LED LYNN AND TERESA TO THE HOUSE AND SAT them down at the kitchen table. "Let's get you cleaned up and make a damage assessment." Both were dirty, bruised, and shaken. "Any cuts? Anything broken?"

"I don't think so," Lynn said. "Just sore."

Teresa nodded wearily. "Me, too."

Like a doting mother, George offered them ice water. "Would you like anything else?"

"No, this is fine. You're sweet," Lynn replied.

"Go ahead and get cleaned up. You'll feel better."

Lynn motioned to the bathroom. "Go ahead, Teresa."

Teresa accepted the invitation, washed up, and brushed herself off. Lynn followed. And when they were all back at the table, George opened the subject of next steps.

"This is what we were worried about. Now what?"

"We're taking Teresa to the Catholic church in Elk," Lynn said.

"Have you talked to them?"

"No, but Father Mike at the Guerneville church told me he would do that for us."

"And where does that stand?"

"Hank is in Guerneville talking to him right now."

"Okay, that's good, but I think we should move you and your car to my place, Teresa. I don't think anyone is going to come up here today. The law doesn't move that fast. ICE will want to go the winery, confirm whatever Juan Carlos tells them. But we should move you right now, just to be safe."

Lynn helped Teresa pack her things, and they followed George a mile south to his place, another historic Sonoma ranch house, nearly identical to her Bella Vista cottage. George hid Teresa's car and showed her to his guest room. They put her things down and stepped outside.

"As I was saying, Teresa, you should pack your car and be ready to go," Lynn said. "We may not have much warning." She turned to George. "This would have turned out very differently if you hadn't showed up. I'll find some way to thank you." She reached up and hugged him.

"You asked me to keep an eye out, didn't you? That's all I was doing."

"It was a lot more than that. We're in your debt." She smiled, turned, and took a step toward the driveway.

"Can I give you a ride back to your place?" he asked.

"Do you need to go back?"

"No, but I'm happy to take you."

"Thanks, George, but I think I'll walk. I have some things to sort out. It'll help me get my bearings."

Lynn walked out to the road, disoriented. She had committed herself to Teresa's cause, acknowledging the danger, but she had not prepared for the reality of it. She knew that this was just the beginning, that more danger loomed. But for now she chose not to analyze or parse that danger. Instead, she let her reasoning mind go. *I can't plan this, no matter how I try to map it out.* She appealed, instead, to her intuition, putting her trust in it, hoping it would bring her the clarity she sought—and the strength and confidence she had felt a few hours earlier under the night sky.

CHAPTER 9

RETREAT AND DEFEAT

Juan Carlos sat in his truck in front of the Cazadero General Store. His jaw throbbed. He touched it. It was hot and swollen. He looked in the rearview mirror. Already, it was taking on the ugly colors of bruising—red, purple, black. The pain sharpened when he tried to move it.

Inside he asked the man behind the deli counter for ice, just enough to hold against his face.

"You okay, fella? That looks pretty bad."

"It feels pretty bad."

"I'd have that looked at."

He thanked the man for the ice, bought ibuprofen, and returned to his car. He slumped back in his seat, pondering the immediate future. *You stupid fuck! If only you hadn't gone up there!* He knew that impulsive act would change the course of his life. Events would take on their own self-propelled trajectory beyond his control. All he could manage now was damage control. *Think! What do you need to do?* He held the ice against his jaw. Condensation ran down his fingers and dripped onto his pant leg.

He might not be able to save himself, but he could save his family. The throbbing intensified. *The damn thing is probably broken.* He tried to pull his thoughts together. *What should I tell her?* He called his wife.

"Juan Carlos?"

"Olaya, listen to me carefully. I'm in trouble."

"What kind of trouble?"

He had gotten her attention. "I don't have time for that now. Just listen. Take the kids and go to your sister's in Watsonville. Today!" He knew his request sounded crazy.

"What?" Olaya asked as though it *were* crazy.

His words accelerated. "I can't explain it all now. It's about Rico. He's gonna be looking for me."

"Rico? Rico, who?" she insisted, frightened now.

"Rico Guerrero, a gangbanger in Roseland. It's serious."

"Why don't you come home and go with us?" Her question was more like a plea.

"I can't risk it, not in broad daylight. You go. I'll catch up with you."

"Juan Carlos!"

He hung up, backed out into the road, and headed south toward the river. He wished he had been able to tell Olaya in a different way, face to face, with more time. He consoled himself with the knowledge that she would be safe.

Now what? Teresa. As badly as her friends had beaten him, he couldn't imagine Rico catching her. She'd be better off detained by ICE, even deported. At the River Road junction, he pulled over on the shoulder and searched for an Immigration and Customs Enforcement number. There were several. *Should I use this phone? They'll trace it. What difference does it make? I have no secrets anymore.* He called the closest, in San Francisco.

"Enforcement. Officer Swenson," sounded the calm, confident voice of authority.

He hesitated. *Do I want to do this?*

"Enforcement."

I do. "I want to report an undocumented immigrant."

"And who are you, sir?"

"I'd rather not say."

"Then we don't have much to talk about."

What the hell. They all know. Juan Carlos gave the officer his name and address.

"And who are you reporting?"

"Her name is Teresa Alvarez."

"And what should I know about Ms. Alvarez?"

A truck roared by, rocking him and spewing road dust through the open window.

How much should I tell him? There are hundreds of undocumented grape pickers in Sonoma County. What will get his attention? No, he would tell the officer the whole story. *I'll be implicated, but I'll be implicated anyway. What do I have to lose?* It was Rico he feared most. ICE might be his salvation.

He brushed away the last of his reluctance and eased into his story. "Her name is Teresa Alvarez, and she worked at the Valley Run Winery on the Russian River, near Mirabel Park. She's on the run, at a ranch on Mountaintop Road north of Cazadero."

"That's it?"

"No. She's stealing wine and selling it to a gang in Santa Rosa. They're Sureños. And she's collecting protection money from other undocumented workers and passing it on to them."

"Sureños, huh?"

"Yeah."

"And how do you know this?"

Juan Carlos had known this question was coming, but even so, he found it hard to answer. He had reconciled himself to giving himself up by opening this conversation. But he was not prepared to seal his guilt by saying the words.

The officer was patient. "Take your time."

Juan Carlos's jaw throbbed harder. His teeth hurt. Rico hovered over him. "Okay, I know because I'm her supervisor, and I've been doing it with her."

"Ah! I see. Mr. Hernandez, give me a minute. I'll be right back with you."

That was all Juan Carlos needed to hear to melt down. His face was half crushed. His job was history. He feared for his life. He had sent his wife into panic. He began to hyperventilate.

After what had been only a couple of minutes, the officer returned. "Mr. Hernandez?"

"Yes."

"We'd like to talk with you more in person."

Juan Carlos balked at the idea, but he took it as a sign that ICE was interested in his story. "When?"

"That's not clear yet. We'll be in touch. Don't leave the area."

Again, Juan Carlos reasoned that he was better off with ICE than with Rico. "Okay."

HANK HAD NO TROUBLE FINDING THE LITTLE CHURCH, just two blocks north of Main Street on the road to Armstrong Woods. It was a simple, hundred-year-old structure built entirely of redwood, distinguished only by a low bell tower on one side, a white cross on the roof above the entrance, and ornamental white trim on the gables and portico. The sun had just risen above the redwoods behind the church. It was a few minutes after nine. Mass had begun. He found a place to park on the street beside the fire station and waited.

At ten, the dark wooden doors opened. A silver-haired priest appeared, as Lynn had described Father Mike. Congregants filed out, pausing to greet him and shake his hand. When it seemed the last had left the church, Hank ascended the stairs and approached the priest. "Father Mike?"

"Yes."

"I'm Hank Peterson, Lynn's husband. I'd like to speak with you."

"Of course. Come in." Father Mike ushered him into the sanctuary and offered him a seat in the last row of austere straight-backed pews.

"We were wondering if you'd had a chance to speak with Father Angelo in Elk. Things are moving. We're getting nervous."

Mike listened attentively. Hank felt the same comfort in his presence that Lynn had a few days earlier.

Mike beamed. "I have, and I have good news. Father Angelo tells me his congregation is concerned about the plight of immigrants and wants to help."

A flash flood of relief washed away Hank's anxiety. He wanted to support his wife, but she had gotten out ahead of him, taking risks for which he was not prepared. Father Angelo's invitation might bring their lives back to normal. "Oh, that's great! Thank you so much!"

"No, son, thank you. And bless you for your work. Blessed are those who hunger and thirst after righteousness."

"I'm not sure what that means, but I don't feel righteous."

Father Mike smiled again. "That's a pretty good sign that you are."

Hank rose to leave. "How do we proceed?

"Call Father Angelo. The church probably isn't ready for her yet, but that's all right. Sanctuary isn't about being ready, having all one's ducks in a row. It's a response from the heart to a pressing need. Don't worry."

HANK HAD REACHED THE RIDGETOP. HE WAS FEELING good, looking forward to giving Lynn and Teresa the news, when he saw the figure walking far off down the road. A pedestrian was an odd sight here. It was a perfect day for a walk—warm, but not hot, clear, and breezy—and it was a beautiful byway, of course. But it was a long way from town, and dwellings were few and far between, so Hank was surprised to see someone out there, striding with purpose, swinging her arms, holding her head high. He knew who it was. He had lived with Lynn long enough to identify her simply from her bearing, no distinguishing marks necessary. It was as if she emitted an aura only he could see, by virtue of their long relationship.

"Fancy meeting you here," he said as he slowed to a stop.

Lynn stepped to the car. Through the open window, she threw an arm around his shoulders and burrowed her face against his neck. Silent tears grew to chest-heaving sobs.

Hank placed a hand on her shoulder and let her cry. Her sobbing ebbed. She took a few deep breaths, and he spoke. "What happened, honey?"

"I'll tell you when we get back to the house. Let me get myself together." She walked around to the passenger's side of the car and got in.

Back in the kitchen, she told the whole story. "Hank, it was awful. I don't know what I was expecting, but nothing that horrible. I fired a *shotgun* at him and couldn't stop him! Thank God George showed up!"

"And he was there because you talked to him. Give yourself some credit." Then regretfully, he stated the obvious. "I told you this was dangerous."

"Hank! Come on! That's not helpful. Of course I knew it was dangerous. Let's focus on what we do next." She sank into a chair at the kitchen table.

Hank stood behind her and rubbed her shoulders as she leaned her head back against his arms and breathed, pulling in the air of safety.

He walked around the table, and sat opposite her, engaging her eyes in love and admiration.

They planned. Lynn would call Father Angelo. They would make sure Teresa was ready to leave. And they would take her to Elk as soon as the church was ready for them.

"What do we do about ICE?" Lynn asked. "You know they're coming."

"Yeah. We'll tell them she left."

"And what if they come before she's gone?"

"George will save us again. They'll never check his place."

LYNN WALKED OUT THE BACK DOOR INTO THE GLORY OF late summer, an unlikely setting for the drama of the morning. Fear dogged her—fear of Juan Carlos, who was still out there, fear of ICE, and fear of the gang. *If they didn't know where we are by now, they will soon.* Planning the next step had been helpful, but it could not erase her anxiety.

The barn door was open. Reluctantly she stepped through. The only signs of struggle were a pitchfork lying askew on the floor and a few indistinct drops of blood. But the event played vividly on the screen of her memory—in technicolor and full stereophonic sound—and with it, the attendant trauma. The comfort of the space had vanished.

The breeze blowing through the open doors nudged her out into the back pasture, where she climbed to the top of a knoll and sat in the majesty of the top of the world. She longed for Karen's wise counsel. *What would she tell me? Would she blame me if I delivered Teresa to Father Angelo and moved on?*

She called Karen's cellphone. It went to voicemail. She called the hospital and asked for her. A nurse answered. "Hello, this is Lynn Peterson. May I speak to Karen Boyd?"

"I'm sorry, ma'am. She's asleep. Try later in the afternoon."

What would she do? She wouldn't mess around. She'd say this thing is bigger than Teresa; she'd go after the gang. I don't know if I can do that, whatever she says. Oh, I wish she were well.

But she knew she had already taken that step—taken on the gang—when she'd met with Nicki Simpson. *I need to let her know. It's Sunday.*

She texted her. *This is Lynn Peterson with the undocumented worker, Teresa. Hernandez found us this morning, attacked us. We're okay. Neighbor beat the hell out of him. I turned him in to his boss. But he's still out there. So is the gang. I'm worried.*

The reply came quickly. *Hope you're okay. Thanks for telling me. Will talk to my contacts in the gang unit. Be safe.*

I'll try. Thanks.

Lynn was struck by the power of Karen's spirit, manifested here through the mere suggestion that she find the reporter of a months-old incident. Now, magically, Nicki Simpson was imbued with that power. And Lynn felt less alone.

Juan Carlos drove around Guerneville looking for a place he could wait until it was nightfall; someplace where he wouldn't be conspicuous, where he could sit in his truck all afternoon and not draw attention to himself. Somewhere away from town, like Armstrong Woods. The woods would be a perfect place to hide, even on a Sunday. No one would look for him there. He would park and stay until dark.

From River Road in the center of Guerneville, he turned north on Armstrong Woods Road. He passed the old wooden Catholic church; the long, low fire station across the road; the elementary school complex; a trendy spa. The trees—redwoods and Douglas fir—grew taller. The small one-story houses beneath them grew fewer and farther between until two miles from town the road ended at a wall of green—the park. He swung into the parking lot beside the gate attendant's booth, found a spot in the shade, and waited.

Watching visitors coming and going, seemingly carefree, he fantasized about a new life far from Sonoma. Surely, there was some place in the vast agricultural valleys of California where he could catch on as a supervisor of migrant and seasonal workers—the Sacramento Valley, Salinas, Fresno, Bakersfield. He knew people. They would help him. Maybe his brother-in-law in Watsonville. But what about Kelly? He could never use her as a reference. No matter. He wouldn't need it. What about ICE? Would they report him to the cops? It was all too much to contemplate. Too many ifs. And it all paled beneath the frightening image of Rico.

After an hour, he got restless. He picked up a trail map at a rustic information kiosk and walked into the deep shade of the grove, following a thin line of other visitors. The giant trees, the cool damp air, and the sunlight-dotted darkness worked their magic, soothing his physical and psychic pain. He moved along the woodland paths as though pulled by an unseen spirit—a wizard—happy to let go of any need for agency. He sat on a wooden bench beside a mammoth named redwood and watched limber reeds swaying in the current of a gravel-bottomed brook. Birds sang—thrushes. He didn't know their names, but he liked their music. Time went by. The line of visitors thinned. The light changed. He stirred, rose, and resumed his walk.

The path brought him back to the entrance and his truck. The sun was down. Within an hour it would be time to leave. Only a few cars remained in the parking lot. He called Olaya.

"Juan Carlos, where are you?"

"In Guerneville, waiting. Are you in Watsonville?""

"Yes, what are you waiting for? Aren't you coming?"

"I am, but I need to stop at the apartment first to pick up a few things. We may not be back for a while."

"Oh?"

"We can talk about it later. I'll call you when I leave Santa Rosa." He hung up and drove warily through the cover of darkness to his duplex apartment on the north side of the city. He parked and looked around. Nothing seemed out of the ordinary. He stepped from the cab and walked to the door, scanning his surroundings as he went.

Inside, he filled a duffel with clothes, retrieved his checkbook and a wad of cash from his top dresser drawer, turned off the lights, and pulled the door closed behind him, then twisted the knob to make sure it was locked.

He opened the door of the truck, tucked the duffel behind the driver's seat, and as he swung himself up behind the wheel, the passenger's door opened. A man climbed in, one hand pointing directly at him as the other closed the door. Gunmetal glinted in the dim yellow light of a streetlight down the block.

"Just drive. And don't say a fucking word." It was Jorge, Rico's compadre.

Panic rushed in. It was all Juan Carlos could do to breathe, to mutter a weak, "Where?"

"River Road."

"I can tell you where she is."

"We know where she is. Shut up and drive."

"What?"

Jorge snorted an evil laugh. "We put a GPS tracker on your truck, man. You think we're stupid?"

In minutes, they were beyond the city limits. Juan Carlos brought the truck up to speed and stared into a hellish, unfathomable darkness.

Minutes later Jorge grunted, "Turn here, right."

Juan Carlos slowed and turned. He knew the spot well. They were east of Mirabel Park, where the river turned north, on the road to Valley Run.

Jorge barked orders. "Slow down when you get to the bridge, and listen to me."

Juan Carlos slowed where the road turned west to cross the river.

"That's it. Now drive past the turn slowly, and back up under the bridge, along the bank. Wait for that car to go by."

He did as he was told. Under the bridge, his headlights lit a rutted dirt track. He inched the truck forward.

"Stop there in the trees."

Juan Carlos brought the truck to a stop and turned the engine off.

"Get out."

Escape entered his mind, even with the barrel of a gun pointed at his head. He would ease out of the truck, duck and run into the darkness. What did he have to lose? He opened the door and swung his left leg to the ground. His right leg hit the ground. *Now!*

A hand reached out of the night and clamped his left shoulder. Cold steel tickled his throat, and he felt nothing as blood poured from a massive gash below his chin. In one brief second, a razor-sharp hunting knife had severed the major highways through which life had moved within him—arteries, windpipe, esophagus. That life drained away from him and pooled on the bare ground. He felt nothing ever again.

Without a word, Rico dragged the body into dense bushes on the riverbank and threw the knife far out into the river. He took the seat Juan Carlos had vacated, and with the lights off, as Jorge stood by the road to watch for passing cars, he backed up under the bridge. When the coast was clear, Jorge climbed in, and they headed north, past Valley Run toward Healdsburg, where they turned south on the 101.

Ten minutes later, they exited the freeway on the north side of Santa Rosa. They drove a few blocks through a funky district of hot-tub outlets, emissions-testing stations, and cheap restaurants, and turned up a deserted dead-end side street where Rico had parked his car. The apartment Juan Carlos had lived in lay just a block south across an open drainage canal. They locked the doors of the truck, threw the keys in the bushes, and drove south to Roseland.

CHAPTER 10

FLIGHT TO SAFETY

At daybreak Lynn trudged to the barn and let the goat and chickens out. They shuffled and waddled happily to the barnyard, seemingly unaffected by the noise and confusion of the previous morning, unlike Lynn, for whom the barn would be forever disquieting, threatening. Within the barn's walls, Lynn had once felt like a new-born chick—warm and safe. No longer. Once mother hen, the barn was now only inanimate roof and walls.

Lynn collected eggs and climbed the worn stairs to the loft. She threw open the heavy west-facing door, inviting in the scent of the sea, and texted Kelly. *Juan Carlos found us yesterday. We fought him off, with help. The gloves are off.*

Before she reached the house her phone chirped. *Sorry! But thanks! I'm on it.*

———————

Kelly parked her aging turquoise Ford pickup behind the barn in the shade of a tall second-growth redwood—a spot all at the winery knew as hers. She had been thinking of Juan Carlos, of how or whether she would confront him. She wanted to be rid of him immediately—and with him, the danger of the gang. She didn't need cause, but she needed to know what he had been doing. She would take a deep breath, talk to Julia, her tasting room manager, compare notes, gather evidence.

She noticed the absence of his shiny white truck. It was always there when she arrived. *Maybe Lynn scared him off, did us all a favor.*

As she peered into a vat of fermenting wine and poked it with a stirring paddle, her phone rang. She answered. "Olaya?"

"Kelly, I'm so worried. Juan Carlos didn't show up last night—in Watsonville. Is he there?"

"No, he's not. Watsonville? He didn't tell me he was going to Watsonville."

"He is worried about some guys who are after him. He thought he'd be safe here at my sister's."

"Some guys?"

"Yes, a gang, Sureños from Santa Rosa, a guy named Rico."

The clomping of heavy boots on the barn's wooden floor pulled Kelly's attention away from Olaya. "There's someone here, Olaya. Let me call you back."

"I'm worried, Kelly. Call me!"

"I will."

From the open door at the far end of the barn, three men approached with intention and purpose. They were dressed alike, in uniforms of a sort—blue jackets with white lettering, blue baseball caps with a white insignia of some kind, and khaki pants. *This must be ICE.* She put down the paddle and faced her visitors, steeling herself for an interrogation that she expected to be invasive and unpleasant. *I'll bet this is about Teresa. Be cool. Be polite. Don't volunteer anything.*

Indeed, when they reached her, her suspicion was confirmed. The lettering read "Police ICE."

"We're looking for the owner."

"I'm the manager. The owner's not here. You can talk to me." She extended her hand to the apparent leader, a tall fellow with angular, Marine-like features and close-cropped blond hair. "I'm Kelly Ahearn."

"I'm Officer Swenson; Tom Swenson, Immigration and Customs Enforcement."

"What's this about?"

"We've had a complaint about a Teresa Alvarez. Does she work here?"

"She did. She quit about a week ago. May I ask who lodged the complaint?"

"Of course. A mister Juan Carlos Hernandez. Is he here?"

"He's not. I don't know where he is. His wife called a few minutes ago, looking for him, said he didn't show up last night."

The officers exchanged glances, and Officer Swenson continued. "He's not answering our calls either. Do you have his address?"

"In my office."

They walked back to her office at the other end of the barn, and Kelly retrieved his address. "Maybe he's there. His wife said he planned to meet her and the kids at her sister's place in Watsonville. But, as I said, he didn't show up there."

"Watsonville? That's a hundred and fifty miles from here." Officer Swenson glanced at his colleagues again. "A couple more questions, if you don't mind."

"Okay."

"Did you know Ms. Alvarez is undocumented?"

"No. I didn't." The interview began to feel more like the interrogation she had expected. Kelly grew uncomfortable.

"How do you check your workers' status?"

"We check their papers. We checked hers. They looked fine to us." Yes, Kelly had checked Teresa's papers, but Kelly knew she had no way of authenticating them. In fact, she really didn't care if they were authentic or not. She was happy to hire anyone with a decent reference who was willing to do the hard work of picking grapes and pruning vines.

"Okay. Did you know that she and Juan Carlos were stealing wine from you?"

She lied. "No."

"Selling it to some gang in Roseland. And did you know they were collecting money from other undocumented workers for the same gang?"

She lied again. "No, I didn't know that either."

"Well, thank you for your time, Ms. Ahearn. We'll get out of your hair." Officer Swenson shook her hand, and they left.

It occurred to Kelly that she might never see Juan Carlos again, which would be fine with her. But what of these Sureños who were extorting her workers? Would they continue without him? And how else had they infiltrated her vineyards?

By the time the black SUV reached the road, Kelly had texted Lynn. *ICE just left here; three guys, one SUV. Will check Juan Carlos's apartment first, but they're on the way. By the way, he hasn't shown up this morning.*

LYNN LEAPT TO HER FEET, KNOCKING OVER HER COFFEE. The brown liquid flowed across the table like thin molasses, and when it reached the edge, cascaded to the floor.

Damn. I don't have time for this. She mopped it up and ran to the pasture behind the barn, where Hank was repairing a fence.

I can't believe we didn't send her up to Elk yesterday. What were we thinking?

"They're on the way!" she yelled from a distance.

He looked up and waited until she got close enough to hear him. "What was that?"

"ICE is on the way! Kelly texted me. They just left the winery."

Hank dropped his tools, and he and Lynn ran back toward the house as fast as the uneven surface of the pasture would allow.

Hank probed for details. "How long ago did she call?"

"Five minutes ago."

"Then we've got an hour, maybe a little more."

At the back door, they paused to catch their breath. They had known this was coming, and they had planned for it. The task now was to set the plan in motion.

"I'll call George. You call Teresa," Hank said, still panting. He dialed. "George, where are you?"

"Right here, in the equipment barn. What do ya need?"

"It's happening! ICE is on the way. I'll be right there." Hank put his phone in his pocket and jogged to the big metal barn.

Meanwhile, Lynn had reached Teresa. "Pack your car, honey. They're on the way."

"ICE?"

"Yes, we've got time, but we need to get moving. Just pack your car. I'll be right there."

She hurried to the barn, where she found Hank and George standing just inside the doorway. George was grinning.

"What's so funny, George?" she asked.

"I've got a little plan to slow 'em down." He chuckled and pointed out into the barnyard. "I'm gonna hook that big old cattle trailer out there to my truck and take it down the road toward town. When I get into the woods, I'm gonna swing the truck around like I'm trying to turn it around in the middle of the road, and I'm gonna wait for 'em. When they get to me, I'll start working it back and forth, back and forth, 'til I get it headed back uphill. But it'll take a good fifteen minutes, maybe more, if we're lucky."

Lynn shook her head. "You didn't dream this up right now, did you?"

"Nope." George was still grinning.

"Good, get on it. I'll go check on Teresa. Hank, stay here and get ready for them. Remember, you and I need to play dumb."

———————

Lynn called Father Angelo as she walked toward her car, which was parked under the big oak, as always. His phone went to voicemail. "Father Angelo, this is Lynn Peterson in Cazadero, calling about our friend Teresa. We need your sanctuary today. The authorities are coming now. Please call me back."

At George's place, she found Teresa in front of the house, loading her car. Lynn helped, and in a matter of minutes, the job was done. Lynn found an old envelope and a pen in her glove compartment, and using the floor of the front porch as a desk, scratched out directions.

"You might be able to get these on your phone, but just in case, here they are." She pointed to the back of the envelope. "Drive five miles north on this road until it tees. There's an old metal barn on the corner. Turn left on Henson's Bridge Road, toward Point Stewart. There's a yellow sign that says something like, 'Narrow road. RVs and trailers not recommended.' Next, follow the road into the woods and up to the top of hill for about a mile, past a Buddhist Retreat Center. Descend two miles or so, and turn right on a very narrow dirt road— Simpson Ranch Road—again, toward Point Stewart. Follow it down-hill about three miles, until it ends at the Coast Highway. There's a little state park across the road, Sentinel Rock State Park. Go there and wait for my call. You got that?"

Teresa nodded. She looked like a scared kindergartner waiting for the bus on the first day of school.

"Are you okay?" Lynn asked. "You'll be fine. Call me if you get lost, if you need anything."

"Okay."

"They're going to take care of you in Elk. They're good people."

"I know."

"We'll get through this."

"I'm scared."

"I'm scared, too, but I know we're going to be okay, you and me." Lynn reached out to Teresa and hugged her. "You'd better go."

Teresa climbed into her car and closed the door, then started the engine.

"Wait in the park. I'll call you as soon as I've talked to Father Angelo. Now go."

Teresa pulled out to the road and turned north. Anxiety welled up in her as Lynn watched the car disappear over the first rise. She tried to suppress it, drive it back down, but couldn't. *Will she be okay? Of course she will. What can go wrong? We've thought of everything. Have we? That's the thing; what goes wrong is what you least expect.*

———————

GEORGE BACKED HIS OLD BRICK RED F-350 TO A TWENTY-four-foot aluminum cattle trailer, climbed out, and secured the gooseneck coupler. Then he got back in the truck, swung the rig to the road, and raced east and south, toward town, pushing the speedometer to sixty, well beyond cautious on the narrow, winding road. Within a mile, the road left the ridgetop and began its descent through the forest of tall Douglas fir, twisted orange-barked madrone, and ancient live oak.

At the first hairpin turn, he swung wide as if to head back the way he had come. But as he knew, the road was too narrow to allow that maneuver. He climbed down from the cab of the truck to better assess his position and plan his exit from it. Would it be possible to reverse his direction here?

He walked to the front of the truck, where a steep twenty-foot embankment rose above him. He had no more room to move in that direction. He walked to the back of the trailer. It was five or six feet from a precipitous drop-off. He looked over the edge, examined the distance between it and the trailer wheels, and returned to the cab.

I think I can do this. It will just take time, which is exactly what I want. He believed he had just enough room to turn around, pushing back and pulling forward repeatedly, turning the steering wheel just so. Backing a long trailer up was a skill he had learned as a boy. To the uninitiated, the process was counterintuitive; to back a trailer in a certain direction, one had to turn the wheel to the other. For George this had long since become second nature.

He sat in the cab waiting, listening for the sound of a whining engine climbing the steep mountain road. For twenty minutes, there was no such mechanical sound, only the nagging scolds of Stellar's jays, with their regal purple crests, the eerie screams of a red-tailed hawk soaring high above, and the rush of wind through leaves and branches. George slipped into contemplative appreciation of the stillness, a benefit of his occupation—until his purpose returned, pulling him back into attention to his task.

At thirty minutes, the laboring whine of a powerful engine far down the slope invaded his solitude. George focused on the coming event, practicing his lines. *I'm sorry, officer. I don't know what I was thinking. Just give me a few minutes and you'll be on your way.*

As the whine became a roar, George climbed down from the cab and walked to the back of the trailer, as though examining his predicament for the first time. He was gazing down the slope below the road, when the unmarked black SUV rounded the bend and screeched to a stop.

Officer Swenson, the driver, stepped out of the vehicle and approached George. His two colleagues followed. "What's the problem?"

"I thought I had enough room to swing around here. Got myself in a little jam." Already George was enjoying playing stupid.

"Do we need to call somebody? A wrecker?"

"No, I can do it. I just need to take it slow. You can let me know when I'm getting too close to the edge, if you don't mind."

"Sure." Officer Swenson walked to the edge, positioning himself where George could see him.

George began the tedious process of working the rig back and forth, with Swenson's earnest assistance, which he really didn't need. Several times he climbed down from the cab, pretending to reassess his situation, adding valuable minutes to the delay.

With skill, he dragged out the maneuver to the fifteen minutes he had predicted. When he finally had the rig pointed uphill, he pulled as far off the road as he could, and the SUV sped by. George waved and texted Lynn: *They're by me now. Look out.* He pulled back on the road, worrying about her readiness to deal with them.

Teresa glanced at Lynn's directions on the seat beside her. They were little comfort. She was leaving a strange new place for even stranger territory, without a guide. She peeked in her rearview mirror. It made no logical sense to think she might see ICE coming up the road. There was no way they could arrive in less than an hour, but her fear overpowered logic. Gripping the wheel with both hands, she raced along the open ridgetop, taking the tight curves on the narrow road like a Formula 1 driver. Herds of black cows hugged the fences, heads to the ground, tails swishing. Their peacefulness seemed cruel, magnifying her stress.

At the tin barn, she checked her directions, sneaking a peek over her shoulder. No, ICE was not there. But they would be. Of that, she was sure.

She turned left. The road narrowed further, as the bright yellow sign had warned. She entered the forest, then crested a hill at the

Buddhist Retreat Center. It was gated. Teresa thought it odd. *Such a place should welcome people, not shut them out.* She descended for several miles, worrying about the next turn. *What if I miss it? Then what? What will happen to Lynn when ICE arrives? She can't help me then. I feel so alone.*

Simpson Ranch Road appeared to the right—the northwest—as Lynn had written. She turned. It was a dirt track just wide enough for one vehicle; steep and twisting. The four-mile drop to the coast would take her a full twenty minutes. It was a wild passage through dense thickets of rhododendron, madrone, and redwood. The unknown crowded in, threatening to swallow her. Strange birds called. She concentrated on the road and the reassuring rumble of tires that signified progress toward safety. She held fast to her trust in Lynn's guidance.

The road leveled, the sky lightened, and she reached the Coast Highway. There was a sign for the state park fifty yards to the left.

Oh my God. Thank you. Thank you.

She followed the entrance road to the end, and parked. A trail led toward the water. She followed it and collapsed on a grassy bluff high above the ocean.

LYNN AND HANK ERASED ALL TRACES OF TERESA'S PRESence. Short of fingerprints and DNA evidence—a stray hair, perhaps—there was nothing in the house to suggest she had ever been there.

Hank picked up his fence-mending chore where he had left off, and Lynn went to the vegetable garden to weed and hoe. Wheels crunched on gravel. Car doors thudded. She looked up to see the three ICE men on the porch, one knocking on the door, the other two peering through the front windows.

She froze in fright, like a new actor on a big stage. She breathed and straightened her shoulders. *This is it. You can do this.* Her well-practiced lines returned.

She approached the men, feigning confidence. "May I help you?"

Officer Swenson took the lead. "Are you Ms. Peterson?"

"I am."

"Is Mr. Peterson here?"

"He is, in the pasture behind the barn. Shall I get him?"

"No, that's not necessary. We'll do that."

Lynn gestured toward the barn, and the other two officers went off to fetch Hank.

"May I ask what this is about?"

"Let's wait until your husband gets here."

When he appeared in tow, Hank asked the same question.

"Let's not play that game. I think you know why we're here," Office Swenson said.

"And what is that?" Lynn asked.

"We have reason to believe that you have been harboring an illegal immigrant, one Teresa Alvarez, and we are here to detain her."

"She's not here."

"We have a warrant to search the property."

"It's not ours."

"We know."

Lynn motioned toward the door. "Go ahead. You'll find she's not here."

They swept through the tiny house like a SWAT team, combing it in minutes.

Outside, they got down on their hands and knees and checked the crawl space with flashlights.

They searched the barn, poking through the hayloft with a pitchfork. They checked the equipment barn, where George might have been on a normal morning. But he had taken the cattle trailer back to his place and stayed there to avoid suspicion. It didn't take them long to determine that Teresa was not there either.

"We know that she was here as recently as yesterday morning."

"And you know that, because?"

"Because we have an eye witness."

"Well, if she was, she's not here now," Lynn said.

"We see, but now we have more questions. You'll need to come with us."

Since Teresa's arrival at Bella Vista, Lynn's focus had been to protect her from Juan Carlos and ICE. She had not considered—or perhaps she had suppressed—the threat that ICE also posed to her and Hank. Eye to eye with them now, her vulnerability became obvious. She resumed the role of the innocent.

"On what grounds?"

"Knowingly concealing, harboring, or shielding from detection an alien. Teresa Alvarez is an alien."

"You have no proof that she was here, other than the word of a thug."

"Whether we do or not, you'll be coming with us. Ms. Peterson, you ride with me. Mr. Peterson, my two associates will ride with you in your car. Follow me."

"Where are we going?" Hank asked.

"Santa Rosa."

———

THE RED LATE-MODEL CAMARO GROWLED LIKE A MOUN-tain lion, its nose low, haunches high, as it climbed through the curves of Mountaintop Road. Rico was out of his element here in the outback of Sonoma County. He was a city boy with city ways. No interest or need had ever brought him to any part of Cazadero, let alone its remote highlands. But the one who knew enough to make his life miserable could not escape him here. The snaking blue line on his phone led him closer to her with every turn of the road.

Jorge tapped his foot to the beat of the music competing with the roar of the engine. "We've got her now, boss."

Rico slowed at the crest of the ridge, jolted by a strange new world of light and grass that lay on the dark, mysterious forest below like a shock of golden hair. He inflated himself for the coming assault, a snake coiling to strike.

Bella Vista appeared on the back side of a gentle rise in the road a mile beyond the Nicholson ranch. Jorge nudged Rico, as two uniformed men stepped into a black SUV that was parked in front of the caretaker's cottage, and the SUV began to move toward the road.

"Shit. It's the feds. Keep going."

To avoid suspicion, Rico brought the Camaro back up to speed. The SUV stopped at the end of the drive to let them pass, and as they did, both he and Jorge peered at it. Dark window tinting hid its occupants.

"Damn." Rico slammed the palm of his right hand against the steering wheel. "Motherfucker." He couldn't know for sure whether ICE had apprehended Teresa, but it was a safe bet. She had been at the ranch the day before.

Jorge voiced what they were both wondering. "Do you think they have her?"

"Probably, she was here yesterday. Where would she have gone?"

"Maybe somebody tipped them off?"

"Who?"

"If they have her, we're fucked."

"No shit. Let's get the hell out of here, back to town, and lay low."

He sped up and turned left at the tin barn, but stopped at the intersection with the narrow, unpaved Simpson Ranch Road.

"What are you doing, boss?"

"Checking the GPS." Rico pointed to the right. "It looks like that's the quickest way to the Coast Highway."

––––––––––

LYNN FRETTED FOR THE ENTIRE NINETY-MINUTE TRIP TO the Santa Rosa Federal Building. She kept silent, working to keep her head together. Her mind churned, imagining what further questions the authorities would ask, what pressure they would apply, what threats they would make. *What case do they have against us? Only Juan Carlos's testimony. His word against ours. And why didn't he show up at Valley Run this morning? Did he run? What tack should I take? What would a lawyer counsel? To offer nothing. That's it. I'll offer nothing. They'll have to take me to court. And then what? If they can't find Teresa, they've got nothing.*

It was strange to be driven on this route that was so familiar to her, that represented her emerging strength and advocacy. She felt caged, disempowered, but not defeated. Mentally, she paced, anticipating freedom. Landmarks on the route evoked milestones on her new journey. When they passed the Cazadero General Store, she recalled her first meeting with Karen; at Rio Bravo, her unfortunate confrontation with Juan Carlos; at the turn-off to the winery, her first glimpse of him. Crossing the 101 Highway to the east side of Santa Rosa, she thought of Karen again.

But two blocks shy of the hospital, on Sonoma Avenue, in a prosperous neighborhood of quintessential suburban ranch houses, Officer Swenson turned into the parking lot of the Santa Rosa Federal Building, a long, low modern structure with a face of menacing black windows. Internal Revenue Service and US Bankruptcy Court, the sign read.

Lynn reflected on the irony of her appearance here. *Does it matter to these guys that immigrants like Teresa are paying payroll taxes for benefits they'll never collect? And bankruptcy? This whole lousy immigration system is bankrupt.*

Swenson led them down a long hall, institutional green, to a small office identified with a crude handwritten sign reading ICE. "A few months ago, we would have taken you all the way into the city, but we're expanding our footprint," he said as he ushered Lynn and Hank into the cramped, drab, cell-like office, a virtual museum of government-issue furnishings—a brown metal desk, scratched and dinged; three gray file cabinets with hand-lettered labels on the drawers; a portrait of President Trump; a framed print of the Declaration of Independence. Overhead, fluorescent lights flickered.

Lynn bit her tongue, resisting the impulse to call out his euphemism, but she got right to the point of their predicament. "Are you detaining us?"

"That is yet to be determined. We have sufficient reason to bring you in for questioning, as I said before. Now, for the questions. Please sit there."

He motioned to a metal chair at a rectangular wooden table. The chair's cushioned seat was torn, revealing the stuffing. It fed the room with the musty aroma of stale sweat. Swenson placed a handheld recording device on the table, and adjusted a video camera. Then, to Hank, he said, "Please step outside while I question your wife."

The space intimidated her. Her body shrank. She slumped in her chair. But she pushed back. *I know my rights. I'm not answering. As a citizen, I don't have to answer.* She stiffened her backbone. With Hank still in the room beside her, she said, "I'm telling you right now before you get started, I'm not answering any of your questions, not without a lawyer present."

"Do you know how that makes you look?"

"It doesn't matter. I'm not answering."

"Do you know a Ms. Teresa Alvarez?"

"No comment."

"Was she at your residence yesterday morning?"

"No comment."

"Were you aware of her immigration status?"

"No comment."

"Okay, step outside, both of you." He opened the door.

They stepped out into the hall, and he closed the door behind them. Guarded by Swenson's two associates, Hank and Lynn waited while the unintelligible cadence of conversation seeped through the door.

The door opened and Swenson stepped out. "We are not detaining you for now, but we will continue to consider you persons of interest, suspected of harboring an illegal immigrant—a crime. We will continue to investigate, and we will be contacting you again, rest assured. And do not leave the area. You are free to go."

Without a word, they stepped around their handlers and walked back down the long hall of bureaucracy.

TERESA PEERED INTO THE FOAMING WAVES THAT CRASHED and washed to shore with the hypnotizing regularity of a heartbeat. Her hair waved in the stiff, unrelenting wind. Gulls cried overhead. But nothing about the wonder of the place lightened her. No smile came to her face. Instead, fear and uncertainty weighed on her like a too-heavy blanket, compressing her lungs. She struggled for breath.

She tried but failed to imagine the way ahead. Sanctuary was welcome and vital. It would be her salvation now. But sanctuary in a tiny church, in a remote village, far from anything she knew, could never be her future. Beyond it, was only forbidding darkness.

She had crossed the border as a young woman full of hope and optimism. She had found joy. She had found meaningful work. She had launched two children into responsible adulthood. But that life—and all its possibilities—was gone, erased by one man's cruelty.

That cruelty filled her consciousness, pulsating like a strobe light, allowing no room for joy or hope. The raw violence of that night haunted her again, bringing back the pain, terror, and humiliation of the brutal rape; the rough grape bin, mean hands, her utter exposure, the hateful force of his angry phallus.

He had cornered her in the dark vineyard after picking had ended for the night.

"Come here," he said. "You know you want me."

"No. Please leave me alone, Juan Carlos."

He walked toward her, his arms out. She retreated, backing into a grape trellis—trapped. He grabbed her arm and pulled her to him. She struck him with her free arm. He grabbed it, tried to kiss her. She recoiled.

"Bitch." He hit her, spun her around, and threw her face-first against a wooden grape bin. With his left hand in the middle of her back, he held her hard against the bin. She struggled to breathe. With his right, he tore down her pants.

"Don't say a word, bitch." He rammed his engorged penis into her, slamming her against the bin. He came in seconds but held her by the waist in triumph. Then he backed away and left her there, sobbing.

Now, days later, the fear that always accompanied that memory chased her off the open bluff. She retreated to the cover of the trees, where she watched the little parking area. She remained alone, but she imagined searchers swooping in to haul her away; ICE, the police, even vigilantes. *Where is she? Why doesn't she call? I can't stay here like this.*

After an hour, she called Lynn. It went to voicemail. *That's it. I'm going to Madera to be with my daughter. They won't find me there. Yes, they will. Help me, God. What am I going to do?* She paced, walked to the car, climbed in, sat behind the wheel, and stared out into the blank blue sky.

She started the car, backed out of her parking spot, and drove back to the park entrance with no sense of a destination. At the Coast Highway, she stopped, unable to move out onto the highway. Overcome by futility, she sat at the intersection.

Across the highway, a car appeared at the base of Simpson Ranch Road. It turned toward her, accelerated up to speed, and roared by.

Teresa gasped. The car was red, a red Camaro. Shaking, she watched it disappear around a bend. Then she turned around, returned to the parking area, and waited, her eyes on the entrance.

CHAPTER 11

SOLACE AND SETBACK

"Teresa must be frantic," Lynn said as they reached the car. She tried Father Angelo again.

"Father Angelo," he answered.

"I'm so glad to reach you, Father. This is Lynn Peterson. I met you last week. We stopped so my friend could pray. I'm calling about sanctuary for the woman who was with me then, Teresa Alvarez. I understand you've talked with Father Mike in Guerneville."

"Yes, I remember you well. I'm sorry I haven't gotten back to you. I was with a parishioner. I have spoken with Father Mike. I told him we are eager to help."

"That's wonderful. We so appreciate that. I'm calling because the situation has gotten critical. ICE raided our ranch this morning. We were tipped off, and managed to get Teresa out before they arrived. We would be grateful if you could take her in now."

"We have a few loose ends to tie up, but that's not a problem. Please bring her."

"Oh, thank you, Father. You're a godsend. She'll be coming alone, and I'll follow as soon as I can."

"We'll be waiting for her."

———————

Low in her seat, Teresa huddled behind the steering wheel. Another hour went by. Wild projections of her future—none of them pleasant—surfaced in her mind, played themselves out, morphing into deportation, the discovery of her dark secret, jail, death at the hands of Rico and his cohorts. She closed her eyes to erase the disturbing images, in vain.

The sound she had all but given up on chased her thoughts away. She answered. "Lynn?"

"I'm so sorry, Teresa. ICE took us in to Santa Rosa, the bastards."

"Are you okay?"

"We are. They can't prove we were hiding you. All they have is Juan Carlos's word. We're on our way back."

"Oh, that's good. What about Elk?"

"That's the good news. Father Angelo is waiting for you. You can go there now."

Teresa felt a lightness in her chest. She sighed. Out of the corner of her eye, the vast ocean suddenly appeared truly pacific—a friend. She smiled. For several hours she had fretted about the temporary nature of the Elk sanctuary. Now it glowed in her mind's eye like Shangri-La. She sighed again. "Oh, thank you, thank you. That's so wonderful."

"I'm so sorry we worried you, but I couldn't call while we were with them."

"That's okay. It's good news."

"Leave now. I'll catch up with you as soon as I can."

"I will." Teresa hung up and left the park.

Even in her anxious state, the fifty-mile drive to Elk, through Sea Ranch, Gualala, Point Arena, and Manchester, was soul-nourishing. The sun, the sparkling water, the wind carrying the salty, primordial essence of the sea, the incessant waves erupting in towers of foam among the stubborn sea stacks—all of these phenomena fed Teresa with new hope. *How can I be sad or afraid in the midst of such beauty?*

Near Elk, the road dropped from the broad, grassy plain high above the sea into a wooded gulch. It crossed a narrow creek there, and rose through wispy, windblown Monterey cypress, back up onto the bluffs and into the village. Squeezed between a long pasture and wooded hills on one side, and the dramatic bluffs on the other, were a few dozen buildings, large and small, a few as old as the town—the Elk Store, a tiny clapboard building advertising picnic supplies, groceries, a deli, and wine; a weathered, shingled storefront decorated with a peace sign; the Elk Garage; a gallery; a small, white, nineteenth-century community church, complete with bell tower; an inn; and a bed and breakfast.

A sawmill had been the town's original raison d'être, and for seventy years it provided employment and livelihood. But in the late 1960s, when the old-growth redwood and Douglas fir were gone, the mill closed, and the town became a sleepy escape for lovers of remote, rustic simplicity. It was a simplicity Teresa found comforting, taking her back to her rural Mexican roots.

Blessed Sacrament Catholic Church, at the far end of the village, epitomized that comfortable simplicity. It felt like sanctuary to her; safety and relief from the fear and tension of the previous nine days.

No sooner had she parked at the modest rectory, when the door opened and the familiar figure of Father Angelo emerged; slight, pixyish. Two others followed, a man and a woman, graying. The man's shaggy hair flowed over his ears and collar, the woman's long hair tied in a ponytail.

Father Angelo greeted her with arms spread wide. "Teresa, we're so glad you're here. Meet Ted and Mary Jernigan. They're members of the congregation and coordinators of the team that will be caring for you while you're with us."

They smiled, and Ted offered his hand. "Welcome to Blessed Sacrament. You're safe here. Let us help you with your things."

"Thank you. It's not much." Teresa opened her trunk and Ted pulled out her canvas duffel.

"Please come in." Father Angelo gestured toward the house. "It's not much. We live simply here," he said as he ushered her through the front door. "But they take good care of me, and they'll take good care of you."

There wasn't much to the place—a kitchen, living room, bathroom, and two small bedrooms—orderly and spare.

He led her to the spare bedroom. "As you can see, we don't have much room here, but we hope it will do. This will be your room."

Ted followed and put her bag on the narrow bed. The room was the simplest space that Teresa had ever been in. The walls were white. A cross hung above the bed. The furnishings were a small oaken dresser, a wooden captain's chair, a rudimentary stand that held a porcelain bowl and matching pitcher, and a bedside table and lamp. Teresa had never been in a monastery, but it struck her that this space was the definition of monastic. In it, she felt the kind of peace that one seeks in a retreat, monastic or otherwise. Its stark plainness lacked the stamp of another person, allowing her to imagine it as hers. And in that way, it was comforting. "This is perfect. I'm so grateful. Thank you so much."

Angelo explained that Ted and Mary ran the little inn down the road. They would do her laundry and bring two meals a day: breakfast and dinner.

"Thank you so much. You're very kind."

"It's nothing. Trust us," Mary said. "We want to help, and we don't want you putting yourself in danger. ICE is looking for people even up here in tiny Elk. And besides that, we're not doing this alone. There are lots of us in the congregation pitching in."

Teresa was overcome. *How can people be so nice? They don't even know me.* Yes, she had suffered cruel indignities, but she struggled to comprehend the empathetic kindness of these strangers. The contrast with her barbarous treatment at the hands of Juan Carlos—and through him, Rico—could not have been more dramatic. "I don't know what to say."

"We understand," Mary replied. "You don't have to say anything." She hugged Teresa, saying, "You're our guest."

"This is a small space, like a cell. I know," Angelo said. "But you don't need to be confined to it. As far as we're concerned, the entire property of the church is a sanctuary. By law the police have the right to come and take you away, but they won't. They know it would be foolish. People wouldn't stand for it. Even in these strange times, you are safe here. I've got to call on an ailing parishioner, but Ted and Mary will show you around."

Teresa bowed ever-so-slightly, acknowledging her gratitude. "Gracias."

Ted and Mary showed her to a back door that opened onto a grassy lawn. A line of shrubby oaks on the property line provided privacy. Monterey cypresses provided shade. And a lone California palm clattered in the constant sea breeze. They walked to the edge of the bluff at the back of the lot, where the Pacific extended beyond her imagination, and above the whirring of the wind, the waves announced their arrival on terra firma.

From the lawn, they showed her the twentieth-century addition to the old church—two offices, the pastor's and a church administrator's, a meeting room, and a common room for functions and gatherings. A door in that room led to the church itself, the place Father Angelo had opened to her so kindly just the week before.

"I imagine you might like some time to rest and get your bearings," Mary said.

Teresa nodded.

They led her back to the rectory and took their leave. "We'll be back at dinner time. See you then."

Teresa entered her room and closed the door. A window looked out on the ocean. She turned the chair to face it and gazed into the blue distance. Like the lands far beyond the horizon, her future was out of sight, unknown and unknowable. She was safe in this tiny space, but she longed for her loved ones. It felt like years since she had seen them or talked with them. Her weekly calls were overdue. What would she say when she did call? She had not wanted them to worry. *But I can't keep this from them forever. They have to know. I need them to know. I want to be with them.*

As Lynn and Hank worked their way from Sonoma Avenue to the Guerneville Road on the north side of Santa Rosa, the relief Lynn might otherwise have felt was tempered by the knowledge that ICE would not end their pursuit of Teresa—or of them. They had found sanctuary for her, but Lynn fretted about its temporary nature.

"I need to get up there, Hank. This won't be over until we've helped her find a safe place to live and work. We can't leave her there."

Hank slowed, and turned north on Cazadero Highway. Now, well into the dry season, the stream was a trickle. "She's safe, Lynn. Take a breath. We've got time."

"I don't think so. It's not just ICE. It's Juan Carlos and Rico, too. Those bastards aren't about to quit."

"I hope you aren't back to thinking you—or we—can take them on by ourselves."

"I'm not. I'm going to call that number Nicki gave me—the detective—Maria something-or-other—Sandoval, I think."

"When?"

"After I've gone to Elk and checked on Teresa."

They passed through Cazadero and crossed the creek on Mountaintop Road.

"Are you sure you need to do that? Don't you think they can take care of her?"

"I know they can, Hank, but she's my charge now, and I need to see her."

"That's what I'm talking about, Lynn. She's not in your charge. She's in theirs. She'll be fine. Why can't you let this go?"

The road left the stream and started up the ridge. Hank accelerated. He was a good driver, skillful on these twisting roads. But Lynn often wondered if he wasn't reliving boyhood fantasies as he took the turns faster than she would have.

He seemed to be driving faster than usual, Lynn thought. *He's upset with me. Should I back off? Stay at the ranch? Go up to Elk tomorrow?*

Turning to her, he said, "I really think we need to pause and reassess. This is starting to feel like—"

Lynn screamed, "Watch out!" A deer—a buck, massively brown, with antlers like branches—stood in the middle of the road.

Hank swerved to the left. The car skidded and drifted off the pavement. As Hank struggled for control, the agony of helplessness filled Lynn. *No, no, no, no. This is so wrong.* The car moved on its own trajectory. Hank spun the wheel and pressed the brakes to the floor in vain. His tires scraped and squealed, broke loose. The forest leaped toward them.

Lynn lost connection to space and time, spinning like a rider in a mad tea cup, until all motion ceased, when the car slammed into a mammoth redwood.

Surreal silence followed, settling upon the mayhem. Lynn lay in her seat with her eyes closed. As if observing from above, she wondered what had happened. *Where am I? What is this?* Steam hissed. Glass clattered from broken windows, invading the silence, providing a clue. The air smelled of burnt rubber and dust.

She opened her eyes. The world had changed. *Is this real? A dream?* Lynn moved her head, her arms. *I'm alive.* She breathed in deep relief, ran her hands over her body, feeling for pain, and feeling none, knew she had escaped unharmed.

She turned to Hank. The dashboard had collapsed toward him. *Oh my God. He's hurt.*

His breathing was slow and labored, like an exhausted runner's.

"Hank, are you okay?" There was no response.

"Hank!"

He stirred.

She shook his shoulder. "Hank."

He groaned.

"Hank, are you okay?"

"I don't know. My knee is killing me—my leg." He touched it. "Ahhh, it's fucked."

Lynn feared that it might be trapped.

"Can you move?"

"I think so, but I shouldn't. I know I can't walk."

Lynn called 911, and then George.

He answered.

"We've had an accident, George—a bad one. Can you come?"

"Are you hurt?"

"Hank is. His leg is broken—pretty bad. I called nine-one-one."

"Where are you?"

"Not sure exactly. A mile, maybe more, below your place."

"I'll be right there."

In minutes, he was, pulling off on the other side of the road. He braced his arms against the roof of the car and peered across at Hank. "You gonna make it, buddy?" he asked as Hank grimaced.

"Yeah."

"Bleeding?"

"I don't think so, but it hurts like hell."

"I can take you down to Guerneville. Whatya think? It'll be half an hour before the EMTs are here."

"No, I'm messed up enough, I think I should wait for them."

"Fair enough. How 'bout you, Missy?"

"Shook up."

"I bet." He straightened up and looked down the road. "I imagine they'll take you into Santa Rosa. Lynn'll need a ride back. I'll follow you."

Those details had escaped Lynn. "Thank you, George. You've come to the rescue again."

She opened her door and climbed out gingerly. The car looked worse from the outside. It had struck the tree just to the right of the left headlight, driving the bumper back, crumpling the hood and left fender, knocking the left front wheel askew. A headlight dangled. Pieces of plastic trim littered the road. Orange coolant dripped from a cracked radiator hose and sank into the earth.

"Damn, we're lucky," she said.

"Yeah, you are."

Lynn leaned back against the car, waiting for help. A soaring raven croaked overhead. A squirrel chattered in the distance. *What now?* She had no idea.

———

GEORGE WAS RIGHT. IT TOOK THE EMTS ALL OF THIRTY minutes to arrive from Guerneville. They pulled Hank out through the passenger door, slid him into the ambulance on a folding gurney, and made for Santa Rosa Memorial. George followed with Lynn.

At the hospital, the medics wheeled Hank directly into the emergency room, leaving Lynn and George in the waiting room.

They had been there only a few minutes when Lynn's phone chirped over the babble to herald an incoming text. It was Nicki. *Big news. Need to talk.*

Tough right now. In ER waiting room.

She replied with a question mark.

Hank's leg. Pretty bad car accident.

May I come over? It's important.

Okay.

Lynn tucked her phone in her pocket. "That was the reporter I met the other day. She says she has big news, can't wait. She's coming over. Tell me, George, what more can happen?"

"With what you're mixed up in, it could be anything. We'll find out."

A cross-section of the county filled the room; a sampling of ages, colors, ethnicities, physical conditions. Mothers comforted crying children. Wheelchair-bound elders waited beside their caregivers. A laborer held a bandaged, bloodstained hand against his chest. The receptionist called names. Patients rose in response. Nurses greeted them. The ill and injured streamed through the front door, replacing them.

Nicki appeared at the door and motioned to Lynn.

"That's her," Lynn said. "I'll be right back." She stepped outside.

"What is it?"

"Juan Carlos Hernandez is dead. A fisherman found him by the river this morning, with his throat slit."

Lynn's breath stuck in her throat. This had been the stuff of her wildest imaginings, which she had suppressed as just that—remote, crazy, wildly unlikely. But here it was, grizzly and real.

"His throat slit?"

"Yeah, nasty."

"How did they identify him?"

"His wife did. She reported him missing this morning. Then they found his truck a few blocks from his house. Weird—blood on the inside of the driver's door, no prints except his."

Lynn struggled for air.

"Have you talked to the cop?" Nicki asked.

"No, I haven't had time."

"I think you should. This has to be gang related, and Teresa might be able to help."

"How?"

"You told me she knew the ringleaders, Rico Guerrero and Jorge Sanchez."

"Yeah."

"So maybe she can connect the three of them, provide some piece of the puzzle."

Yes, maybe she could. But the events unleashed by Teresa's flight were becoming so frightful that remaining within range of them seemed like suicide—for her and for Teresa. "I don't know how we make that happen. It seems so dangerous."

"They might offer immunity."

"For what? Deportation? I don't think the police can do that."

"Yeah, you're right."

"I don't know. I'll think about it."

"Stay in touch."

"I will." They parted.

Lynn returned to her place beside George. "What more can happen, George? You won't believe it. Maybe you will. They killed Juan Carlos, slit his throat. And she wants me to talk to the cops, get Teresa to talk to the cops. I can't do that."

"You don't have to. Not right now. Give yourself some time to think it through."

"That's what Hank was telling me—just before the accident."

"Good advice."

She heard her name above the multiple conversations around her.

"Lynn Peterson!" called a nurse in lavender scrubs from the door to the emergency room.

"Come on, George. I might need the moral support."

Hank lay on a gurney with an inflatable splint covering his leg from ankle to thigh. He managed a smile.

A white-coated doctor greeted Lynn and George. The doctor's gray hair and calm air inspired confidence. "Your husband was lucky, Mrs. Peterson. He has some bad fractures, but he'll make a full recovery. His tibia is fractured in two places. He'll probably need pins to hold it in place. And his patella—his kneecap—is fractured. That will require surgery, too. And there may be ligament damage in the knee. We'll admit him and call in the orthopedic surgeon."

Lynn squeezed Hank's hand and kissed him. "You're not going anywhere in a hurry, are you?"

"No, I guess not."

The doctor confirmed it. "He'll be laid up for a while—a couple of months, at least."

Karen was in the hall, finishing her evening circuit of the hospital's third floor, when Lynn and George stepped off the elevator. They walked with her past the nurse's station to her room.

"He had it coming," she said, when Lynn told her about Juan Carlos.

"Really? He didn't kill anybody."

"No, but he made plenty of people's lives miserable, including you."

"Yes, he did."

"What are you going to do now?"

Karen's hospital room offered itself as a quiet eddy in the furious torrent, a place to consider that question. "I don't know, Karen. There are so many pieces to this mess. Teresa is safe for now, but she can't stay in Elk forever. ICE is still after her—and us. And we're not safe as long as Juan Carlos's killers are loose. I'm sure they know where we live. It's too much for me right now."

"I get it, honey. They're releasing me tomorrow. You can stay at my place."

Karen's offer was attractive, but she had a responsibility to the Tillsons, who were paying her and Hank to care for the ranch. As long as that was the case, she needed to be there. "Thanks, but for now I need to stay at the ranch. Maybe we should quit. It's not a whole lot of fun right now."

"Maybe you should."

"And then there are the cops."

"What do you mean?"

"Nicki Simpson, the reporter, thinks I should talk to them. She thinks Teresa can help them get to the gang."

"She probably can."

"That's what I mean, Karen. I've got so much to sort out." Her voice cracked. Tears slipped down her cheeks. "I don't know if I can do this alone."

"You don't have to, honey. You've got me. And you've got Hank."

"I know. That helps, but you're both out of commission. I just feel so alone right now."

"And you've got me," George said.

"I know, George, and I appreciate it. Forgive me."

"I got some ideas," he said. "For starters, you should stay at my place tonight. The gang—if that's who killed your guy—has no idea I'm involved. Second, we'll put up a security camera on the house. You can buy 'em on Amazon for two, three hundred bucks, maybe four.

The Tillsons would be glad to have it. And talking to the cops is a good idea, wherever it goes. It's not gonna make you any less safe. The cops need to nail those guys."

At the mention of "those guys," Lynn remembered Teresa. *I need to tell her about Juan Carlos. She'll be relieved—or will she?*

CHAPTER 12

MARIA INVESTIGATES, ICE CLOSES IN

LYNN POPPED AWAKE—TENSE AND SHAKEN. THE DREAM had plagued her for years: A raging woman, wailing, "You killed him! You killed him! You killed him!" Dropping to her knees and collapsing, her shoulders heaving with sobs, Lynn kneeling beside her and stroking her back, the accusations continuing. "You killed him, Lynn. You killed him. Why?" Years elapsed between episodes, but the dream would not leave her.

In the dark, the room looked different. *Why? What's different?* The window was in an odd place. A curtain fluttered. Cool air wafted over her face. She came fully awake. *Of course—George's house.*

She summoned the mantra she had repeated often through the years: *You were young, still a teenager, and afraid—with good reason. It wasn't your fault.* But she had never believed it. She didn't believe it now. She had failed her best friend, Ellie, whose fiancé, Randy, eventually came back from Vietnam in a body bag. Prior to that, he'd gotten wounded, and was sent back to the States for recovery. The army ordered him back to the war. He balked, and chose, instead, to desert. Lynn agreed to drive him across the border into Canada. But she'd lost her nerve. At the appointed time, she failed to pick up him up from his safe house in Cincinnati. The army picked him up and sent him back to Vietnam, where he was killed a few months later in an ambush near the demilitarized zone. *No, I didn't shoot him. I just failed to save him.*

She reached for her phone. It read 5:58 a.m. She closed her eyes, rolled over, and wrapped her arms around her pillow. She squeezed her eyelids. The image went away, as it always did.

Another replaced it: another safe house, another hunted soul hiding from a predator, another trusting friend. This image stayed with her, waiting, waiting for her to muster the courage to say, *I won't let you down. Trust me. Please trust me.* Then it, too, faded.

Must get up. Lynn rose—and teetered. At the accident scene, she'd told the EMTs she was fine. They'd checked her, given her a clean bill of health, and for the rest of the day, she'd felt no ill effects. But now she was stiff and weak. Muscles ached. *What do they say? Been through the wringer? Yes, that's it. Or hit by a truck.* She sat back on the bed.

How am I going to get through this day? She would, she told herself, the same way she had for years when she'd dragged herself out of bed, feeling lousy, to get her daughter ready for school. She stood and shuffled into the bathroom. Ignoring the exhausted visage in the mirror, she splashed cold water on her face, brushed her teeth, and ran a comb through her hair. Then she pulled on the jeans and chamois shirt that still wore yesterday's drama, and left the house.

A faint glow on the eastern horizon hinted of dawn, but overhead, the sky was still filled with stars. The air was cool. Birds chirped, warming up their vocal chords. She tried to warm herself by lengthening her stride.

She would walk to Bella Vista, where the goat and chickens awaited her, then take Hank's car to the hospital to consult with the orthopedist about his surgery. She would check in with Karen, if she was still there. And Teresa—she needed to call Teresa. The thought alone tired her.

And check on the car. How could I forget the car? I'll do that on the way home. Yesterday on the way to the hospital, George had called his friend Doug at the garage in Cazadero and asked him to pick up Lynn and Hank's car. She would need to file with the insurance company. Surely, they would total it. She wondered what she'd get for it. Whatever it was, it wouldn't be enough.

———————

At Bella Vista, the barn loomed in the dim twilight. As much as it now distressed her, the animals lightened Lynn's spirit. Clucking and bleating greeted her when she opened the squeaky barn door and flipped on the light, bringing a smile to her face, easing her tension. "You are my therapy animals," she told them as she made her morning rounds.

The sky was lighter when she finished. She fetched Hank's car keys from a hook in the back hall of the house, splashed water on a wilting plant by the sink, and picked up Hank's iPad and put it in her purse. When she left the house, she locked the door behind her.

She adjusted Hank's seat and mirror, checked the fuel gauge, and turned the key. The engine responded with a throaty, diesel rattle; catlike. She preferred her Prius, but Hank loved his VW, a ten-year-old station wagon that served him well hauling loads from the lumber yard and the feed store.

The sun was up when she turned out of the driveway toward Cazadero. Cresting the first rise in the road, she met a car approaching from the south. Odd, she thought, for so early in the morning. Mountaintop Road was not a thoroughfare. She moved toward the shoulder to make room for it.

She knew most of the cars that used the road, but not this one. The red Camaro passed without slowing or yielding to her, the way a local would. *Asshole.* She went on.

On the valley floor, mist rose from the shallow creek. She lowered her window just enough to feel the cool moisture on her cheeks. Like the animals, it cheered her.

Across the bridge in Cazadero, she stopped at the general store to buy coffee and a breakfast sandwich. The coffee, advertised as the best in Cazadero, was the only coffee in the village. And the sandwiches were homemade. Lynn liked the unpretentious hominess and authenticity of the place.

The cashier greeted her as always with "Mornin', Miss Peterson."

Lynn was thankful to be recognized and acknowledged, no longer anonymous, but *this* morning the words sounded more than perfunctory. She appreciated their unvarnished sincerity. "Good morning, Alison."

In the car Lynn spread a paper napkin across her lap to catch the crumbs. Another day, she might have eaten at a table on the store's front porch, but today she was in a hurry.

As she turned east on River Road, her phone rang. She put her coffee down and put the phone on speaker. "This is Lynn."

"Lynn, this is Detective Maria Sandoval in Santa Rosa."

Damn, I should have called her. "Yes, detective."

"I need to question you about the murder of Juan Carlos Hernandez."

The idea alone rattled her. *What? Surely, I'm not a suspect. Be polite.* She pulled over and picked up the phone. "I understand, detective. When?"

"This morning, if possible."

I really don't need this. "My husband's in the hospital, Santa Rosa Memorial. I'm on my way there to meet with his surgeon."

"I'm sorry to hear that."

"Thank you. He'll be okay."

"Can we talk when you're through?"

Lynn wanted to push back, put it off, but what else could she say. "I guess so. Where?"

"At the hospital, if you don't mind. I could speak with your husband, too, if he's up to it."

Lynn wasn't sure he would be. She wasn't sure *she* would be.

———————

HANK WAS SITTING UP IN BED WATCHING THE MORNING news when Lynn arrived. On the screen, angry protesters waved signs and chanted slogans as they encroached on a line of stern-faced policemen at the White House fence.

"It's the same old thing every day. Mind if I turn it off?" she asked.

"No, that's fine. It's depressing."

She took his hand and kissed him. His left leg, still wrapped in a full temporary cast, looked uncomfortable. "How is it feeling?"

"Not bad. They've got me drugged up."

"I was afraid of that. Have you seen the doctor?"

"He was in last night, wants to let the swelling go down some." He looked up. "Here he is."

A handsome young black man walked into the room. Lynn took notice of his obvious fitness. She might have been put off by his youth, but he'd come highly recommended. She would hold judgment.

"We'll put pins here, and here," Dr. Montgomery said, pointing to each of the two white lines on the X-ray, both of which indicated fractures of his tibia. And with a simple drawing, he showed them how he would stitch together the three broken pieces of his kneecap. "This is all common, normal stuff, Hank. You're going to be fine. It will just take some time to heal."

"What's the schedule?" Lynn asked.

"I'd like to operate tomorrow morning."

"When?"

"We'll bring him down at seven o'clock."

He explained the pre-operation protocol, and excused himself.

Lynn reassured Hank that she would be there bright and early.

"You don't need to. They're just going to knock me out."

"Yes, I do. I'll be here." He might have been just fine facing the operation alone. But she wouldn't be. She had to see him, touch him, wish him well, kiss him. She would be there to send him off.

———————

"Lynn Peterson?" came a woman's voice from the doorway. A Latina in a long-sleeved khaki shirt, jeans, and flashy neon-green sneakers opened her wallet to reveal a detective's badge. She adjusted the sunglasses propped on the top of her head and flipped her long jet-black ponytail off her collar.

"Yes, that's me, and this is Hank."

"I'm Detective Sandoval—Maria. Do you mind if I sit?"

"Of course not," Lynn replied. She motioned to a chair by the window.

"You know about the murder of Juan Carlos Hernandez?"

"Yes, I heard about it yesterday."

"I'd like to ask you a few questions."

Lynn took a deep breath. "Okay."

Detective Sandoval closed the door. "Did you know him?"

"No, but I know who he was," Lynn said. "And I know he attacked me at the ranch."

"When was that?"

"Sunday morning—two days ago."

"Why do you think he did that?"

"I was hiding a woman from him."

"And this woman, who was she?"

"Her name is Teresa Alvarez."

"How do you know her?"

"A friend of hers brought her to me the week before last, about ten days ago. He had just raped her, and she needed a place to hide."

"Why didn't she report it to the police?

"Because she's undocumented."

"Ah. A common story, unfortunately. You know, there are protections for cases like hers."

"Yes, I do know. We told her, but she said she couldn't pursue them. She wouldn't say why."

"You've talked with Nicki Simpson."

"Yes."

"Can you tell me what you told her?"

Lynn related everything Teresa had told her about Juan Carlos and his schemes—the wine theft, the extortion, the connection to Rico and Jorge, the stabbing in Healdsburg, the smuggling pipeline. "But I have no direct knowledge of any of this."

"But Teresa does."

"Yes, most of it."

"Where was she on Sunday night?"

"Staying with our neighbor, George Nicholson, for safety."

"And where were you two?"

"At the ranch on Mountaintop Road, Bella Vista, where we're the caretakers."

"Where is Teresa now?"

"I'd rather not say."

Detective Sandoval looked surprised. "You don't have to worry about us working with ICE. We aren't, and we won't."

"That's good to hear."

"We could offer her immunity."

"Not from deportation."

"You're right—we can't do that."

That galled Lynn. *What a screwed-up system.* "You know ICE is looking for her."

"Yes, I do." The detective turned to Hank. "And you, Mr. Peterson?"

"I only know what Lynn's told me."

"I understand. May I ask what happened to you? That's a pretty big cast."

"A deer stepped out into the road, and we hit a tree on the way home from the ICE office."

"They told me they brought you in. Trust me, we're not doing their work for them." She rose to go. "You worried about Guerrero and Sanchez?"

"Yes, we are," Lynn said.

"Teresa can help us get to them before they get to her—or you."

Lynn knew that was the bottom line. As long as Rico and Jorge were free—and as long as she and Hank stayed in the area—they weren't safe. "I'll try to talk to her."

But that was the last thing she wanted to do. Her resolve had stalled, paralyzed by the collision on Mountaintop Road. Teresa's plight wore on her. She wanted to help. But the accident had thrown her off balance and weakened the sense of direction and purpose she had gained since Teresa's arrival at Bella Vista. She could not be in two places at the same time—physically or mentally. The hospital was the place she needed to be—both for herself and for Hank. Elk would have to wait.

———

NEWS OF THE MURDER TRAVELLED QUICKLY THROUGH the vineyard and the winery. Kelly Ahearn, the general manager, had learned of it late Monday, the day Juan Carlos's body was discovered, about the same time Lynn was told. Kelly had been investigating Juan Carlos's wine theft scheme with Julia, her tasting room manager, when Jessica had come in to tell them.

Kelly was not surprised the next day, Tuesday, when Detective Maria Sandoval came to see her, but she was not eager to talk. She was stressed, shaken by the murder and overwhelmed by the loss of a key employee at the busiest season of the winery year. She had neither the time nor the equanimity for conversation.

Kelly was in the barn at eleven, where she liked to be in the heat of the day. A batch of fermenting pinot noir needed testing for dryness. She was reaching into the vat to retrieve a sample when Sandoval arrived and introduced herself.

"I hope I'm not disturbing you," she said.

She was, but Kelly tried not to show her irritation. "No, it's fine. This can wait."

"I have a few questions about Juan Carlos Hernandez."

Kelly set her beaker and hydrometer aside. "Okay, but I don't have a whole lot of time."

"I'll try to respect that. When did you last see Mr. Hernandez?"

"Saturday afternoon, when he left for the day."

"Did you know if he had enemies—people who might want to see him dead?"

"No, I didn't, not until I heard about the gang he was involved with."

"When was that?"

"Last week sometime."

"And you heard that from whom?"

"Lynn Peterson told me he was involved with the gang. ICE told me the same thing; Swenson was his name, I think. And Juan Carlos's wife, Olaya. She called me yesterday morning, told me he was afraid of them."

"Do you have any evidence that he was engaged in illegal activity here?"

"I know a lot of wine is missing. My tasting room manager and I confirmed that yesterday. I was told he took it, but I can't prove it."

"Are you aware of any other illegal activity?"

"Only what Lynn told me."

"Have you noticed anything else unusual?

Anything else unusual. "Anything?"

"Sure, we'll see if it's relevant."

"Well, one of my full-time workers, Jessica Martinez, didn't show up this morning. That's unusual, and my tasting room manager told me two young guys came asking for her."

"Did she describe them?"

"Just that they were young, Latino, and driving a red sports car—a Camaro."

KAREN LEFT THE HOSPITAL AT NINE THAT SAME MORNING, her surgeon having dismissed her on his rounds. She was under strict orders to exercise moderately every day; walking, bicycling, spinning. But she was not to go back to work for at least four weeks. Most likely it would be longer.

As her Uber made its way along River Road and then Cazadero Highway, she wondered how she would spend that time. She was not accustomed to inactivity. She spent her days in active busyness until the end of the day, when she'd run out of steam, sink into bed, and fall asleep. As much as she looked forward to being back in her colorful house on the creek, she was already itching to get back to work. *What am I going to do with myself?*

But her musings gave way to curiosity when the Uber rolled up her narrow driveway. A strange car sat in her parking place, an old brown Toyota Corolla with the remnants of a UCLA decal in the back window and a bumper sticker that read "If you can read this, you're following too close."

Hmm. She thanked the driver and started toward the house. It was good to be home, where the wind talked in the treetops, needles of redwood and fir cushioned her steps, and sunlight played on the riffles in the creek. But what of this car she didn't recognize?

The driver's door opened, and a woman stepped out, looking somber, grim. It was Jessica Martinez, the vineyard worker whom Juan Carlos had pressured for information about both Karen and Lynn.

"Jessica, what are you doing here?"

"Can you help me, Karen? I need a place to hide. I didn't know where else to go."

Karen took her hand. "Honey, you don't have to worry. Juan Carlos is dead."

"I know. I'm not worried about him. I'm worried about Rico Guerrero and Jorge Sanchez. A friend in Roseland called, said they're looking for me."

"Well, come on in, honey. We'll make you safe here."

CRASHING WAVES AND CRYING GULLS WOKE TERESA EARLY. She dressed and walked across the wet lawn to the edge of the bluff. She settled on a wooden bench and stared out into the blue-black morning, watching the stars fade and the world take form.

Lynn had called her the night before as she was climbing into bed. "Juan Carlos is dead," she said. *Juan Carlos is dead.* It had taken Teresa a while to absorb that idea. It was still unreal. *Juan Carlos is dead. Thank God!* She had never wished anyone dead, but she was convinced this man wanted to kill her. She was not unhappy that he was gone.

Juan Carlos was dead, but others still pursued her; ICE, Rico. The church felt safe, but it could not be forever. She would have to return to the world. Her prayer was that she might do so without fear, that her life might once again be peaceful and secure.

Lynn said she would get here as soon as she could. She has a lot to deal with. I'll be patient. Teresa trusted Lynn in a way that she trusted no one else.

When the first rays of sunlight lit the waves far from shore, Teresa returned to the rectory, where Father Angelo was making coffee. The aroma woke her appetite.

"Buenos días, senõra," he said, rolling the *r*. "Cómo estás?"

"Muy bien, senõr. Gracias, y tú?"

"I am well. Thank you," he said. "Forgive my Spanish."

"Thank you for trying. It makes me feel at home."

"You're welcome. It's the least I can do. Did you sleep well?"

"Yes. The room is very comfortable."

When the coffee had finished dripping, he carried the pot to the table in the living room, and with it, a plate of breakfast tacos that smelled of sausage, egg, and peppers.

"A taste of home, I hope," he said. "Ted and Mary delivered these while you were out there welcoming the morning. They said they're authentic. They have a Mexican chef."

Teresa took a taste. "Mmm, perfecto." The gesture of gracious hospitality moved her.

"We have orange juice. Would you like jugo de naranja?"

Teresa giggled. "Very good, Father. Sí."

He went to the kitchen. At the refrigerator door, he paused and stared toward the street. He moved closer to the window. "What's that?" she heard him say. His tone worried her. She got up and joined him at the window.

A black SUV slowed, turned off the road, and pulled up to the church. Three uniformed men climbed out and walked to the office door. They knocked and waited. Getting no response, they turned and started toward the rectory.

"Teresa, hurry, back to your room—now. This looks like ICE," he said, sounding like her father warning of imminent danger, calm but decisive. Father Angelo scooped her plate and cup off the table, as a loud knock reverberated through the little house. "Just a minute," he said as he slid the plate and cup into the refrigerator.

"Oh my God."

"It will be okay. I won't let them in."

Teresa ducked into her room and closed the door. Through it, she heard the front door open and Father Angelo address them.

"May I help you?" he asked.

One of the uniformed men spoke. "I'm Officer Swenson. We're with Immigration Control and Enforcement. We're looking for an undocumented immigrant, Teresa Alvarez. We have reason to believe she's here."

"And what reason is that, may I ask?" Father Angelo said.

"I'm afraid I can't say."

"And I'm afraid I have to say she's not here."

She couldn't believe Father Angelo had lied for her. *Oh, thank you, Father.* Her hands clasped, she prayed he could resist their authority.

"May we look around?"

"No, you may not."

Oh, thank you, Father. Thank you, Father. Thank you, Father.

"Well, I'm telling you I don't believe you. We know she's here. And you can tell her we'll stay right here until she gives herself up."

"You can wait as long as you want, but I'll have to ask you to move your vehicle from our property."

Teresa was petrified.

Soon a knock came on her door. "May I come in?" It was Father Angelo.

"Sí."

Teresa had closed the blinds; the room was dark. Unlit, and without connection to the outside world, it was more a cell than a room; lifeless and depressing. She sat on her bed with her hands clenched in her lap. Shaking, she said, "How could they find me so soon? I thought I was safe here."

"You are safe."

"No, Father. They will keep coming back. What good is being safe if I'm only safe here? You can't keep me safe out there. You are like David, the shepherd boy, without a slingshot."

CHAPTER 13

WE HEARD IT THROUGH THE GRAPEVINE

HANK'S HOSPITAL ROOM WAS A REFUGE FROM THE FRIGHT-ening drama of the previous ten days. It was light and airy. Threats were walled out. The pace of life slowed. Fear ebbed. Uncertainty abated. For days, the world had torn at them, diminished them. Here they would be restored.

They spent the afternoon in a way they hadn't for years—in the same space, engaging each other without distraction—just as they'd done during the Blizzard of '78 in Boston, where they lived the first few years of their marriage. Four feet of snow had brought the city to a halt for weeks.

They played double solitaire with two decks of cards Lynn bought at the hospital gift shop. They read and shared interesting tidbits from their news feeds.

"Did you ever look for another caretaking opportunity, Hank?" Lynn asked as she moved a string of cards to an open king.

"No, I never did. That was just a threat."

"Maybe we should."

"Where would you like to go?"

Lynn was about to say "Alaska" when her phone beeped with an incoming text.

It was Karen. *Jessica is here at my house. Rico has been asking for her. I'm making room for her. Stop by when you can.*

"Who was that?"

She relayed the text message.

"Do you really want to get involved?"

"No, not really." She texted back, *Will try. Can't say when.*

Lynn stayed through Hank's dinnertime—six o'clock—when an aide brought a tray of lasagna, a green salad, and fresh strawberries.

"That doesn't look like the hospital food I remember," she said.

"It's California. They grow it here."

Lynn took the elevator down to the cafeteria and returned with two slices of pizza decorated with fresh basil and strips of mozzarella. "Margherita," she said. "Who knew?"

"I should just stay here with you," she said as they ate. "Sleep in the chair."

"No, you can't do that. You'll be a wreck. Go back to George's and get a good night's sleep."

"Okay, I will, but I'll be here before you go to surgery."

She left and began driving the now-familiar route as if on autopilot, through Mirabel Park, Hacienda, Korbel. In Guerneville, the shops had closed and the restaurants were filling. A woman held the door of the Sawmill Grill for a man. Her husband? They entered, smiling. At the gas station, a teenage boy with a black Giants cap on backwards pumped gas with one hand and held his smartphone with the other.

She knew these people had cares. But she doubted they were her cares. Who else could be caught up in such a wild intrigue? Who would understand? How would they respond if they did?

As she approached Karen's place, she slowed automatically. But she didn't really want to stop. She wanted to see Karen, but she couldn't add Jessica's burden to hers. She brought the car back up to speed and went on.

Warm light welcomed Lynn from the windows of the house when Lynn pulled to a stop at the end of George's driveway. Hank was right; for a good night's sleep, she needed a comfortable bed. A load of care and tension lifted from her shoulders as she climbed the two short steps to the back door and opened it.

The radio in the kitchen was tuned to the Giants game, but George was not in evidence. She laid her purse on the table, pulled out a chair, and called, "George!"

There was no answer. Footsteps sounded in the front of the house—and voices. She pushed the chair back under the table and listened.

The voices stopped.

George appeared in the doorway. "You've got company, Lynn."

I've got company? "Oh?"

"Two families. They came to the ranch this afternoon looking for you; four adults, six kids—all undocumented. They say you're the one who can protect them from ICE."

Lynn stared at George in disbelief.

He waited—with the hint of a smile on his face—for some reaction from her.

"You've got to be kidding. This is not happening."

"I'm afraid it is, missy. They're not bad folks, just scared. But they're sure you're gonna save 'em."

"How am I going do that?"

"If anybody can figure that out, you can."

"Right." As soon as the words were out of his mouth, Lynn discounted them, but they hung in the air like smoke, impossible to ignore. She reconsidered them. *Maybe he's right. Maybe I can.* "What are we going do with them now?"

"You have room at Bella Vista. Maybe they sleep there tonight, and we deal with it tomorrow."

"We" deal with it. The pronoun was not lost on her. This was still her issue, her responsibility, but George was offering the firm ground she needed to stay calm, to assess this new reality without panic. "What about the gang?"

"They're looking for you, not these people."

"What about the security camera?"

"I ordered it today. Should be here tomorrow."

"That doesn't help us tonight."

"What else are we gonna do? I don't have room here."

"Okay, let's take them down there."

Lynn followed George around the corner into the front room, where ten apprehensive faces greeted her. The runaways filled every seat; a threadbare couch, two wooden rockers, a footstool. Three children sat on the floor, and one on a brown leather La-Z-Boy, her legs barely protruding beyond the edge of the seat. "Hola," she said.

Eyes lit up, and a few thin, tentative smiles brightened their otherwise dreary visages. "Hola," came the multiple replies.

"I'm Lynn. Lynn Peterson. I'm curious. Why did you come *here*?"

A short, round-faced woman on the couch stilled a child fidgeting at her feet, and spoke. "We heard you were hiding Teresa Alvarez. So we thought you could help us, too."

Oh my God. That's not good. "How did you hear that?"

"How do you say?—through the grapevine. At the winery, Valley Run. I can't remember, exactly."

"And how did you *find* me?"

"You lived on a ranch on Mountaintop Road—Bella Vista, they said. We looked it up on the internet."

Some secret. Take a deep breath. Deal with this. "What's happening at the winery?"

"ICE are coming. They plan a raid, we hear," said the man beside her on the couch.

Lynn was in no position to think beyond the night ahead. But like a platoon leader facing an enemy incursion, she found the strength and presence of mind to focus on the immediate challenge. "First, tell me your names."

"I'm Martha Garcia," said the woman on the couch. "This is my husband, Manny." He nodded. "And these are our children. This is Patricia," she said, introducing the squirmy girl at her feet.

"Hola," said the girl.

Martha continued. "This is Margarita," she said, and the girl in the La-Z-Boy waved in response. "And this is Miguel," Martha finished, looking at a shaggy-haired boy sitting cross-legged on the floor.

A woman on the other end of the couch—husky, with a weathered face—introduced herself and her family—Gabriela Cruz, her husband Jose, and her children Rosa, Daniel, and Pedro.

"Okay, here's what we're going to do."

There wasn't a sound in the room—and barely a twitch—as Lynn spoke. "We are going back down to my house at Bella Vista. You can sleep there tonight. Tomorrow we will talk about the future, but tonight you will be safe."

The migrants piled into their cars—a twenty-year-old blue Ford Explorer with a deep dent in the right front fender and a once-silver, now-gray Honda Civic—and followed Lynn down the road. When they reached Bella Vista, she directed them to the barn and instructed them to park out of sight behind it. The moon had not yet risen. The sky was alive with stars, but the night was dark. Lynn took a flashlight from Hank's glove compartment and lit the way back to the house.

She opened the back door and turned on the light in the back hall. "This is the bathroom," she gestured to her left, "And this is my bedroom," she said, stepping into the room to her right, directly across the short hall. She turned on the overhead light.

"I have two beds, this one and another upstairs in the loft. Martha, why don't you and Manny stay here. The girls will probably fit on the bed with you."

Patricia and Margarita, holding Martha's hands, looked up at her and smiled.

"For Miguel, I have some heavy blankets we can fold and put on the floor for a kind of mattress. Will that be okay?"

"Of course. We have squeezed into smaller places than this. You are kind just to put us up, senõra."

Martha, Manny, and their children stayed in the room and began to arrange themselves for the night, while Lynn led the Cruz family through the kitchen to the front room. She turned on two black wrought-iron floor lamps with yellowing shades; one on the near side of the room beside the couch on the wall facing the front door, and another in the opposite corner of the room by the stairs leading to the loft.

She put a hand on the back of the couch. "Will this work for the boys, one on each end?" she asked Gabriela.

"Sí, yes."

Daniel and Pedro eased onto the couch and stretched out, as if to test it.

"The loft has a smaller bed. If your daughter—Rosa, is it?"

Gabriela nodded.

"If Rosa won't fit on the bed with you, we can make another blanket mattress. Is that okay?"

"It will be fine. Gracias."

Rosa tip-toed up the stairs, peered into the dark, unfamiliar space, and scurried back down to take a position of safety at her mother's side.

Lynn gathered the adults in the back hall, and the children followed. The two families stood before her like new campers away from home for the first time, scared and desperate to learn the ropes, but also brave. "This is wonderful. We will be fine. You are very kind," Martha said.

"I'll be staying at George's house tonight," Lynn said. "You won't see me in the morning. My husband is having an operation at Santa Rosa Memorial, and I'll be leaving early. But I'll have someone check on you. There's food in the kitchen and the pantry—enough for breakfast, I'm sure. Use whatever you need."

"Gracias," Martha said.

"You understand?"

"I do."

"Your English is good. That's helpful for me; I don't speak Spanish."

"Thank you. It's nothing."

"Will you be okay?"

"Yes, ma'am. Don't worry about us. Just worry about your husband."

"Thank you. You're kind to say that. Give me your number, just in case."

They exchanged numbers, and Lynn called Martha to make sure they had them right. She answered.

"We're good. I'll see you tomorrow. Call me if you have any trouble." She opened the back door, but stopped and turned around. "One more thing." She stepped into the pantry and came out with the shotgun. "Do you know how to use this?" she asked Manny.

"I think so."

"It's easy. You load it like this." She opened it, slid the two shells from the side-by-side barrels, and reloaded it. "Then just aim and pull."

They looked at her wide-eyed and open-mouthed.

"Just in case. You never know. Oh, and check the doors and windows. They should be locked, but check them. Good night."

"Buenas noches," Martha replied.

Lynn drove back to George's. She was tired when she returned from the hospital. Now she was exhausted.

George was nursing a beer at the kitchen table. The room was dim, lit only by a low-wattage bulb over the sink. "All tucked in bed?"

"It'll be tight, but they'll be fine." She opened the refrigerator door and took out a beer. She looked at the label. A sea lion propped up on its front flippers looked back at her. *Red Seal Ale. That'll work.* She pried off the cap with an opener screwed to the door frame. It dropped into a tin bucket hanging from it. She settled into a chair. "What are we going to do with them, George?"

"Ya got me."

"There's no way Becky will put up with them there, and she's due up here any time now."

"You never know. Isn't she one of those Nancy Pelosi liberals?"

"She may be. But does she want to tangle with ICE? They've been up here once already. What's to say they won't come back?" She yawned.

"So what does that leave us?"

"A choice. We send them away, or we try to help them." She yawned again. "If I'm going to be at the hospital at six thirty, I need to go to bed." She went into the guest room, changed into pajamas decorated with Valentine's Day candy hearts—the ones with the cute expressions on them—and crossed the hall to the bathroom. Over the sound of running water she called out to him. "Do you think you can put up the security camera tomorrow?"

"I will if it shows up. It shouldn't be hard."

She turned off the water and the light, and stepped back into the hall. "I don't know when I'll see you tomorrow. It's going to be a long day."

She climbed into bed, checked email on her phone, and called Karen. "You awake?" she asked.

"I am now. What's up?"

"You won't believe it."

"What?"

"There are two undocumented families up here. They heard I could save them from ICE."

"Maybe you can."

"Come on, Karen. No, really, how am I going to do that?"

"Get them out of the valley."

"Where?"

"What about that congregation in Elk? You said they're all over this sanctuary thing."

"They are, but this is a lot bigger."

"Ask them. What harm can it do?"

"Maybe I will. I need a favor, Karen. Can you check on them for me tomorrow? I may be gone all day. See if they've got enough food. See if they slept all right."

"Yeah, I'll do that for you, honey. I'll have Jessica drive me up."

"Thanks a million."

Lynn turned off the light and let her head sink back into her pillow. *What have I gotten myself into? I've invited two families into a house that's not mine. I'm not there to oversee them. And I gave them a shotgun to protect themselves from a gang that could show up at any time. This is crazy.* She rolled over and wrapped her arms around her pillow.

But what else can I do? Send them away?

AT FIVE MINUTES TO SEVEN, TWO ORDERLIES IN BLUE scrubs transferred Hank to a gurney and wheeled him out of the room. Lynn walked beside them as they pushed him down the hall to the operating room elevator. She held his hand as they waited for it and kissed him when the doors opened. They wheeled him in. She blew him another kiss and walked back to his room.

It would be several hours before she could see him in recovery. What would she do? She took a book from her purse and opened it. She read a few lines and closed it, not that it wasn't good. She couldn't sit still, not while there was so much swirling in her life. What about Teresa? What of these ten runaways? No, she couldn't sit here. She needed to check in with Kelly Ahearn. Was ICE snooping around Valley Run? What of the gang?

She went back to the elevator and took it down to the first floor. She bought coffee and a bagel in the cafeteria and looked around for a place to sit. Outside, beyond a wall of glass, was a patio furnished with tables and chairs, behind it, a backdrop of thick, green woods; the oak and madrone and redwood of the Northern California forest. *That's what I need right now.* She stepped out into the delicious air of a late summer morning, found a seat, and called Kelly.

"How are you, Lynn? It's crazy, isn't it? Juan Carlos dead."

"You don't know the half of it. I don't know how it could get any crazier." Lynn told her about the accident and Hank's surgery.

"I'm sorry to hear that. You've got a lot going on."

"That's what I wanted to tell you. I got home last night to find two undocumented families looking for sanctuary, worried about ICE raids. Their names are Martha and Manny Garcia, and Gabriela and Jose Cruz. I got the impression they had worked at Valley Run."

"They might have," Kelly said. "I don't know the names of all the pickers."

"But what about ICE? Are you hearing anything about raids?"

"No, I'm not. I'm worried about the gang. A couple of guys came here looking for Jessica. And now she's gone."

"She's hiding from a couple of guys—Rico and Jorge. What did these guys look like?"

"I don't know. My tasting room manager just said they were young Latinos driving a red Camaro."

Lynn gasped. "Oh my God."

"What's wrong?"

"A car like that nearly drove me off the road yesterday morning near the ranch." Lynn told herself it was only coincidence. But it didn't feel like it. It felt like Rico and Jorge were closing in, circling.

"Did you get a look at the driver?"

"No, it was probably someone else."

"I hope so."

Lynn hoped so, too, but she was shaken. Kelly's comment had compounded her fear, given it new life. She had to do something with it. "Will you let me know if you hear anything more about ICE—or the gang?"

"Sure, and you do the same."

"I will."

Lynn hung up, her renewed fear weighing on her. She called Detective Sandoval.

"Yes, Ms. Peterson, what can I do for you?"

"I have some information about Guerrero and Rodriguez."

"MRS. PETERSON, YOU CAN SEE HIM NOW." DR. Montgomery held open the door to the recovery room and ushered her in. Patients in various states of grogginess lay on beds separated by floor-length curtains. Nurses clad in blue and lavender shuttled about the room like honey bees, hovering, checking, moving on. He led her past several still-sleeping patients to one just waking up—Hank.

The room was quiet, and it had the antiseptic smell and the whiteness of a place worried about infection. Lynn was glad for that.

"It went well," the doctor said. "Nothing out of the ordinary. I stitched the kneecap back together and I put some pins in the tibia. He'll be sore, especially the knee, but he'll make a full recovery. It will take a while, but he'll be fine with time."

"When can he go home?"

"Tomorrow."

"Really?"

"Yes, his leg will heal as fast there as it will here." He turned to Hank. "How you doing, champ?"

"Fine, I guess."

"Good. You did well. Just pay attention to the physical therapist." He shook Hank's hand and left.

In forty-five minutes, when he was fully awake and his vital signs were stable, the nurses released Hank to his room. Lynn was working a crossword puzzle and Hank was dozing, when Detective Sandoval knocked on the door, sunglasses propped on her raven hair and neon-green sneakers on her feet as before. It was just before noon.

"May I come in?" she asked.

"Please do," Lynn replied.

"How's the patient?"

"The doctor said it went well, but it's going to be a long slog."

Hank stirred, opened his eyes. His bed had been adjusted to let him sit upright.

"Detective Sandoval is here, honey. I told her I had some information about Guerrero and Rodriguez."

"What's that?" He sounded half asleep.

Lynn turned to the detective. "Another one of the Valley Run workers has run away. I know her. She heard through the grapevine in Roseland that Guerrero and Rodriguez were looking for her. Then this morning Kelly Ahearn, at Valley Run, told me two young guys showed up asking for the girl. She said they were driving a red Camaro.

I think it was the same red Camaro that nearly drove me off the road on Mountaintop Road yesterday morning."

"Red Camaro?" Hank asked, now sounding fully awake. "One drove by the house Monday morning when we were leaving the ranch with ICE. I thought it was odd. It's the kind of car you don't see up there."

"You didn't mention it to me," Lynn said.

"No, I just thought it was odd."

"It is odd," the detective said. "But it's also significant. Guerrero drives a red Camaro. You're right to be concerned. What else can you tell me about them? Anything that connects them to Hernandez?"

"No, but don't you think it says something that they drove by the ranch the morning after he was killed? He would have told them where Teresa was, and they would have come after her."

"We need to talk to Alvarez—Teresa. Any luck with her?"

"I haven't talked to her since Monday."

"Can you try?"

"Yes. By the way, two undocumented families showed up at the ranch last night."

"So, you're Mother Teresa now."

"It's beginning to feel that way. They're hearing that ICE is about to make some big raids. What are you hearing?"

"The same thing. You know," the detective said, "they might be able to help us."

"How?"

"If we can't pin the murder on Guerrero and Rodriguez, maybe we can get them on immigrant smuggling. These people at your place might be able to connect them to a pipeline from Mexico. Can I talk to them?"

"That'll be tricky. How are you going to keep from spooking them?"

"I don't know. Again, I'm going to need your help."

CHAPTER 14

THE RESCUE

THE MORNING FOG DRIFTED OFF THE OCEAN AND HUNG over the village, waiting for the rising sun to burn it off. Teresa watched it as she washed the breakfast dishes. Father Anthony had left for his morning rounds, reminding her she was safe, that things would work out. It's hard, but try to be patient, he said. It was now Wednesday. Lynn had not called since Monday evening. Teresa worried.

The black SUV was gone, but another suspicious-looking government-issued car was parked on the road in front of the rectory. She wondered if there was some agent there around the clock, how they spelled each other, where they slept. *Why am I so important to them? Maybe they will get tired and leave.*

Teresa was grateful for this sanctuary. It was comfortable. Father Angelo was kind and gentle. She *could* stay here forever, she supposed. But she was not monastic. This was not her life. She wanted hers back.

She finished the dishes, dried her hands, and hung the towel over the cabinet door below the sink. She walked out the back door and across the yard to the church office. Margaret, the part-time church administrator, had just opened it.

"Good morning, Teresa," she said. She was a slight, gray-haired woman, retired—and friendly.

"Good morning, Margaret. I'd like to go into the church for a few minutes."

"That's fine, dear."

Teresa opened the door to the sanctuary and entered. It was quiet and dim, the sunlight filtered by stained glass, yellow and green and red. She crossed in front of the altar, made the sign of the cross, and took a seat in the second row of hard wooden pews where she had been just a week before. She knelt and prayed. First, the Lord's Prayer, Padre Nuestro.

Padre nuestro, que está en el cielo, santificado sea tu nombre.

And then Ave Maria, Hail Mary.

Dios te salve, María, llena eres de gracia. El Señor es contigo. Bendita eres entre todas las mujeres, y bendito el fruto de tu vientre, Jesús.

She prayed for strength. She prayed for guidance. And she prayed for mercy. *Forgive me my trespasses. And give me peace. I don't ask for much, Father. I just want to be able to see my daughter and my son and my grandchildren. I want to live without fear.*

With eyes closed, she felt her heart slowing down, her lungs filling and emptying. She saw her loved ones. She held them, blessed them, and let them go. She rose, walked back through the office, and out into the back yard.

The fog had retreated out over the water, a filmy translucent curtain obscuring the infinite, and confining Teresa's thoughts to the here and now, magnifying her predicament. She sat on the bench at the edge of the bluff, vacillating between patience and desperation. There was no escaping her sense of confinement. She was well-fed and cared for. Her surroundings were pleasant, even beautiful, but she was walled in. Not all of the barriers were visible, but they were all real.

There must be a way out of here. She surveyed the limits of her space: the dramatic bluff in front of her; the road behind her, where ICE sat; the church to her right, and the deep cove beyond it with its own impassable bluffs; and to her left, a thick hedge. *That's the only way. What's over there? What will I do if I go there? Lynn said she would help me. Where is she?*

———————

DETECTIVE SANDOVAL HAD BEEN GONE FOR ONLY A FEW minutes when Lynn's phone chirped an incoming message. *ICE is here. Watching the house. I can't stay. Help me.*

Lynn put aside her crossword puzzle and closed her eyes. Her shoulders sagged.

"What is it?" Hank asked.

"Teresa. It's too much, Hank."

"What?"

"ICE has found her. She says they're watching the church."

"Damn. How did that happen?"

"Who knows? They've got eyes everywhere."

"What are you going to do?"

Lynn walked to the window and looked out over the houses below, where people were living unfettered lives, coming and going as they pleased, engaging with their community. "I don't know, Hank. I need some time to think."

"Take a walk. Get some air. I'll be fine."

"I think I will. Thanks." She kissed him and walked out into the hall.

At the elevator, she texted Teresa back. *Stay put. I'm working on it.*

Lynn rode the elevator down. She passed visitors asking for information in the lobby, and walked out into the bright noonday sun. With no idea of a destination, she went to the street, Montgomery Drive, and turned left. She turned left again on Doyle Park Drive, into a neighborhood of small ranch houses; tree-lined, well-maintained, prosperous—safe.

She came to a creek, where a sign read Santa Rosa Creek Greenway. A paved ramp led down to a shady creekside path. She followed it. Beneath the leafy canopy, the air was cool. She found a bench where the stream gurgled over gray, rounded stones, and took a seat. A kingfisher chattered and flew off downstream.

Two lunchtime runners came by, chatting in the rhythm of their breathing, millennials, a man and a woman glistening with sweat. A young mother jogged by, pushing a big-wheeled stroller.

Lynn wished away extraneous thoughts, making room for wisdom. She hoped it would come. *Father Angelo and his parishioners are capable people. They will figure out what to do. The Cruzes and the Garcias? They're not my problem. Surely, they have other places to hide. Do they? Would they have come to the ranch if they had?*

Lynn let these competing thoughts play against one another in her mind, not weighing them in a rational cost-benefit analysis, but letting them vie for attention and acceptance. She watched the water weaving through the rocky stream bed, listened to its constant rippling, and waited for an answer.

When it came, she got up and made her way back to the hospital.

"Well?" Hank asked when Lynn walked through the door. He moved an empty food tray to the table beside his bed.

"I'm going to help her."

"I had a feeling."

"I just couldn't abandon her."

"I know. But you said it was too much. What happened?"

"It's a long story."

"I've got time."

"I don't know if I can go there."

"That's okay. You don't need to."

She felt a lump growing in her throat, tears pooling in the corners of her eyes. She tried to hold them back, but couldn't. They ran down her cheeks and dripped on her shirt. She wiped them on her sleeve. "Yeah, I do. It's important."

She stood with her back to the window, her hands on the sill behind her, and told him the story of Ellie and Randy—how she promised to help them, how she got scared and broke her promise, how the MPs picked him up, how he went back to Vietnam, how he was killed there.

He listened with a long face, somber and serious. "Wow, no wonder. Come here."

She moved to his side. He reached out and pulled her toward him. She buried her face against his neck. He held her tight, as tears moistened his shoulder. "That's a lot to carry by yourself, honey. I wish you'd told me years ago."

She raised her head and looked at him. "I wasn't proud of it. I just wanted it to go away."

"But still."

"I know. That was useless. It wouldn't leave me alone. And now it's back, with Teresa. I think, 'She'll be okay. Father Angelo will take care of her. ICE won't grab her,' and I remember I thought the same thing about Randy: 'The army won't find him. He'll find a way. Someone else will help him.' But they didn't, and the army did."

She sniffled. A little sob rippled her chest. "I just can't let that happen again. I can't."

"I understand."

"I can't. I promised people. They need me."

"It sounds like she needs you *now*. What are you going to tell her?"

"That I'll be up there this afternoon."

"ICE will recognize you."

"I know. I'll figure something out. Will you be okay?"

"Don't worry about me. This leg won't know you're gone. Do what you need to do."

Lynn hugged him again, gave him a long, tender kiss, and left.

TERESA STIRRED SLICES OF SIZZLING ONIONS, PEPPERS, and chicken in a cast-iron frying pan. The aroma filled her nostrils, smelling of home. In another, she heated fresh tortillas—lunch for her and Father Angelo, back from his morning rounds. She looked out the front window. The car was still there. It wore on her. *I could go crazy here.* Cooking was a welcome distraction. She returned to it.

She scooped a tortilla from the pan, added it to a stack on a plate beside the stove, and placed a cloth napkin over them to keep them warm. She turned off the burners, and brought the tortillas and the strips of meat and vegetables to the table.

"Gracias. May I?" Father Angelo asked.

"Please do, before they get cold."

He took a tortilla, filled it, topped it with fresh tomatillo salsa, folded it, and took a bite. "Mmm, excelente."

"Gracias, senõr." She reached for a tortilla. And her phone rang.

"Teresa, it's Lynn. I'm on the way."

"Oh, thank you. Thank you so much."

"I can't drive directly to the church. ICE will recognize me. Is there a back way?"

"I don't know, but Father Angelo might. He's right here."

"Can you put him on speaker?"

She did, and placed the phone on the table between the two of them.

"This is Father Angelo, Lynn. How may I help you?"

"Father, is there a way to get into the church or the rectory without coming through the front door?"

He turned in his chair, as though to look at the back yard. And then turned back to the table.

"Maybe there is. There is a house next to us, with a thick hedge in between. On the other side of that house are three cottages and the inn—Blue Cove Inn. Ted and Mary Jernigan run it. They also head our sanctuary committee. You could drive there. Tell them I sent you. If there *is* a way to get safely here from there, they will know—and they will help you. I'll call them and tell them you're on the way. How are you coming?"

"I'm not sure. What's the quickest way? I'm in Santa Rosa."

"Take the 101 to 128 in Cloverdale, 128 through the Anderson Valley to Navarro, and then south a couple of miles on the Coast Highway to Elk. It will take you about two hours."

"I'm on my way."

Teresa looked at Father Angelo and managed a smile. "I don't know where this is going, Father, but I feel better. I can't stay here. Not with them out there."

"I know, dear." He reached across the table and squeezed her hand. "I know."

US 101, THE REDWOOD HIGHWAY, RAN NORTH FROM Santa Rosa through the heart of Sonoma's wine country—Healdsburg, Geyserville, and Asti—following the Russian River. Vineyards fill the valley, squeezed between steep hills alternately wooded and cleared. All was radiant in the bright, clear light of early September, the deep green of summer leaves and the golden brown of dry California grass.

The scale of grape-growing and winemaking was not lost on Lynn as she sped toward Cloverdale. *Who picks all these grapes?* It was a rhetorical question. She knew who picked them: Mexican-Americans and Mexicans; some documented guest workers, others undocumented, like Teresa and Martha and Manny, and Gabriela and Jose. Kelly Ahearn and the other winemakers were not interested in the status of the workers. They needed hands—eager, hard-working, and skilled. Wine required grapes. Grapes required picking. On the vine, they were useful only to birds. Any ambivalence Lynn might have felt about her mission dissolved in her contemplation of the unfairness and inequity of this modern-day land of milk and honey.

At Cloverdale, she turned northwest on CA 128, as Father Angelo had instructed. The landscape of the Anderson Valley became famil-iar—Boonville and Philo—Mendo Wines.

She wondered about Amy Henderson. *Does no news mean good news? Probably not.*

Her progress slowed where the road followed the Navarro River through redwood-covered hills to the coast. She became more atten-tive. But when she turned south on the Coast Highway five miles north of Elk, any stray thoughts of landscape or history or inequity vanished. She entered a new place of hyper-focus, a place tinged with wariness and fear, and emboldened with courage and purpose.

She entered the village like a commando behind enemy lines, slow-ing to the speed limit at Blessed Sacrament Church, scanning the road-sides for ICE, and checking her rearview mirror as she turned in to the inn, trusting that Hank's VW had provided cover.

A colorful, handcarved sign read Blue Cove Inn: Since 1901. Elements of the building's original form remained. Renovations and additions had updated and repurposed it, but it retained the charm of an historical landmark. Lynn parked behind the inn, well off the road, and entered by a side door guarded by a rose-covered arbor.

She rang a bell at the front desk.

"Just a minute," came a woman's voice from around the corner. "I'll be right there." In no time at all, a tan woman with a long gray ponytail came through the parlor-like lobby. "May I help you?"

"Yes, I'm Lynn Peterson. Father Angelo sent me."

"Of course. We've been expecting you. I'm Mary Jernigan. Come in." She ushered Lynn into an office just large enough for a small wooden desk, two Windsor chairs, and a filing cabinet. Photographs of the Mendocino coast hung on the walls—foam-washed sea stacks, dramatic cliffs, turquoise water.

"I'm sorry it's taken me so long to get up here. My husband and I were in a bad accident, and he's in the hospital."

"Yes, I've heard. You've had a rough stretch."

Lynn smiled. "Yeah, we have. And now we've got ICE out there."

"Teresa is talking about leaving. We don't think that's such a good idea."

"I don't either, not if she doesn't have somewhere else to go, but I don't know if we can stop her." Lynn explained that she had come to respond to Teresa's call, to be supportive, and with Teresa and the sanctuary committee, try to find a way forward. "Father Angelo said we might be able to get to the rectory from here without being seen from the road."

"I think you can staying close to the bluff, but to be safe, you should wait until dark."

"That makes sense. I'll call her and tell her I'm here."

"I'll leave you here," Mary said. "I've got some work to do in the kitchen. Thank you for coming. You're good to be doing this work." She offered her hand.

Lynn took it and responded, "And you, also."

Mary rose and left the office. Lynn remained, previewing her imminent conversation with Teresa. *What will I say when she tells me she wants to leave immediately? She will. How can I keep her here? She's a free person. No, she's not, not now. That's the point. Where do I take her? Can we go back to George's?*

She called Teresa.

"Lynn, thank you, thank you. Where are you?"

"Over at the inn."

"I need to get out of here."

"I know you do, but we should wait until we've found another place for you."

"I can't wait, Lynn. I'm a prisoner here. I want to see my children and grandchildren."

"They can come here."

"I know they can, but it's not the same. It's like a prison visit."

"I'll come over to the rectory after dark. We can talk about it then."

"Be careful, Lynn. These ICE guys never take their eyes off this place. Be careful."

Lynn went searching for the kitchen, admiring the old building, a pleasing combination of old and new, period antiques in bright, modernized spaces. She found Mary in the kitchen with the cook, menus spread out before them on a long stainless steel table. She waited while the two finished their conversation.

"How did it go?" Mary asked.

"About as I expected. She wants to leave."

"But where will you take her?"

"That's the thing. The only place I know is my neighbor's house. ICE has no reason to check there, but it's awfully close to my place. I'm clutching at straws here. Do you have any ideas?"

Mary took a few seconds, then said, "Ted and I have a cabin up in the hills, a few miles from here. Like your place, it's not far from prying eyes. But it might work as an interim solution."

"Can you talk to your husband about it before I go over to the rectory tonight?"

"I will."

Lynn walked across the back lawn to the edge of the bluff and looked out over the cove. Its cobalt-blue water and steep dark cliffs were stunning.

A path worn in the grass led along the bluff to the south. She followed it behind a house, through a grassy nature preserve, to a small park. She crossed the road to the little Elk Store and bought a tall cup of coffee. Locally Roasted in Fort Bragg read the sign on the urn. She took the coffee back across the road to the park, found a shaded picnic table with a view of the water, and sat. It was five o'clock, three hours before dark.

She sipped her coffee, letting the stiff afternoon sea breeze blow back her hair. It whistled through the branches of the Monterey cypress above her, while two hundred feet below her, waves curled in perfect tubes, collapsed, and ran up on the white sand of a small crescent beach. The air smelled of salt and wildflowers. Bees buzzed. Ravens floated above the cliffs on powerful updrafts. Black cormorants flew low over the water to and from their rocky perches. Seals bobbed in the surf. Lynn immersed herself in the scene and waited.

At six, she followed the path back to the inn, where Mary fed her in the airy dining room, with its large western windows that promised an unobstructed view of the sunset. She dined on fresh Klamath River salmon and a salad of local greens, taking her time, waiting for dark.

As she nursed a glass of Mendocino County pinot noir, Mary Jernigan came to her table.

"May I sit?" she asked.

"Please do."

"Ted and I have talked about the cabin. We've decided there's no reason for her not to stay there if she insists on leaving the rectory, at least until you can find something else for her. It's close, but it's out of the way. It might be the perfect hideaway."

Lynn had not realized how wired and tense she had become until the relief of Mary's offer worked its way into her muscles and tendons. In focusing on her own responsibility for Teresa's fate, it had become easy for her to forget that others were prepared to help her. If she managed to free Teresa from the rectory undetected, the cabin would get them over the next hurdle. "Oh, thank you, Mary. I can't tell you how sweet that sounds."

"It's nothing. We're happy to help. We're in this with you."

Should I mention the new refugees? Is that too much? What else can I do?

As the sun set, Mary and Lynn hatched a plan to get Lynn in and out of the rectory under the noses of the authorities. Mary would go out to the road and walk to the rectory, hoping to distract the agents. Lynn would text Teresa and slip along the edge of the bluff, hurrying through the open places to the cover of trees and bushes. Safely in the rectory's back yard, she would slide along the hedgerow to the back door, where Teresa would meet her.

At eight o'clock, Lynn texted Teresa, *I'm on my way. Meet me at the back door.* She and Mary left the inn by the side door, passed under the arbor, and went to their positions. Mary turned right, toward the road, and Lynn, left, toward the bluff.

Under the cypress trees on the bluff, Lynn stopped and looked back. Mary was starting down the road toward the church. The distraction would be short-lived. Lynn would need to move.

"Uno más, compadre, por favor." With his left hand, Rico held out an empty beer bottle toward his friend.

Jorge took it, set it aside, retrieved another Corona from the cooler beside him, and put it in Rico's hand. They sat on the front stoop of Rico's house in Roseland. It was several hours after dark.

"Gracias." Rico squeezed off the cap and flipped it with a snap of his fingers, sending it flying into the night like a tiny flying saucer. He put the bottle to his lips and took a long swig. "We need to go back there tonight. She'll be there."

"Teresa?"

"No, the gringo woman. For sure, she moved Teresa before ICE got there. She knows where she is."

Across the street, a small person raced across a lawn and kicked an empty can. It flew into the street, clattering as it rolled. Children screeched with glee and ran for cover behind bushes and parked cars. One ran into the street to fetch the can. A car stopped to avoid it. The driver hollered out the open window.

Rico went into the house and came back with a jacket. "It'll be cold up there."

"I know. I'm okay."

Rico tipped back his head, emptied the bottle, and handed it to Jorge. "Here."

Jorge took it and set it in a six-pack carrier with the others.

"Let's go." Rico took his keys from his pocket and walked toward the car.

LYNN ROUNDED THE END OF A PICKET FENCE, HUGGING IT for safety, the roar of surf a constant reminder of danger. She shuffled past three identical cottages set side by side on the edge of the cliff. A dog barked. A face peered out a window. She hurried on.

She skirted another fence and searched for the way forward. The fog had returned, rolling off the water and up over the cliff. It was cold on her face. A wide field lay before her, disappearing into the murky darkness. To her left, it met the void. No fence or shrubbery guarded the precipice. Ahead, through moving veils of fog, she made out a stand of trees. She stepped into the field.

To her right, a car turned into a driveway, lighting up the fog. She froze. As quickly as it appeared, the light went out. She hurried across to the trees and stopped to get her bearings. She bent forward, hands on her knees, catching her breath. Her heart pounded. She moved on, feeling safer in the cover of the trees.

On the far side of the grove, she came to a hedgerow and stopped. Waves crashed; louder, she thought, closer. The gap between the end of the hedgerow and the cliff was narrow. *Can I do this?* She hesitated. *What choice do I have?* Through force of will, she calmed her heartbeat, reached into the hedge for a hold, and slipped around it. In front of her was a familiar wooden bench, and across a narrow lawn, an edifice. *The church?* To her right, a light glowed in the window of a small house. A door cracked open. Her phone chirped.

Lynn, I'm at the back door now.

She hurried along the hedgerow toward the crack of light. She called through it. "Teresa?" The door swung open, and she slipped through.

Teresa closed it behind her and threw her arms around Lynn like a young girl greeting a doting grandparent. "Lynn, you made it."

The crossing had been nerve-wracking, but Lynn chose not to go there. She might be taking Teresa back with her. "Of course I did." She held Teresa at arm's length and added, "Teresa, I'm so glad to be here. I'm sorry it took so long."

"I understand."

They walked into the main room, where Mary and Father Angelo sat at the table. The curtains and blinds were closed, and the lights were low; to keep ICE guessing, Lynn assumed. Only a light over the stove and a floor lamp in the corner of the main room were on.

"What now?" Lynn asked, taking a chair.

"Nothing's changed," Teresa said. "I need to go. These people are wonderful, but I can't live here."

"I worry about you getting caught," Father Angelo said with an air of wise benevolence befitting his clerical garb: black shirt and white clerical collar.

"I do, too," Teresa said, "but I'm willing to take the risk. It's my life. I need to live it." She had the look of someone pleading for her life.

"It will probably be underground," Lynn said.

"I know."

"Then you'll need our place," Mary said.

"What's that?" Teresa asked.

"I told Lynn about a cabin Ted and I have up in the hills. It's not far. You can stay there until you find something better."

Teresa closed her eyes and sighed in deep relief. "Thank you, Mary. Thank you."

"It's nothing—what we're doing here, just in a different place."

Teresa looked around the table with smiling eyes. "You all are so kind. I don't know how to thank you."

"You thank us with your courage. That's enough," Mary said.

Should I tell them about the others? Lynn thought. *They didn't sign up for that. What harm can it do?* "We may need the cabin again, Mary."

"Oh."

"I have ten more people in my house right now looking for sanctuary—two families. Rumors are flying about ICE raids in the vineyards. They know you, Teresa—the Garcia and Cruz families."

Mary looked at Father Angelo. "I don't know if we're ready for that. We'll have to talk about it."

"That's all I ask. Thank you."

———

MARY STEPPED OUT THE FRONT DOOR INTO THE FOGGY night. Father Angelo made a show of wishing her goodbye. He closed the door and peered through the kitchen window toward the road. When she reached the ICE patrol car, he gave the word "Go."

Lynn, with Teresa close behind, hustled to the hedgerow and hurried along it to the edge of the bluff. "Just stay with me," Lynn said. "Don't wander, especially toward the cliff. Do exactly what I do." *If I go over, she's going too.* But Lynn was confident, and wanted Teresa to feel her confidence.

Moving only when there were no passing cars to light up the fog, they retraced Lynn's steps. In ten minutes, they were behind the inn. "Get in and keep your head down," Lynn told Teresa when they reached Hank's VW.

Lynn slipped to the cover of the rose arbor over the side door, and tried the knob. It was locked. A pulse of fear shot through her.

The knob jiggled and the door opened. Mary stood on the other side. "I need to check with Ted before we leave. It'll just be a minute. I'll lead the way to the cabin. You'll follow me, but give me a head start—a minute or so. When I get out of sight of the agent, I'll pull over and wait for you."

"What are you driving?"

"A black Prius."

Lynn liked the continuity of that coincidence. It felt right. And she said as much. Then she added, "Do you think Teresa will be all right by herself tonight? I have those ten other sanctuary seekers in my house right now, and I need to check on them."

"Sure. I'll get her situated, make sure she has food."

Mary went to find Ted. In a few minutes, she returned. "We'll turn right on the Coast Highway. At the end of town—about a quarter of a mile—where the road drops down to cross Greenwood Creek, we turn left on the Philo Greenwood Road. It's marked. If you reach the creek, you've gone too far. I'll pull over about a hundred yards down, on the right, under a big cypress. Remember, give me a minute."

They left the inn. Lynn watched Mary climb into her Prius, turn on the lights, and ease out of the driveway onto the Coast Highway. She was operating on pure adrenaline, her body chemistry tuned both for flight and fight. She wondered if Teresa felt the same. She couldn't tell. "Well, this is it, Teresa—the getaway. We're not there yet, but we're close. You okay?"

In the dim light from village windows, Teresa looked jittery. Lynn tried to put herself in Teresa's shoes. Yes, the same hormone flowed in her veins, but she was in a very different position. Teresa was not in charge; she had no control over where she was going or how she would get there. Unlike Lynn, she was not focusing her energy on the car ahead, or an unfamiliar destination. *Teresa has had to surrender totally to the care of others. I don't know if I have that kind of faith.*

"The police want to talk to you about Rico and Jorge," Lynn said when she turned onto the highway.

"I know, but I can't."

"I told them I'd ask. But I understand. The thing is, Rico and Jorge are still looking for you, and they're looking for me, too. We saw their car on our road the other day. They're going after Jessica, too. She's hiding at Karen's." Lynn slowed. A sign read Philo Greenwood Road.

"So far, so good. This is it." She turned.

"Do you think they killed Juan Carlos?"

"I do. And I think they can kill again. You might be able to stop it."

"How?"

"You can tie them to Juan Carlos, and you might know something that ties them to the murder."

"Like what?"

"You never know. It could be something simple."

Mary pulled out onto the road ahead of them. They left the village, skirted a broad pasture, and entered the forest above Greenwood Creek. Lynn lost Mary's tail lights around a bend now and then, but never for long.

"I talked to Detective Sandoval. She said they might give you immunity."

"From what?"

"From stealing the wine with Juan Carlos and taking the payments from the other workers."

"He forced me."

"I know, but they could call you an accessory."

"That's not fair."

"I know." Lynn agreed, but she also agreed with the police that Teresa held the key to prosecuting Rico, Jorge, and the rest of the gang.

They rode along silently for a few minutes. On the hills east of the village, they climbed out of the fog. Stars appeared in uncountable numbers.

"The thing is," Teresa said. "I need amnesty for something much worse."

"Oh?"

"Murder."

Murder?! Oh my God! Lynn was stunned. She drove the next few curves unable to respond. *Tell me there's some explanation, some mitigating circumstance, please.* "What do you mean?" she asked finally.

"Twenty-five years ago when I came across the border with my boyfriend, he got involved with a street gang in San Diego. And I became involved, too, because I was with him. I didn't know anybody else. They were smuggling drugs across the border—mostly marijuana—and some people, too. One night there was a shoot-out with another gang. My boyfriend killed one of them. He was caught, but he wasn't convicted because no one talked. I was there, but I got away and came north. They issued a warrant for my arrest. Like you say, I'm an accessory."

Your boyfriend killed someone? What? Who is this person? Are those questions unfair? The person beside me is not the one living with a gang member. Twenty-five years is a long time. She let that idea sink in. *And who am I to judge someone who risks much to venture into a new land with nothing but the clothes on her back?*

Lynn drove a few more curves in silence. The word *shoot-out* burrowed into her memory and imagination. In the darkness beyond her headlights, she saw a soldier walking a jungle trail with his platoon mates, his uniform soaked with sweat, eyes searching the trees for signs of Viet Cong, scanning the ground ahead for signs of land mines and snares. Flame exploded from hidden muzzles to the fearsome tat-tat-tat of AK-47s. Soldiers groaned, cried out, "I'm hit!" Randy threw his hands high and dropped to his knees, his chest red with blood, his eyes telegraphing his fate.

*Teresa was merely with someone who killed another per*son. *I caused someone's death. Shame on me for judging her.* "It's been a long time, and you were just a kid. You could help them put Rico and Jorge away, and get that gang off the street. That would be a good thing."

"Yes, it would."

Lynn followed Mary when she reached the crest of the ridge and turned north on Cameron Road, and again a few minutes later when Mary braked and turned left down a narrow dirt track that tunneled into thick, dark forest, and ended in a small clearing. Lit only by the stars, a cabin clad in wide rough-hewn boards sat on a steep west-facing slope. Lynn imagined it had a view of the Pacific.

At the cabin door Mary used her phone to find the lock. She turned the key, opened the door, and flipped on a light. "There. They'll never find you here."

AT TEN O'CLOCK, AFTER A BRIEF FAREWELL AND AN ASSURance of returning the next day, Lynn left Teresa in Mary's care and headed south. She texted Martha, *Leaving Elk now. See you in two hours.*

Okay, Martha replied. *Drive careful.*

At several points along the way, straining to follow the narrow, unlit roads—the Coast Highway, and beyond Stewart's Point, the unfamiliar Skaggs Spring Road—she wondered if it might not have been wiser to spend the night in the cabin with Teresa. It had been a long day.

Sometime after midnight, she pulled in under the big oak in front of the cottage at Bella Vista, exhausted. The house was dark, save for the light over the back door. *You're sweet, Martha.*

She stepped out into the cool night and breathed in the scent of sea and fir and grass. The faintest of breezes stirred the leaves above her. *It's good to be back!*

She started for the back door. A low rumble broke the silence. *Is that a car? Now?* She stopped. Motionless, she listened. It grew louder, then stopped. *Maybe not. You're tired.*

She hurried to the back door and unlocked it. It squeaked when she pushed it open and again when she closed it behind her. She locked it.

Through the walls of the house, she heard the muffled but unmistakable thunk of car doors closing. Her heart raced.

Martha emerged from her bedroom, half asleep.

"Did you hear that?"

"Sí."

Lynn called George. *Please answer, George. Please.*

"Lynn?" he asked. "What's wrong?"

"George, there's a strange car here. We heard the doors close. Hurry!"

"I'm on my way."

She shooed Martha back into the bedroom and reached behind the pantry door for the shotgun. She checked to see that it was loaded, turned off the outside light, and stood back from the door.

The knob rattled. Voices murmured.

These fuckers are not going to get in here. "I've got a gun," she barked.

The voices went silent. Then came a thud. The door shuddered. It held.

If that door opens . . . Another thud, the splintering of wood. It flew open. Two forms stood in the darkness. She fired.

CHAPTER 15

STANDING HER GROUND

LYNN STOOD IN THE HALLWAY WITH THE SHOTGUN AT her shoulder, aiming at the two figures in the darkness beyond the open back door. Every ounce of her energy and will was focused on holding the gun steady, as steady as the most seasoned hunter ever held one. The acrid smell of gunpowder filled her nostrils. The blast of the weapon still reverberated in her ears. *Did I hit them? Are they coming at me?*

"Don't try me, assholes! I'll shoot again!" she shouted into the night, not so much from bravado as from the fear she might have to shoot again. *I don't want to kill anybody. Tell me this isn't happening.*

Outside a man groaned and staggered. His accomplice threw an arm around him and dragged him into the darkness. Lynn slammed the door shut and leaned her back against it, panting with the extraordinary exertion of self-preservation.

The bedroom door opened a crack. Martha peered out with terrified eyes. Behind her in the dark room, children sobbed.

Lynn stood up, straightened her back, and swung the back door open. She stepped to the corner of the house and fired again toward the fleeing phantoms, guided by the crunch of gravel beneath their feet.

A car engine sounded; the lights came on, lighting up the house, and swung away as the car sped out to the road and headed north, just as George's truck came over the rise from the south.

She was reloading when George pulled up beside her.

"What in the name of God?" he asked, climbing out of his truck. "Did you use that thing, missy?"

"You're damn right. Hit one of them. Might have killed him." *Might have killed him. I might have killed him.* Adrenaline had been coursing through her veins for hours, since she'd first crept along the edge of the bluff to rescue Teresa from the rectory. Now it drained away, leaving her limp. She drooped, exhaling fear and tension, inhaling relief. The shotgun dangled from her right hand.

"Should I chase 'em?" George asked.

"I doubt you'll catch them. But I'm calling the cops."

George took the shotgun from her hand. He wrapped an arm around her and pulled her close. "You done good." He guided her to the dark house.

Lynn slumped against him, her energy spent. Without him she might have withered to the ground.

In the kitchen, she flipped on a light, revealing the stunned, frightened faces of all ten of her new charges. They watched as she pulled out a chair and collapsed into it. She pushed it back with her legs. It creaked. She sighed. Outside a whippoorwill called a melancholy, "Whup, whup, whup, whup."

Five-year-old Patricia peeked out from behind her mother's legs, sniffling. "Did you shoot them?" she asked.

"Yes, I did." Those three little words sounded as foreign to her as anything she had ever said. She had never wanted to shoot a gun. And she had never in her wildest dreams imagined she would ever fire one at another person. But she had. *I need to call Maria Sandoval.* She took her phone from her pocket and called. The phone rang so long she expected it to go to voicemail.

But it didn't. A voice said, "Yes, Lynn."

"They're coming for me, detective. Two guys just tried to break into my house up on Mountaintop Road in Cazadero. I shot one of them. They drove north toward Tin Barn Road."

"How long ago?"

"Five minutes."

"Could you identify them?"

"No."

"How about the car?"

"Not sure. It was long, low; a sports car, maybe. Hard to say. It was dark."

"Is everyone okay there?"

"Yes."

"Good. I'll call you back." Detective Sandoval hung up.

The children huddled behind their parents, clinging to them, staring at Lynn and George, like their parents.

"We can't stay here, Lynn." Martha's voice quivered.

"Who those guys?" Manny asked. "Rico and Jorge?"

"I don't know. It was dark, but who else could it be?"

Martha stepped forward. "We need to leave. I don't know where we'll go, but we need to leave."

Lynn looked up at George, who was leaning against the sink with his arms folded across his chest and his brow wrinkled.

"You don't need to worry about them coming back tonight," he said. "Who knows, one of them might be dead by now."

Gabriela gasped. Her eyes grew wide, and her mouth fell open.

"Dead?" Margarita asked.

"Maybe. The cops are on this. They'll be up here soon, I'm sure."

"What about us?" Martha asked.

"They aren't ICE," George said. "But it might not be a good idea for you to be here. You can go back to my place. But you better hurry."

Lynn roused herself into action, mustering energy from some deep interior well. *Hurry. Yes, must hurry.* She went to the counter and took a flashlight from a drawer beside the sink. "Hurry, get your things," she said to the group.

Martha went into the bedroom, and Gabriela, to the loft. In a few minutes they returned with the few small bags they had brought.

"That's everything?" Lynn asked.

"Sí," Martha said.

Gabriela nodded.

"Okay, then. Let's go." Lynn opened the back door, and one after the other, the two families followed. With her light she led them behind the barn to their cars, the beat-up Explorer and the faded Civic. "Just follow George. You'll be safe at his place."

She watched as the three-car caravan crept to the road and disappeared over the rise. *They ought to be safe there. But God, I thought they were safe here. When is this going to end?*

Back in the house, Lynn collected blankets and returned them to the chest in her bedroom. She straightened up the bed in the loft and rearranged the covers on hers to hide the fact that more than one person had been sleeping in it. Then she fell back on her bed, arms spread wide, and closed her eyes. As she had feared, Rico and Jorge had found her, but they had not prevailed. The police would arrive. She would tell them what happened. She had nothing to hide, aside from her new guests, who were, for the moment, not her guests, and she had nothing to fear, she told herself.

———

THE CAMARO SCREAMED NORTH. JORGE SAT SLUMPED over against the door in the front passenger seat, moaning. "I'm hurt bad, Rico, bad."

"I know, compadre. I'm driving as fast as I can." He looked over at his friend, whose right shoulder and arm were red with blood. He turned left at the tin barn as he had a few days earlier, but whereas before he had turned right on Simpson Ranch Road, he went straight, staying on the paved road.

The road brought him to the Coast Highway a few miles north of Jenner. He raced through the curves on the winding road, slowing as he dipped into ravines, accelerating as he climbed out of them to the treacherous bluffs high above the water, repeatedly looking over at his friend whenever he could risk taking his eyes off the road.

How am I going to do this? They'll ask questions. I could drop him in the lobby and take off, refuse to answer questions, say I don't know what happened, that he was shot on the street and came to my house. I don't know. Rico debated these options as he drove. He couldn't leave his friend on the side of the road to die—or could he? *The police will question him in the hospital. What if he talks?* Could he finish his friend off, or dump him in some remote place? No, he could not, he decided. He would trust in the honor of the brotherhood of thieves.

"Tell them you were shot on the street in Roseland," he said as they made their way into Santa Rosa on the 101.

Jorge moaned.

Rico glanced at his friend. "Can you hear me, Jorge?"

Jorge moaned again.

Rico exited the highway at College Avenue, turned right on Brookwood, and then left on Montgomery Drive. "How you doin', Jorge?" he asked as he pulled up to the emergency room entrance at Santa Rosa Memorial.

Jorge did not answer.

Rico jumped out of the car and signaled for help. Medics raced out with a gurney, pulled Jorge out of the car, and wheeled him into the hospital. Rico got back in the car and put his hands on the wheel. He hesitated, watching the gurney disappear into the hospital. Then he turned the key and drove out onto the street.

———

LYNN DOZED, AND SHE DREAMED—OF ELLIE AND RANDY. They were hiding in the basement of her parents' home in Cincinnati. She was sitting in the living room—on guard—a shotgun on her lap. A car stopped on the street in front of the house. She peeked out through the living room curtains. Two men in army uniforms got out and slammed the doors behind them. They walked to the front door, carrying a battering ram. They pounded on the door. "Go away," she said. "Give us that commie coward!" they yelled. "Over my dead body!" she screamed. The battering ram crashed against the door. It splintered and flew open. She fired. They stepped through the doorway. She fired again. They kept coming. The phone rang louder, louder still.

She woke. It rang again. She reached for it.

"Hello," she said, too groggy to note the caller ID.

"Lynn, it's Maria Sandoval. A county sheriff's deputy is on his way. He'll ask for a statement, and he'll want to inspect the scene. He'll probably stay there all night. I told him you need protection. I'm sending people to check the hospital emergency rooms."

"Okay."

"Did you talk to Teresa?"

"Yeah."

"What did she say?"

In her half sleep, Lynn tried to bring herself into the present. *What did Teresa say? Oh yeah.* "She understands, but she's not there yet."

"Maybe this will change her mind."

"It might, but then again, it might scare her more."

A broad swath of light beamed through the kitchen window and swept across the wall above her bed. The sound of an engine grew louder and stopped. "I think he's here, detective," she said. "Let me check."

Still in her clothes, Lynn got up and walked to the kitchen. A man stepped out of a police car. *This is way too much like my dream.* "He's here, detective."

"Let me know what he says. I'll check with you in the morning."

The officer walked to the front door and knocked. Lynn turned on a light in the front room and opened the door for a burly man, thirty-ish, in a khaki uniform. His bulging biceps overfilled its short sleeves. With a Marine Corp haircut—close-cropped above the ears, longer on top—he looked serious, disciplined. Somehow that, and the sidearm in a black leather holster on his hip, inspired confidence.

"Mrs. Peterson?"

That simple question rattled Lynn. She told herself again, she had nothing to hide, nothing to fear. *But I did shoot someone. He might be dead. That's something to worry about.* "Yes," she replied.

"We've had a report of a shooting here."

"Yes, sir."

"First, is everyone all right?"

"Yes. It's just me."

"Does anyone else live here?"

"My husband, but he's in the hospital in Santa Rosa."

"Can you tell me what happened?"

She described hearing the car, the rattling of the doorknob, the smashing of the door. She told him she'd warned them, the door flew open, and she fired a shotgun. She walked him past the kitchen to the back hall. It still smelled of gunpowder.

He inspected the cracked door and broken frame, took pictures. The double-barreled shotgun leaned against the wall. He picked it up. "I assume this is the gun."

"It is, sir." Seeing the shotgun in his hands, she felt a surge of pride in her quick-thinking, steadfast defense of the house.

He opened it and dumped the spent shells into his open hand. He examined them like specimens of precious gems. "Twelve gauge. That bastard is hurting if he's still alive."

She nodded.

"We'll need these. Do you have any live shells?"

Lynn opened the door to the pantry, took two shiny red shells from a box on the shelf, and handed them to him. "Is that enough?"

"Sure." He scanned the ground by the back door with his flashlight, revealing numerous partial, overlapping scuffed footprints in the dust, some pointing in, some pointing out.

She worried about the story he might piece together from those prints. Could he tell ten people, large and small, had recently left?

"You heard their car," he said. "Do you know where they parked it?"

"Not exactly. It was probably halfway to the barn, over there." She pointed toward the equipment barn.

"We'll leave that to the forensics guys in the morning. Hopefully they'll find tire tracks. That's all I need now, ma'am. You're free to get some sleep, if you can. I'll stay here in the squad car until morning. Good night, ma'am." He tipped his cap. "You done one helluva good job protectin' yourself."

Lynn watched as he walked to his car, turned on the roof light, took the radio microphone from the dashboard, and began speaking into it. Then she stepped inside and closed the door. It sagged open a crack, letting a gentle stream of night air through. *One more maintenance job.* The thought reminded her of Becky Tillson. *How am I going to explain this to her?* She began to put together the story. *I have to tell her the whole thing, and she won't be happy with it. Karen brought Teresa to me. Her abuser found her here. George chased him off. He turned Teresa in to ICE. They came. She escaped. They took us in to Santa Rosa. We hit a tree on the way back. George is in the hospital. Oh, this sounds great. She's going to love it. Juan Carlos was murdered. And now this. I shot someone here. Oh my God, what a story. It's too much.* She sat on her bed, pulled off her shoes, and without removing her clothes, lifted the covers, and slid under them.

IT WAS STILL PITCH BLACK WHEN MARIA SANDOVAL pulled into a space marked Emergency Room Parking Only, and hustled into the admittance room of Santa Rosa Memorial. The colleague she'd sent to check for a male shotgun victim had called. Now he stood in his blue uniform by the door to the emergency room. She stepped toward him past a gaunt man with a long, untended Ho Chi Minh beard and a bloodied forehead, the stale, pungent smell of alcohol rising from him.

"We may have our man," he said, "but he's in pretty bad shape."

"Is he going to make it?"

"Don't know. He showed up about two. The orderly at the door said the guy who brought him in drove off as they were wheeling him in."

"Did he notice what the guy was driving?"

"Yeah, a Camaro."

"Fits."

"The ER security camera confirmed it, got the plate number."

"Good."

"He's been in there a couple of hours. No telling when he'll be out. Like I said, he's messed up good."

"Did you get a description?"

"Better than that. They took a picture for me." He opened his phone and showed her a young, bare-chested Hispanic male with a right arm and shoulder that looked like tenderized meat.

"That's Sanchez, the sidekick. That means the other guy was probably Guerrero. Stay here until he's out. Then confirm his identity, and guard his room. No one who isn't hospital staff gets in. I'm going over to Roseland."

She strode back to her car and drove the mile and a half to the Hispanic enclave, west of the 101 and south of the 12, feeling a heightened sense of urgency. Rico meant business. He had upped the ante, challenging her to take him off the streets. It was a challenge she intended to meet.

When she reached Rico's block she slowed. The activity of the previous evening was long since over. The street was devoid of traffic. No windows were lit. No music played. No children darted from behind parked cars. A camouflaged cat prowled through the cover of overgrown shrubbery. A fat raccoon rattled a garbage can by the curb. But Rico's car was not in his driveway—or on the street.

Maria drove the quiet streets of the neighborhood, one after another, looking for the red Camaro. Not finding it, she drove home to catch a few hours of sleep.

LYNN SLEPT FITFULLY. AFTER ANY OTHER LATE NIGHT, her weary muscles would have kept her asleep until eight or later, but that morning she woke before sunrise. The last traumatic event of the previous evening sat on her shoulder and whispered into her ear a not-so-gentle reminder of its existence. *You shot someone. You shot someone.* She stirred. *I shot someone. I can't believe I shot someone.* One half-open eye took in the hint of light in the east, beyond the barn. She shut the eye and savored the soft comfort of her pillow. *Not now. Later.* The bed held her for another moment, but the ingrained discipline of the school teacher overpowered it. She pushed herself up on one tired elbow and opened her eyes. Then she rose and looked for her clothes on the chair beside the bed. They weren't there. She looked down at herself. She was wearing them. *Of course. No point in changing them now. The chickens won't mind.*

She staggered out into the cool of the morning, still waking. *Need to check on the families. They were terrified, must still be. And those poor kids.* Over her shoulder, the sheriff's deputy was sitting upright in his squad car, awake. She nodded and opened the barn door.

The animals brought her back to the present with their charm. She ran her hand over the goat's soft white fleece. It twitched its ears and bleated. The earnest chickens clucked as they scurried about her feet.

She opened the big back doors and let the goat out into the pasture and the chickens into the barnyard. Fresh, cool air poured in. *Oh, wouldn't it be nice just to stay here all day and be a caretaker?* But she couldn't. Forensic examiners would be arriving soon. Hank would be released from the hospital, and she would pick him up. Teresa was in a new temporary sanctuary in Elk; she would need attending to. And there were the ten scared refugees at George's house. They couldn't stay there.

The first rays of the rising sun burst over a dark, distant ridge like sharp golden swords. A white-crowned sparrow called from the edge of the forest. The air was filled with the intermingled scents of fir and dried grass that identified this place for her as surely as her sight. The newness of the day delighted her, called her to welcome it. And she did. But she could not tarry. She had things to do; chores, duties, responsibilities. And there was still Rico, the ongoing threat she was determined to defeat. *I'm not backing down.*

She walked back toward the house energized by the dawn, but wary. The policeman saw her and climbed out of his car, stretching his arms, clasping them behind his head, yawning.

"Thanks for staying last night. I would have been crazy here by myself," Lynn said when she reached him. She brushed straw off the sleeves of her chamois shirt. *I need to wash this thing.*

He dropped his arms. "You're welcome, ma'am, but that's my job." He shrugged.

"I couldn't have slept."

"I'm sure."

"I'm going to fix myself some breakfast. Can I get you something?" Her tone was one of genuine hospitality, the eager repayment of a debt.

He looked as though he'd been waiting for that question. "Coffee would be nice, ma'am."

"That's all?"

"Yes, thank you."

By ten o'clock, two police investigators had come and gone. There wasn't much to investigate, and not much evidence. They took pictures, as the deputy had a few hours earlier, and dusted the door for fingerprints. The footprints and tire tracks in the dust of the dooryard and drive were inconclusive, corrupted by the dust of more recent comings and goings.

Lynn was happy to see George when he pulled up to the equipment barn in his old pick-up a few minutes after the investigators had left. With puffy bags under his eyes, George looked as tired as she felt. "How did they sleep last night?" she asked.

"It didn't take 'em no time to settle down. Just glad to be out of the line of fire, I figure."

"Now what?"

George kicked at the barnyard dust with his old leather boot, so formed to his foot he could have been born with it. "I can put up one person—you or Teresa—but I can't handle ten, I hate to tell ya."

"I know, George. Can you keep them for another night?" She tried not to sound needy and desperate, but her words were more plea than question.

"What do you have in mind?"

"The church in Elk might take them. I'll ask again when I go up to check on Teresa, but that will have to wait until after I pick up Hank."

"They're letting him out?"

"Yeah, they don't keep them long these days."

"Gonna stay at the ranch?" George looked over at the scene of the assault.

"Don't know. I'd rather not."

"I don't have room for ya, not with those others." He kicked at the dust again.

"I know," she said. *What are we going to do? I'm not spending another night there until Rico's in jail.*

Lynn left Bella Vista and headed south toward Cazadero. Two minutes later, she turned left down George's long driveway. Midway along its length it bent behind a stand of firs, hiding it from the road; an advantage, she thought. Lynn knew her new charges would be anxious, afraid. *It wouldn't surprise me if they wanted out of here now.*

She parked beside the house and walked toward the back door. Now and then a leaf on the gnarled old apple tree in the front yard quivered in a phantom breeze, but otherwise the air was still and hot. A pensive face peered through the kitchen window—Martha's. *I don't blame her. Every car could be ICE or Rico.* She opened the back door. Its dry hinges squeaked. *Good, he's got an early warning system.* The four adult refugees sat at the kitchen table. They smiled at her, relieved.

"You slept okay?"

"Yes, senõra," Martha replied. The others looked down at the table when she continued. "We are wondering about Canada. We think we might be safer there. Can you tell us anything about that?"

Lynn could not. She had heard about Syrian refugees crossing into Quebec, walking through deep snow in the dead of winter, and being accepted there, but she knew nothing about the fate of undocumented Mexican immigrants crossing into British Columbia—or anywhere else along the border. "No, I can't, but I promise you I will find out. And I promise you I will help you if that is what you want to do." Her promise was sincere.

"Thank you, senõra."

Canada. What do I know about Canadian immigration? I'm in way over my head here. But right now I need to deal with this. "We need to find another place for you. Mr. Nicholson can't put you all up here for long— maybe just one more night. I have some ideas. Please be patient."

"We understand, and we're grateful," Martha said.

"I'm going to Santa Rosa now to pick up my husband from the hospital. We'll talk more when I get back."

———

LYNN WOUND DOWN THROUGH THE FOREST ON THE treacherous Mountaintop Road, passing the hairpin turn where George had blocked ICE's progress and the site of the accident, where small, jagged fragments of plastic and glass still littered the shoulder and the redwood stood unscarred, its thick bark more than a match for the light Prius.

When she reached Austin Creek, her phone chirped an incoming text. It was Detective Sandoval. Lynn pulled over to read it. *Found Sanchez at Santa Rosa Memorial. Call me.*

Lynn had known the invaders were Rico and Jorge. She did not wish them well, but she was relieved to hear she had not killed someone. She slowed at the narrow, rusting bridge and crossed into the village. On her left, a muddy Jeep was on the lift in the auto repair shop. On her right, the Cazadero General Store was busy with lunchtime traffic. Cars and pickups filled its half-dozen parking spaces. When the road reentered the woods, she savored the shade of the redwood canopy, marveling at the way the giant trees dwarfed the houses beneath them.

She turned into Karen's simple dirt drive and pulled up behind Karen's green Subaru. *Good. She's home.* Even without a breeze, the air in the deep shade was cool and refreshing. And as low as it was in this dry end of the summer, the creek still gurgled and sunlight still sparkled on the riffles.

"Good morning, if it's still morning," Lynn said through the screen door.

"Come in, honey!" Karen called from around the corner in the kitchen.

Lynn opened the door and stepped into the living room. Magazines littered the coffee table. Stacks of books, some leaning precariously, left little room for anything else on end tables. A poster hung on the far wall—a horse and rider in native dress on a desolate, snow-covered plain. Above the photo, a heading read "Healing Hearts at Wounded Knee." And below it, the words "The 125th Anniversary Big Foot Ride: December 22-29, Bridger to Wounded Knee. We Can End the Transmission of Wounding."

Karen emerged from the kitchen, her long silver hair draped forward on her chest, her face radiant, the bluebird tattoo on her cheek seeming to wink at her visitor. She hugged Lynn, squeezed, and held her at arm's length. She looked straight into her eyes with a warm, penetrating gaze. "It's so good to see you. How have you been?"

"It's still crazy, Karen."

"Have a seat." Karen motioned to the couch that faced a plate-glass window overlooking the creek. She ducked into the kitchen. A cupboard door slammed, and she returned with two glasses of iced tea. She gave one to Lynn and took a seat in a brown reclining chair. "There. Tell me about it."

Sitting forward on the edge of the couch, Lynn related all that had happened since they'd last talked; her rescue of Teresa from the rectory, the Jernigan's assistance, the cabin, and the shooting.

"Look at you!" Karen said. "You're a hero."

"I don't know how I feel about that. I'd rather they never showed up."

"But still. The barbarians were at the gate, and you repelled them. You should be proud of yourself."

"I guess I am. The thing is, Rico is still out there."

"They'll catch him."

"I hope so, but I don't think I can stay in that house until they do. I'm on my way to the hospital to pick up Hank. I know this is a lot to ask, but can you put us up here for a little while until they catch him, or we can figure something else out?" Lynn leaned toward Karen in an unconscious attempt to pry a yes from her friend.

"Of course, honey. Jessica's gone. She went to work yesterday and didn't come back."

"That doesn't sound good."

"No, it doesn't, but there's not much I can do about it."

Lynn looked at her phone to check the time. "I can't stay too long, Karen. I need to get to the hospital. But I do want to ask you about Teresa."

"Okay."

Lynn stood up and walked to the window. The creek, at its dry season ebb, wound from bank to bank through brilliant white sandbars, pooling in the turns, running through quiet, shallow riffles between them. "She's safe in the Jernigan's cabin right now, but that's only temporary. Where do we go now? What do we do?"

Karen leaned her head back, then sat up. "In the end, she's going to have to keep herself safe. One enemy is gone—Juan Carlos. That leaves Rico. If you can keep her away from him until the cops can nail him, you've done your job."

"She's desperate to see her family."

"I know. Maybe that's where she should go. She might be safest there."

"But she says she wants to stay in la uva."

"Maybe there's a way for her to do that there. Where does the daughter live? Madera?"

"I think so."

"They grow grapes down there."

"I know, but it's not Sonoma. She's lived here a long time. It's her home." Lynn stood up. "I should go." She took her glass into the kitchen and put it in the sink. Returning to the room she stopped in front of the poster. "What's the Big Foot Ride?"

"We've done it for twenty-five years to commemorate the Wounded Knee Massacre. I helped organize it."

"From here?"

"Yeah."

"I'm not surprised, you fierce lady, you."

Karen rose and stood next to Lynn. She pointed to the bottom of the poster. "See those lines? That's what you're doing—ending the transmission of wounding."

"I don't know about that. I'm just helping a few people."

"And that's enough, honey. That's where it starts."

———

Lynn stopped at the first of the two traffic lights on Main Street in Guerneville—the one at the intersection with

Armstrong Woods Drive. Watching an elderly woman with a broad-brimmed straw hat crossing the street with a two-wheeled shopping basket, Lynn called Detective Sandoval.

"Lynn, you saw my text. Jorge Sanchez is at Santa Rosa Memorial. Guerrero dropped him off in his Camaro and took off. They have it on closed circuit TV. We're looking at the prints on your back door, and we're comparing the shot the surgeon removed from Sanchez with the shells the officer took from your place."

The light turned, and she pressed on the accelerator. "I'm worried, detective. Am I in trouble?"

"For what?"

"For what? I shot someone."

"It was self-defense. You have nothing to worry about."

Lynn wasn't so sure. *How can you have nothing to worry about when you shoot someone?* But she would try to set that worry aside. "What about Rico?"

"I have an all-points bulletin out for his car. We'll find him."

The next light—at the Route 116 Bridge—was green. "It can't be soon enough," Lynn said as she went through it.

"We're closing in. We recovered Hernandez's truck on Airway Drive, just north of Piner Road. Tire tracks by the bridge show it was there. There aren't any prints on the truck, but we have CCTV footage from an auto glass shop on Piner showing Guerrero and Sanchez cutting through the lot toward Sanchez's house Sunday night—before the coroner says he was killed. We've got enough to bring him for questioning. But we don't have a murder weapon."

"That was a knife, right?"

"Yeah."

Lynn reached the outskirts of town and passed the Stumptown Brewery, a repurposed roadside tavern. "If found, please return to

Stumptown Brewery" read the sign on the funnel-bottomed grain hopper on the side the building. "And Teresa? You still need her?"

"She could help establish a connection between them and Hernandez."

"I'll talk to her." But Lynn was still not confident Teresa would cooperate. She hung up and pulled into the brewery parking lot. She called Teresa.

"Lynn?"

"How is it going, Teresa?"

"Much better, Lynn, thank you. Mary has been very kind. But I can't stay here either."

"I know. We're working on that." *I should tell her about last night.* "Something happened when I got home last night, something you need to know. Rico and Jorge tried to break in. I shot Jorge. He's in the hospital, and Rico is on the run."

"You didn't!"

"I did. Jorge is lucky he's still alive. And the cops are closing in on Rico."

"He's a bad dude. That's not going to be so easy."

"They could use your help."

"How can I help? It's not like I witnessed anything."

"But you know Rico. Maybe you can tell them something about him they don't know."

"Like what?"

Lynn didn't know, but grasping at straws, she recalled an innocent piece of her previous conversation with Detective Sandoval. "Did you ever see him with a knife?"

"Yes, he used to wave around a long hunting knife to show he was boss. It had a wooden handle with a mountain lion carved on it."

Lynn was stunned. "That's exactly what I'm talking about, Teresa. I'll tell the police."

"I still don't want to talk to them face to face."

"I understand. I'll come up tomorrow morning, and we'll work on a plan. Maybe we'll get you out of there."

"That would be nice." Teresa's voice was light, almost cheerful.

In her change of tone—from desperation to hope—Lynn was reminded of all they had endured and accomplished since they'd met. "Good," she said, "I have an idea."

CHAPTER 16

MARIA CLOSES IN; LYNN MAKES A CHOICE

Rico conjured images of a man lying dead by the river, his throat slit, a bullet through the back of his head—not Juan Carlos—Rico saw himself. *I wish I could blow this place, disappear, start over.* But he couldn't. He was in too deep. Others up the chain, the chain of human smuggling, would never let him. *They would find me anywhere.* He knew what he needed to do.

It was shortly after eleven the morning after his raid on Bella Vista. He opened the front door of his house and stepped out into the dry heat of late summer, squinting into the dense blue sky.

He looked up and down the street, checking for anything out of the ordinary; strange people, strange cars. Seeing none, he turned back to the door and reached for the knob. "Let's go," he said.

Jessica Martinez emerged from the darkness of the unlit front room. "How far is it?"

"About a mile." He pulled the door shut and locked it.

He walked her to the street, focusing on what he had to do. His crimes were piling up; immigrant smuggling, extortion, theft, murder, home invasion. The authorities were after him. Jorge might talk. *I should cut my losses and get the hell out of here. But I can't.* He knew his only chance for survival was to prevent Teresa from exposing the network. That meant finding her. *That gringo bitch knows where Teresa is, and she's going to tell me, if I have to pry it out of her.*

With the long strides of a man on a mission, he led Jessica down the sidewalk to the end of the block, where he turned north on West Street. Cars passed in the normal unhurried pattern of midday Roseland. The manicured grounds of the elementary school were quiet; children were in class. Modular classrooms surrounded the neat, brick post-war building, attesting to the recent influx of immigrants.

Dogs leaned their forepaws on the sills of front windows and barked. Otherwise there was little activity in the modest, single-story bungalows along the shady street. Most people were at work.

A mile to the north they reached Sebastopol Road, a busy commercial strip lined with shops hawking ethnic food, hamburgers, tires, furniture, groceries, insurance. They turned west and walked one block, past the donut shop and the RV dealership, to Jose's Body Shop.

"Follow me," Rico said to Jessica. He led her through the cramped front office to the shop itself, where cars and trucks in various states of repair sat side by side. The big overhead garage doors were open. Sunlight and the warm air of a late summer day filled the space. Mariachi music played background to the random clanging of metal tools and parts and the shouted calls and responses of mechanics.

"Hey, compadre." Rico signaled with two fingers of his right hand to a man bending over the crushed fender of a late-model Mustang and pointed toward the back door.

The man in grease-covered overalls straightened up and signaled back. "Como estás, compadre?"

"Bien. Gracias, man," Rico replied. He led Jessica through a back door and out into the day, where his red Camaro sat waiting for him out of sight of the road.

"Get in," he said.

She complied.

Rico opened the driver's door and climbed in. He reached under the seat for the keys and started the engine. He revved it for a few seconds, then made his way to the road and turned east toward downtown Santa Rosa.

In a voice of measured control, Rico reviewed the plan. "You told me she's picking him up today. Now tell me what I want you to do," he said, keeping his eyes on the road.

"I don't like this, Rico."

"But you'll do it—unless you want me to turn your parents in."

He could feel the hot burn of her glare. She said, "You want me to go to the receptionist and ask if Hank Peterson is still in his room, or if he's already been discharged."

"That's right. That's a good girl. And I'm gonna wait in the visitor's parking lot where I can see the front door."

"They'll see you there."

"No, they won't. They won't be looking for me there."

They passed under the concrete arches of the freeway, traffic whooshing and rattling overhead, and turned right on Third Street through the heart of downtown Santa Rosa, past the fancy Hyatt Regency with its red-tiled roof, and under the Santa Rosa Shopping Plaza. Beyond the Third Street Cinema, they turned right on Montgomery Drive. A short two blocks down the street, across the greenway, they arrived at Santa Rosa Memorial Hospital.

Rico turned in and found a parking place in the shade within sight of the front door. He lowered the windows and turned off the engine.

Lynn completed the hospital discharge formalities and made sure Hank was clear about his recovery and physical therapy schedules. Then she brought his car up the front drive, circling a statue of the Healing Christ, and pulled up under the marquee at the entrance, where Hank waited in his wheelchair. A white-clad orderly stood behind him, his hands on the back of the chair.

Lynn was in high spirits, eager to retrieve her husband and get him on the road to recovery. She hurried around to the passenger's side and moved the seat back as far as it would go. "Is this gonna work, honey?"

"I think so," Hank replied. He stood up, and with the aid of his crutches, backed into the seat. He swung his bad leg forward, under the dashboard. Lynn put the crutches on the back seat and closed the door. With a broad smile, she thanked the orderly, gave him a quick hug, and got back in the car.

"Shall we stop for lunch?" she asked, easing around the circle and down to the street.

"Sure. How about some tacos?"

"Can you wait 'til we get to Guerneville?"

"Sure."

She turned right onto Montgomery Drive and merged onto Brookwood Avenue, heading north. She crossed Third and Fourth Streets, and stopped for a red light at College Avenue. The accident was traumatic—and Hank's injuries, no small matter. But getting him back to the ranch felt to her like the end of a bad chapter. She trusted Hank's presence would make the next chapter a better one.

"It's a big day, Hank," she said, waiting for the light to turn. "How do you feel?"

"I'll feel a lot better when I can walk again."

Lynn swung between opposing emotions—heartfelt sympathy, and the cold knowledge her husband would be of little practical help for months. Finding safety for her immigrant friends would fall to her alone. "I get that."

"Don't get me wrong. I realize I could be a lot worse off."

Lynn was about to reply when she glanced in her rearview mirror. *Oh my God.* "Hank, there's a red Camaro behind us."

"Don't do anything crazy. Stay calm."

Lynn took her phone from her pocket and handed it to her husband. "Find Maria Sandoval and call her. I think that's Rico behind us."

Hank called.

The light changed, and Lynn turned left—west—toward Guerneville. The Camaro followed. *Okay. Stay calm.* College Avenue was two lanes in each direction. She moved into the right-hand lane and held her speed at the limit. Again, the Camaro followed.

The detective answered. "Lynn?"

Hank put the phone on speaker. "No, this is her husband, Hank. We just left the hospital, and that son-of-a-bitch Rico Guerrero is following us."

"Where are you?"

"On College, just passing Humboldt."

"Can you read his plate number?"

"I'll try. Slow down, Lynn. It's tough, detective," he said, squinting. "I'm not sure, but it looks like it's 'three, *A, L, N,* two, seven, six.' It's a white plate."

"Stay on College, Hank. Don't get on the 101. Drag it out, if you can. Where are you headed?"

Lynn said, "Detective, I was planning to jog north on Marlow to the Guerneville Road."

"If it's our man, I'll set up a roadblock," Sandoval said. "Just don't get in a race with him. Stay on the phone while I check the plate number."

Lynn slowed, and the Camaro slowed and fell back, but not far enough to allow another car between them. Near the 101, the road became more congested. Cars pulled in and out of gas stations and changed lanes, weaving, maneuvering toward the northbound on-ramp, or away from it. Lynn turned on her blinker and moved left to stay on College, just ahead of a gray Honda CRV.

The Camaro sped up and forced its way in front of the Honda. A horn blared. Tires screeched and metal crunched as the Honda braked hard and a white delivery van slammed into it from behind.

Through the rear window, Hank watched cars swerve left and right to avoid the van. Ahead, a truck coming toward them ran up over the curve, chasing people from a bus stop. Traffic in all lanes came to a stop.

But the Camaro stayed with them.

Lynn felt her muscles tightening, control slipping away. "What the fuck? This guy's a maniac. He's going to kill us!" Lynn bellowed at the windshield.

"No, he's not. I'm with you. Just drive," came the voice from the phone.

They passed under the 101, and Lynn squeezed the steering wheel harder.

"It's him," the voice confirmed.

"What the hell are we going to do?" Lynn blurted.

"Just listen," the detective said. "Follow your plan. Get on the Guerneville Road. Take your time as slow as you can, but not so slow you spook him. Stop at the yellow lights. Don't race through. We'll set up at the Route 116 junction. That's about seven miles. We'll get there before you do."

"Don't go away, Maria," Lynn pleaded.

"Don't worry. I'm with you."

Lynn made her way to the Guerneville Road, as planned. It led directly west, as straight and flat as a draftsman's steel rule. Driving it was simple, allowing her to focus on evading the predator behind her.

The outer neighborhoods of Santa Rosa gave way to vineyards and pastures. Now and then a road went off through the fields at a perfect right angle. But Guerneville Road was the thoroughfare in these parts. Lynn prayed to some unknown force for safe passage through them.

The road seemed endless, like an asphalt treadmill. Lynn's breathing became shallow and forced. She tried to bring it back to normal, to concentrate on the road ahead, to block out the menace behind her. But she couldn't.

Her eyes were drawn to the rearview mirror and the image of a man she had never seen in broad daylight, smirking through the glare on his windshield. She forced her focus back to the road ahead. But it wouldn't stay there. Her eyes returned again and again to the car and the man behind her. *Is that a gun in his hand?*

Three miles out, there was a traffic light at Willowside Road—green. She drove through, and Detective Sandoval's voice came alive again on her phone. "Lynn."

"Yes."

"Listen carefully. At the stop sign at 116, there's a lane on the right that turns toward Guerneville. Take it. Stop. Then hit the accelerator and pull away fast. We'll have 116 blocked on the left. He won't see us because of the trees. We'll surround him. Just keep going. He won't be following you."

Trees hugged the road as it crossed Santa Rosa Creek and began a long, gradual climb out of the stream valley. Lynn wasn't as confident as the detective sounded. "What if he does follow us?"

"He won't," she said, "but if he does, just keep driving the speed limit. Don't get in a race with him. We'll get him. Trust me."

"I'm trying."

"Keep cool," Hank said. "They've got us covered."

At the crest of the hill, they could see the intersection about a mile off.

"Here we are," Hank said. "Be cool."

Lynn checked her rearview mirror again. The woman next to Rico seemed animated, as though she were shouting at him. She saw him raise his arm and slap her across the face.

"Watch out!" Hank yelled as wheels ground against gravel.

Lynn looked down. The VW had drifted onto the shoulder. The passenger side tires bit into the unpaved surface, sending up plumes of dust. The right side of the car rose. Something hard smacked the underside.

She pulled the car back on the road, breathing hard, concentrating on maintaining control. She snuck a peek in the mirror. The Camaro was still there, relentless.

As they drew closer to the intersection, a wall of trees rose up on the far side of Route 116. It was either left or right. But the Subaru had begun to limp, pulling to the right. The easy roll of the tires had disappeared. Something resisted. "Oh my God, Maria. I've got a flat."

"You've got three good tires, Lynn. All we need is fifteen seconds. Ignore it and go."

"She's right, baby," Hank said. "Don't worry about the tire. You'll go."

Lynn slowed, turned right, and stopped.

The Camaro pulled up behind her.

Lynn struggled to maintain her composure. *Stay cool. Stay cool. Stay cool.* "I'm there, detective."

"Okay. Remember what I said—quick getaway."

There was no evidence of police presence. Lynn looked right, down 116 toward Guerneville, and then back in her rearview mirror, where a black and white police car pulled out from a side road. She jammed her foot on the accelerator, and the car leapt forward.

The Camaro followed, but not fast enough. As it accelerated, police cruisers closed in, blue lights flashing, sirens blaring. A bull horn barked orders.

Lynn slowed and pulled over on the shoulder, panting, both hands clamped to the top of the wheel. She relaxed her grip, releasing the bungee-like tension, and slumped forward on her limp arms.

Hank put a hand on her back and massaged it in gentle circles. "You were great."

"Maybe, but right now I'm a wreck."

They looked back, glued to the unfolding drama. Officers in blue and khaki uniforms crouched behind their cars with their pistols drawn. One approached the Camaro with both hands clasped on his gun, his arms straight in front of him. Others pulled the doors open, and Rico and Jessica emerged with their hands behind their heads.

As it had so often in the previous two weeks, relief swept over Lynn. *It's over. It's over.* "They got him. I can't believe they got him."

"That changes a lot," Hank said, still watching the scene behind them.

"You got that right."

"Are you okay, Lynn?" It was Detective Sandoval, still on the line.

"I think so. I'm exhausted, but I guess we're okay. I sure as hell don't want to go through that again."

"You shouldn't have to. Go on home. I'll be in touch."

Lynn thanked her, turned the key, and put the car in gear. The car rolled forward, and immediately the flat tire complained.

"Damn it, Hank. I've never changed a tire. You're going to have to talk me through this." Her energy sapped, this challenge felt like a cruel test of her endurance.

Hank hobbled to the back of the car, and pulled the jack from a side compartment and the spare from under the floor of the cargo space. Leaning on his crutches, he hooked the crank to the screw mechanism of the jack and turned it several times to open it up. "You slide this plate on top here into a slot on the frame behind the wheel well. Then you turn the crank until it reaches the ground. Check that it's straight and keep cranking until the tire is off the ground. Use this wrench here to loosen the lug nuts on the wheel."

Lynn struggled with the lug nuts, but she loosened them all, raised the car, and changed the tire. She wrestled the bad tire into the well in the back of the car, put the jack in its place, and started the car again. Then she pulled back onto the highway and headed for Guerneville, negotiating the road like a robot, drained of strength, unable to process thought—spent.

———————

TERESA RAISED THE OVERSIZED WHITE COFFEE MUG. SHE studied the image wrapping around it under the word "Elk"—bluffs and sea stacks in black silhouette—brought it to her mouth, and held it there, lingering on the rich aroma. She took a sip and let it sit on her tongue.

For the first time in days, she could relax, free from the ever-present tension she had felt in the rectory. Here she was safe. Not that she wasn't safe in the rectory. But danger was in full view there, a real and constant threat. Rico might find her here, if the police didn't find him first. ICE might find her here, too. But those possibilities seemed more remote now.

The coziness of Mary's cabin added to Teresa's sense of safety. The rough, unpainted walls were close, and their rich reddish-brown hue, warm. The tiny sleeping loft over the two small bedrooms was a dream of cocoon-like security. And even now, at the end of summer, the black cast-iron stove in the corner evoked comfort. The large picture window on the west side of the room offered her a cloud-like perspective on the world below.

Teresa looked down the slope, over redwood, oak, and fir. It was mid-morning, and the shoreline was still hidden in fog.

She assessed her options. Valley Run was out of the question. Juan Carlos was dead, but Rico and ICE both knew of her relationship to it. There were other wineries and vineyards near Santa Rosa, but ICE felt too close there.

She could go back to the Central Valley and disappear among the thousands of immigrant workers there—documented and undocumented. But she had moved beyond that. She had developed skills in the vineyards, and a relationship with a vineyard, that fed her. She dreaded the thought of returning to the numbing, backbreaking work of picking vegetables for faceless corporations.

She was still a young woman, in her mid-forties, in the prime of life—and also too young to spend the rest of her life housekeeping for her daughter or son and raising their children. She had made a good life for herself, and she would not abandon it without a struggle.

But she missed her children, and she was tired of keeping them in the dark. *I'm going to change that. I need to see them.* It was a Saturday. Her daughter and son might be free the next day. *It's short notice, but maybe they will drive here. If I can get my car, I can meet them somewhere.*

She stood up to diffuse nervous energy. She paced the length of the room. She refilled her mug and stepped out on the front porch, where the nighttime cool still hung in the shadows of the mountainside. The forest was quiet, save for a lone chickadee scolding her from the branch of a nearby fir. She took out her phone and called her daughter.

"Mamà?" her daughter answered.

"Sí, Gloria, it's me. I'm in trouble."

"Oh, Mamá, what's wrong?"

Teresa told the whole story—every detail.

When she finished and paused, Gloria asked, "Mamá, why didn't you go to the police?"

"You know why."

"Why didn't you call me? Or Miguel?"

"I didn't want to worry you. And I thought I could just escape the guy."

"But now you have ICE after you."

"Yes, but I think I've lost them, at least for now." Then Teresa summoned the courage to ask Gloria if she could come to see her the next day. "I could meet you somewhere, so you don't have to come all the way to Elk."

"Of course, Mamá," Gloria replied.

Teresa had no idea where that place might be—or how she would get there. She would need Lynn's help. They left it that Gloria would make plans to leave with her daughter before dawn, to meet somewhere north of Santa Rosa on the 101, and Teresa would find that place and get there—with Lynn's help.

Teresa brushed leaves off a weathered cedar chair and sank into it, her nervous energy gone, drained into the long-overdue conversation with her daughter. She closed her eyes and summoned the faces of the loved ones she would see the next day—Gloria and little Rosa. It had been way too long.

She picked up her phone to text Lynn.

———

LYNN HAD LOST INTEREST IN STOPPING FOR FOOD BY THE time they reached Rio Bravo, wanting instead to get as far from Santa Rosa as possible. But hunger tugged at her. She would get take-out, enough for three, and stop at Karen's. Karen would want to know what had just happened, and Lynn needed to tell her. She turned in and got out of the car. As she started for the familiar restaurant, weak and wobbly, the therapeutic value of that simple act began to work on her. She returned with a sack of tacos, enough for three.

Karen's car was in its usual spot behind the house when Lynn pulled up beside it. She retrieved Hank's crutches from the back seat and helped him from the car. Then, with lunch in hand, she called through the screen door again. "Karen, we're back!"

There was no answer. Lynn called again.

And again, there was no answer.

She opened the door, held it for Hank, and followed him in. She set the bag on the kitchen counter and walked back to Karen's bedroom. "Maybe she's taking a nap." She wasn't.

Lynn returned to the living room, where Hank had claimed the recliner. She looked out toward the creek, and there was Karen, on a sandbar at the water's edge under a broad, white patio umbrella. "Ha, look at that. She's at the beach. Wait here, Hank. I'll go get her."

Lynn scrambled down the bank and crossed a dry pool lined with smooth, gray pebbles. Beyond it was the glistening white tongue of sand where Karen sat in a striped canvas chair facing the lazy channel on the far side of the creek bed. "Karen, you look so comfy!" Lynn called as she stepped up on the bar. The sand squeaked beneath her feet.

Karen swung her face around. "You're back. You got him?"

"I did." The story gushed out of Lynn like air from a balloon, pent up, needing escape. "Rico followed us from the hospital, and the cops intercepted him at the end of the Guerneville Road. It was right out of the movies."

Karen jumped up from her chair. "Damn. They arrested him?"

"Yeah, I assume so. A security camera had him dropping Jorge off at the hospital."

"So he's out of commission."

"For now."

"I don't need to ask you how you're doing, do I?" Karen reached out and took Lynn's hands in hers.

"No, you don't. I'm exhausted."

"I know, honey. You've been through a lot."

"Yeah, I have. Hey, have you eaten? We picked up some tacos in town."

"That would be nice. Thanks."

They made their way back across the creek to the house. Karen put plates, napkins, glasses, and utensils on a tray, added three Lagunitas IPAs from the refrigerator, and carried the tray out to the deck on the front of the house.

Lynn followed with the tacos. She unwrapped them, an assortment; fish, carnitas, barbacoa, carne asada. And they sat down to eat in the deep shade of the redwoods, where the air was still and so perfectly warm it was unnoticeable. Nothing moved. The only sounds were those of enthusiastic eating.

"I had no idea I was that hungry," Lynn said, wiping her hands and mouth with a napkin. She took a long sip of beer and sighed.

"What now, honey?" Karen asked.

"Well, we're probably safe at the ranch. I guess we can pass on the sanctuary offer." Lynn looked over at Hank for confirmation.

He nodded.

"You're welcome any time," Karen said.

"Thanks, but we've got work to do at the ranch, if Becky will still have us."

"I can't imagine she won't," Karen said. She got up and cleared the plates. "Another beer?"

"Sure," Lynn replied. "That's exactly what I need."

Karen returned with the beer. As Lynn poured it into her glass, Rico's chase returned to her, weighing on her already tired body and spirit. *Relax. Rico's in jail.* But ICE still hung over her. Teresa was still in flight, looking for safety in Sonoma or Mendocino. On the other hand, the Cruzes and Garcias were convinced there was no safety in the country. They wanted out. But they, too, still needed her. Her work wasn't done. "What do you know about Canadian immigration, Karen?"

"What do you mean?"

"Are undocumented immigrants safer there than they are here?"

"Only if they're candidates for refugee status, like Syrians. But workers like yours, looking for a better life—Mexicans—no, they're not. They're probably worse off. The police there support the immigration authorities more, even in sanctuary cities. Why?"

"My families say they want to go there."

"That's not the answer. It would be a lot easier if it were. But they either have to make it here or go back to Mexico."

The sad starkness of those choices shook Lynn. She tried to imagine summoning the courage to flee poverty for a better life, risk a dangerous border crossing, and then arriving in the land of milk and honey, having to hide in fear. It depressed her, like the image of Randy hiding in her parents' home.

But it was the courage of her new charges—more than their fear—that moved her now. Like Randy's courage. It inspired and challenged her. *I told them I had some ideas. I am going to find them safety.*

———

WHEN THEY REACHED THE VILLAGE, LYNN'S PHONE chirped. She handed it to Hank. "Would you read that for me, honey?"

"It's from Teresa. She says, 'I talked to my daughter, Gloria, today. She's coming to see me tomorrow. I need your help. Please call.'"

Lynn swung into a parking space in front of the general store. "Well, I told her I had an idea, and that was it. Good for her. It's about time. She's needed to see them."

She took the phone from Hank and called. "Teresa."

"Thanks for calling, Lynn." Teresa described her conversation with Gloria and said, "I want to make it easy for them. It's a long way from Madera—five hours, maybe—too far to Elk. I thought someplace on the 101 north of Healdsburg or Geyserville. Can you find a place for me? And I'll need my car. Can you figure out a way to get it to me?"

Lynn was glad Teresa had finally reached out to her daughter, even as she understood why she hadn't earlier. Teresa would need her daughter's support in the months and years ahead. "Of course I can. Let me work on it, Teresa. There are some motels in Cloverdale, where the 128 branches off to the Anderson Valley." Lynn reasoned Cloverdale would be safe—far enough both from Elk and the ICE office in Santa Rosa.

"Thank you so much, Lynn. It's really important to me."

"I know, Teresa. I'll work it out and call you back."

She handed the phone back to Hank. "See if you can find a motel room in Cloverdale."

She backed out into the road and brought the car up to speed. "I can't put my finger on it, Hank, but I've got a funny feeling things are going to change for her. I think the worst might be behind her."

DETECTIVE MARIA SANDOVAL STOOD ON THE RUST-COV-ered bridge that carried Wohler Road over the Russian River. The air was still. Heat rose from the asphalt, turning the bridge into a slow-cooker. Her shirt grew wet. It stuck to her back. One tiny white cloud hung above the redwood-covered ridge to the west. She peered through her dark sunglasses into the green water making its lazy way toward Jenner, where it would pool behind the bar at the river mouth, awaiting the first big storm of winter that would break the bar and release it to the sea.

The surface of the water swirled. A webbed foot broke the surface, a black-masked head, a back. Acting on Lynn's tip, Detective Sandoval had ordered two police divers to search the bottom of the river—its full width from just above the bridge to a hundred yards below it. They had started at nine that morning. It was now mid-afternoon.

Armed with a warrant, officers had combed Rico's house—and not found the knife. But Detective Sandoval had a hunch. She walked off the bridge and down to the spot on the bank where the fisherman had found Juan Carlos. A team had already searched the bank, the under-brush, the dirt road, the grass, and not found it. Maria imagined the late-night murder scene: Rico slitting Juan Carlos's throat, looking at the bloody knife, realizing he had to get rid of it, and throwing it some-where it wouldn't be found—in the river.

She waded to the water's edge through waist-deep goldenrod and water hemlock, with their broad white flower heads. The river was the color of tarnished copper, pretty in its own way. But she was not there to admire it. She was there to scour it.

She watched as the water swirled again and a black-clad diver stood, chest deep, twin scuba tanks strapped to his back, breathing tube running over his shoulder and into his mouth, eyes masked—a crea-ture from some dark, subliminal place. He took a step toward her and raised his right arm out of the water. In his hand was a hunting knife with a carved wooden handle.

Maria punched the air with her fist. "Yes!"

BECKY TILLSON'S SILVER BMW SUV WAS PARKED IN front of the caretaker's house when Lynn rolled to a stop beneath the long, low branches of the big oak tree. She cringed. *I should have called her. This isn't going to look good.* She turned to her husband. "Moment of reckoning, Hank?"

"Yeah, that's what I'd call it." He pushed the door open and swung his legs to the ground.

Lynn was handing him his crutches when she heard her name. Becky, the owner of the ranch, was calling to her from the direction of the equipment barn. She was standing with George, dressed for the ranch in a stylish blue denim shirt with embroidered pockets, the sleeves turned up halfway to her elbows—just so. The bottoms of her new, deep-indigo jeans flared over classic boots of the supplest, chestnut-brown harness leather, not yet christened by the dust of the barnyard.

"Hi, Becky. I've been meaning to call you."

"I'm sure you have, from what George has told me." Becky folded her arms, straightening her back for emphasis.

Lynn hadn't expected the inquisition to begin so early. "So, what has he told you?"

"He told me about the accident." Becky tipped her head toward Hank.

"We're on the mend." Lynn wanted to stay upbeat, hoping that demeanor might save her from the ramifications of the conversation to come.

"That's good. I see that. He also told me about the shooting."

George was standing a step behind Becky. He winced.

Lynn wasn't upset with him. He was right; he had to tell her. The story was out there. It was truth-telling time. She stayed on the high road. "Would you like to come in? We'll tell you the whole story."

George shrugged in empathy, and retreated to the safety of the barn.

"Yes, I'd like that," Becky said. She and Lynn fell in behind Hank as he shuffled to the back door.

"Damn," Becky said when they reached the door. "It looks like they hit it with a battering ram. You must have been scared shitless." The old six-panel wooden door was cracked and misshapen. The lock bolt had ripped through the door frame. The door no longer latched.

"I was."

Becky put a hand on Lynn's shoulder. "I can't imagine."

Hank pushed the door open. "Looks like we've got some work to do," he said. He hobbled into the front room.

Lynn hurried ahead to turn on lights.

Becky followed, surveying the place like a buyer.

Lynn saw coffee stains on the counter, dust on the baseboards, scrapes on the kitchen floor where Juan Carlos had knocked over a chair. But despite her discomfort, she knew Becky's interest was the natural and normal perspective of an owner.

They went into the front room. Hank lowered himself into the chair by the foot of the stairs and propped his broken leg on the upholstered ottoman. The house was warm. Lynn opened the front door to let cooler air blow through. With it came the low rumble of a tractor, and the sight of George on it, heading for the north pasture. A crow cawed.

Becky moved around the room, taking it all in—walls, floor, furniture. "I'm sorry, dear. It's just that I haven't been in here for months. I really don't like being a landlord, but I should come through more often. I've found it heads off uncomfortable situations. Some people don't take care of the place as well as you do."

"Thank you, Becky. Please, have a seat." She motioned to the couch.

Becky obliged.

"May I get you something to drink?"

"Water would be nice. Thank you."

Lynn fetched a glass of ice water for Becky, and gathered her thoughts. She worried about where to start; what to say to the owner of the ranch, what not to say. She reached back for the arms of a rocker by the front door and settled on the edge of the seat. "It started a couple of weeks ago. A friend of mine, a nurse who works at the clinic in town, brought a woman here who needed protection. She'd been raped by her supervisor in the vineyard, and he was after her."

"Why didn't she go to the police?"

"Because she's undocumented."

"Ah. So you've been hiding her."

"Yes, we were."

"What made you think it was okay to do that here?"

"Nothing, really. I didn't think about it. The woman was in trouble and needed help. That seemed more important."

Becky's face registered surprise. "But it was a disservice. You owed that to me, as the owner of the property."

"I understand."

"She's not here now?"

"No, she's at a cabin in Mendocino County."

"Okay. Tell me about the door and the shooting. Who broke in?"

"*Tried* to break in. Two gang members from Santa Rosa. I shot one of them with your shotgun."

Becky looked as shocked as Lynn expected her to be. "Gang members? You shot a gang member in my house, and you didn't tell me?"

"I know. I should have. But it just happened—last night. A lot has happened—in a very short time." Lynn went back to Teresa's arrival at the ranch and told the whole story—Juan Carlos's raid, ICE, the accident, Teresa's flight to Elk, the murder, the rescue from the rectory, the shooting, the chase, Rico's arrest, and the arrival of the Cruzes and Garcias.

Becky readjusted herself on the couch. "That's quite the story. I have to say, I couldn't have imagined how a simple caretaking job could turn into something so dramatic. Tell me, what have you done on the ranch all this time?"

"I've been taking care of the animals."

"And?"

Lynn saw where Becky's question was going. "I guess I haven't had time for much of anything else."

"And you, Hank?"

Hank thought for a second. "I would say my routine hasn't been affected."

"Until the accident."

"Yes, until the accident."

"But now you're out of commission. For how long?"

"Not sure. Two months, maybe longer."

Becky sat up straighter. Her face lengthened. Any hint of a smile disappeared.

Lynn awaited the verdict.

"I'm sympathetic. I really am. Immigrants have a raw deal in this country. But I need caretakers. Hank's out of service—no fault of his. And what about you, Lynn? Are you still tied up with these immigrants?"

Lynn had faced this question numerous times in the previous two weeks, but now it took on new form for her. It was not whether she would stand with Teresa or the Cruzes and Garcias in a moment of crisis. She had passed that test—again and again. Now the question was whether she would do so in the future. Would she continue to protect them? Was that the role she saw for herself?

Becky was offering her a choice between the refugees and the ranch. Lynn saw her life and work on the ranch as it had been before Teresa—gardening, caring for the animals in a ridgetop nirvana. She saw Teresa and Martha and Manny and the others, hiding in fearful uncertainty. And she saw Ellie, her childhood friend, and Randy, the dead boyfriend.

She looked over at her husband. "I'm sorry, Hank. I can't go back."

He knew what she meant. "I know."

She said to Becky, "These people are important to me. They need my help, and I can't abandon them."

"I understand," Becky said. "I do, but I have a ranch to run. And I can't see how you can do both, especially while Hank's recovering."

"I don't either," Lynn said.

"You can stay until the end of September. That's about three weeks. I'll try to find someone else by then."

Lynn looked around the room wistfully. She would miss the house's simple warmth and charm. An idea came to her. "I know some people who would be good caretakers."

"Your immigrants? Don't go there. I can't get involved with illegals."

That's the point, Lynn thought. *I am involved. And I have to stay involved. There are two families down the road waiting for my involvement right now.* "It was just a thought." She stood.

CHAPTER 17

REUNION

Lynn walked Becky Tillson to the front door and followed her outside. The silvery metal roof of the front porch reflected back the rays of the late afternoon sun, offering some relief from the motionless heat. This place—the entire ranch—was so removed from the valley below that the mad car chase, just hours ago, seemed to have not happened.

"I hope you understand," Becky said. In her spotless clothes, she could not have been mistaken for a rancher.

"I do." Lynn had grown to like Becky in the four months she had known her, but this afternoon, Lynn felt distant from her. As much as Lynn loved the ranch, it was her commitment to Teresa and her new charges that now defined her relationship to Cazadero and Sonoma.

"Let me know if you change your mind, and I'll stop looking for another caretaker. You've been a good tenant."

"I will." Lynn shook Becky's hand and watched her drive off toward the big house, raising a trail of dust. She felt a like a sharecropper.

Her phone rang.

"Lynn, it's Maria Sandoval. We found the knife—in the river. Now I need Teresa's testimony—about the knife and about Hernandez's relationship with Guerrero and Sanchez."

"I'll be with her tomorrow. I'll talk to her." Lynn understood Maria's need, but she also understood Teresa's reluctance to talk.

"I can subpoena her, Lynn."

"I know, but this is complicated."

"There are ways around complications. Do you know about the U visa?"

"Yes, a little."

"She's been the victim of a serious crime—or crimes. All she needs to do is help us prosecute the criminals."

"She says she can't apply for it."

"Why not? She's been abused."

"There's something in her past. I told you it was complicated." Lynn felt herself walking out on thin ice, wanting to explain Teresa's situation without betraying trust.

"A conviction?"

"No, a warrant for her arrest."

"We can work with her."

"How do we know you won't arrest her?"

"Did she abuse a child?"

"No."

"Rob a bank?"

"No."

"Murder somebody?"

Damn. Of course she would go there. What do I say now? "No, but she witnessed one."

"Accessory?"

"That's the charge."

"How long ago?"

"Twenty-five years."

"We can work with her."

Teresa really is the link. "Can you shield her identity?"

"I think so. I'll look into it." The detective hung up.

Lynn knew the importance of convicting Rico. He was a dangerous thug, but more than that, he was the key to a criminal enterprise that victimized thousands of people. It was a long shot, but she would continue to prod Teresa in the detective's direction. She put her phone in her pocket and went back inside.

"Will you be okay for a little while?" she asked Hank, who was still in the chair by the stairs. "I need to check on the families down the road and bring them some food."

"Of course. Just bring me a glass of water, if you would."

Lynn went into the kitchen and filled a glass from the tap. She packed an insulated shopping bag with chicken, packaged tortillas, peppers, onions, lettuce, and salsa, and returned to the front room.

Ice clinked in the glass as she set it on the table beside her husband. A napkin caught the beads of condensation appearing magically like clouds on a summer day. "What are you reading?" she asked.

"That book Lauren recommended, about the young undocumented Indian immigrants in England."

"Hmm."

"Not an easy life."

"I'm sure." She kissed him and headed for the door. "I won't be long."

She thought about walking to George's place, but out in the open sun, the heat convinced her otherwise. She turned back to the VW, parked as always under the big oak in front of the house.

She had reached the road when she heard the throaty rattle of the tractor behind her—George, returning from his excursion to the north pasture. She swung back under the tree, got out of the car, and waited for him.

George pulled up beside her and put the tractor in neutral. He looked down at her from the worn bucket seat. "How did it go?"

"She gave me a choice—the ranch or the immigrants."

"And you took the immigrants."

"Yeah, I did." She softened her tone. "Is there any chance you can do me a big favor tomorrow?"

"That depends."

Lynn liked the sound of that. "Would you help me retrieve Teresa's car from the rectory in Elk?"

"Why do you need *me* for that?"

"I need someone ICE doesn't recognize. I want to take our guests up there tomorrow and then take Teresa on to Cloverdale."

George lifted his straw hat and ran a hand through his shaggy hair. "What's with Cloverdale?"

"She wants to see her daughter and her granddaughter. They're coming up from Madera. I made a reservation for them in the Super 8 in Cloverdale. Who knows? Maybe she'll decide to go back with them."

"And how do I fit into this?"

"I know it's a lot to ask, George, but it would be wonderful if you could drive her car to Cloverdale. I'll pick up Teresa at the cabin. You can meet us in Cloverdale and ride back with me."

"That's an all-day proposition, Lynn."

"I know. It's a lot to ask." The tractor engine clattered and chugged while she waited for his reply.

"I don't know how you get me into these things, missy," he said, "but you do. Okay, I'll help you. Just let me know when you want to leave."

"It'll be early."

"I can handle early."

"Thanks, George. I knew you would." *Yes, good old George. I knew he would.*

He put the big machine in gear, and it crept like an irresistible green monster toward the barn.

Lynn returned to the car. She put the key in the ignition. *Wait a minute. You're not ready for this. Get your act together. Think.* She had so much facing her, so many obstacles so tangled up with each other, she needed time to sort them out. But she couldn't. There was no sorting them out. One action affected every issue. The task immediately ahead of her—moving the Cruzes and Garcias to Mary's cabin—was a perfect example. Mary hadn't agreed to the idea yet, and Teresa was still there. *All I can do is take them one at a time, and deal with what plays out.*

She looked through the windshield toward the house and barn where she had found such peace, and her gaze moved beyond them to the majestic ridges. Their crests glowed golden in the late afternoon sun, even as their forested flanks grew dark and mysterious in shadow. The beauty of the scene rekindled her optimism, inspiring her to believe that one way or another, goodness and will and persistence would prevail.

She texted Mary, *Pardon me for being pushy, but I need a place for my two undocumented families. Teresa will be leaving the cabin tomorrow. May I move them in for a few days?* She *did* feel pushy, but she knew Mary and Ted were sympathetic, and Lynn knew of no other option.

She sent a second text. *I can come by the inn in the morning to talk about it, if you want. Maybe there's another way.* She watched the blank text box on her phone, where a stream of ephemeral bouncing dots told her Mary was typing.

You can bring them to the cabin tomorrow, but we need to talk about it. Stop by.

Thanks a million, Mary! See you tomorrow.

WHEN LYNN ROLLED TO A STOP AT THE END OF GEORGE'S long drive, she found the children darting around the barnyard like sandpipers on a beach. They chased a ball, steering it with abandon toward goals marked with stones on either side of the big yard. Sounds of joy filled the air—screams of glee, shouts and cheers. Dust coated their little feet and legs like layers of youthful contentment.

The adults watched from the shade behind the house; Martha and Gabriela in old folding lawn chairs with sagging seats of colorful nylon webbing, and Manny and Jose on the sparse, withered grass, brown beer bottles in their hands. An iPod played mariachi music, competing with the squeals of the children.

"I brought some food," Lynn said. "I'll put it in the fridge."

"Gracias," Martha said. "You're very kind. We were just thinking of driving down to the village."

"You're welcome. It's the least I can do." Lynn ducked into the house.

When she reemerged, she asked, "Can we talk?"

"Yes, of course." Martha rose and offered her chair to Lynn. "Senõra, please."

"Thank you, Martha, but sit, please. I'm fine over here." Lynn sat down on the grass beside Manny and Jose. "I don't think Canada is a good option. Unless you're seeking asylum from persecution in Mexico, they will send you back."

"Is no safe?" Manny asked.

"No, unfortunately. They aren't hunting for undocumented people, but they won't accept you if they find you."

Jose turned the music off. Even as the children played happily in the dusty yard, the faces of the adults grew long and solemn.

"What we do?" Manny asked.

"I'm not sure." Lynn searched for a better answer. "Did you work at Valley Run?"

"Sí, and other places," Jose replied.

"Did Juan Carlos and Teresa take money from you?"

"Sí, everybody with no papers."

"Did anybody threaten you?"

"Sí. Juan Carlos."

"Do you know about the U visas?"

"Sí, but we no trust them."

"And what if they no take me?" Manny asked. "How do you say it?—I be hanging out to dry."

Lynn stood up and looked at each of them in turn—Jose, Manny, Gabriela, Martha. "I will look into it, without giving anybody's name. I will get a lawyer if I have to. But first we have to leave here—tomorrow."

Their faces grew long again, as their spirits sagged further.

"It's okay. I have a place for you, at least for a little while. It's just that George can't handle so many people here."

"Will we be safe?" Martha asked.

"Of course. It's a cabin in the woods—on a mountain in Mendocino."

Martha resumed the role of spokesperson. "How will we get there?"

"You will follow me—tomorrow morning. Be ready to go right after breakfast."

"Gracias, senõra. Can you stay for dinner?"

"I'd love to, but I need to get back to my husband."

The four stood, smiling again. Lynn embraced them, one by one. "We will find a way. Trust me."

The voices of happy children accompanied Lynn back to her car. Their irrepressible spirits buoyed her. At times ICE's cold, bureaucratic determination felt invincible. But something in these children suggested otherwise.

———————

THE ALARM ON LYNN'S PHONE JINGLED HER AWAKE AT five thirty the next morning. Hank hated the tone—"Ripples," Apple called it—but she rather liked it. It was irritating enough to wake her, but not jarring—just right.

She turned it off as quickly as she could, and still half asleep, reached for her chamois shirt and favorite jeans draped over the chair by the window. She would have worn that shirt and those jeans every day if they didn't soil. But she woke enough to think better of that choice. *Need to be presentable today.*

Using her phone for light, she shuffled through her dresser drawers and found suitable substitutes: another pair of jeans—not as comfortable—and a soft, plaid, long-sleeved work shirt, heathery-green and purple. She pulled on the leather boots that just in the past few weeks had begun to fit like gloves. As an afterthought, she took a silver necklace with a pendant the shape of a maple leaf from the top of her dresser and fastened it around her neck. Hank was still asleep when she pulled the bedroom door shut behind her.

She took the milk pail from the kitchen cupboard and stepped outside, where the crickets still chirped. In the moonless sky, the Milky Way was as bright as ever. Cool air brushed her face like a feather. A great horned owl called from the trees beyond the barn—hoo, hoo, hoo, hoo, hooooo, hoo. She stopped halfway to the barn and took it all in. *This is why I love this place.*

The animals clucked and bleated at her approach, as always. She put her hand on the latch of the barn door, held it there, and looked up into the night sky as the animals serenaded her. The barn had been a complicated place for her—a place of joy transformed in a bizarre flash to a place of fear. But now, as she stood at the door, the fear was absent. Had she driven it away when she repelled Rico and Jorge? She could only wonder.

She went in and flipped on the light. In the goat's stall, she pulled up the stool and milked her, talking softly to her, stroking her soft, white coat when she was through.

The chickens, crowding around her feet like a school of minnows, brought a smile to her face. *I'm going to miss these creatures. Someday, somewhere I'll need to have my own.* She let them out—the chickens and the goat—just as the faintest light was beginning to show in the east. The animals had been good for her these past four months, and they were good for her this morning.

Back in the house, Lynn started the coffee and went back into the bedroom, where she could now see the rough outlines of things. She looked at her dresser, letting her eyes adjust to the dim light. A tawny stuffed animal, Koko the koala, perched there, resting silently against the wall. Her hands recalled its softness. A gift from a child on the day of Lynn's retirement, it had brought her happiness. Perhaps it would bring happiness to another child, Teresa's granddaughter, Rosa, who would be three soon. She picked it up and tip-toed from the room. She would take it with her to the cabin and offer it to Teresa.

———————

THE SHORELINE WAS OBSCURED BY FOG WHEN THE THREE-car caravan drove the Coast Highway to Elk. At nine thirty, Lynn climbed the steep grade out of Greenwood Creek Gulch, passed the Elk Store, the gallery, and the post office, and turned left at Blue Cove Inn. She found a spot at the end of the small lot beside the inn, and parked. The Cruz and Garcia cars followed.

The roar of surf and the cries of gulls greeted her when she climbed from the VW. "Stay here for a minute, George, while I talk to the others."

The Cruz and Garcia cars were parked side by side. Martha, in one car, and Jose, in the other, lowered their windows.

"Wait here while I go into the inn," Lynn said. She had told them about Mary and Ted, and their role in protecting Teresa. She walked back to her car.

"Where's the church?" George asked when she opened the door.

"Just down on the left—a hundred yards. I'll let them know we're here." She called the office number.

"Blessed Sacrament," came the answer.

"Elizabeth?"

"Speaking."

"This is Lynn Peterson, Teresa's friend. I'm down at the inn. We're here for her car. A friend of mine, George Nicholson, will be down in a few minutes, if that's okay."

"I have the key, dear. Just send him to the office."

"Did you hear that?" Lynn asked him.

"I got it. I can pick her up and take her to Cloverdale if you want to deal with the others."

"Okay," she said, "as long as ICE doesn't follow you. I don't know if they're still down there—staking out the place. If they are, be careful. You can't miss them."

"All right then. Let's do it." George got out and walked up the driveway to the road, his dusty black cowboy boots, frayed jeans, tan work shirt, and straw cowboy hat shouting "native."

When he reached the road, he stopped and looked back. He gave her a little salute with his left hand, and set off. The gesture touched her—the gruff old rancher acknowledging the leadership of a woman whose life experience could not have been more different than his.

Lynn returned his salute, went to the side door of the inn, under the rose arbor, and in. She found Mary in her tiny office, just hanging up the phone.

Mary rose to greet her. She hugged her and offered her a seat. "Lynn, I've been thinking about our conversation. Last night I realized I hadn't thought this far ahead. Ted and I and the others in the congregation always knew there might be others after Teresa, but it never occurred to us it would be so many—and so soon. As I said before, we're not ready."

"I just need you to keep them for a couple days—until I can find something else." *Just give us a little time, just a little.*

As though someone had thrown a switch, Mary's face lit up. Her chest expanded. She seemed to sit higher in the chair. "That's not what I mean. We want to help you. You inspire us. You're so relentless. We just don't have a plan yet."

"You're very kind."

"But we will make a plan." A bell rang on the front desk. "Excuse me for a minute."

With nothing but Mary's good intentions to go on, Lynn wondered what that meant—how and where the people of Elk would shelter ten people, and for how long. What about work for the Cruz and Garcia adults? Could they help with that? What about school? But just as *she* was taking her new role one step at a time, she trusted Mary and her cohorts would find their way.

"Are they with you?" Mary asked when she returned.

"Yes, they are."

"Well then, let's go."

Outside in the parking lot, fog wafted up the face of the bluff and through the windblown treetops. Lynn and her charges fell in behind Mary's black Prius and followed her up the Philo Greenwood Road to the top of the ridge and the cabin.

Teresa's brown Toyota Corolla was parked beside the cabin when they arrived. She and George were sitting on the doorstep. Overhead, the sky was pure blue, but the cabin was still in shade. Teresa wore a faded-blue jean jacket against the lingering morning chill.

The car doors opened. The occupants spilled out, sending a huffy raven croaking from the branch of a tall Douglas fir hanging over the dirt driveway. The Cruz and Garcia families hung back while Lynn and Mary approached the house.

"George, you escaped," Lynn said.

He and Teresa stood up to greet the others. "They were there," he said. "In a black Explorer—pretty obvious. They followed me, but I lost them when I turned right on Cameron Road."

"I told George to wait until you got here, Mary," Teresa said. "You've been so kind. I can't thank you enough." She took Mary's hand.

"You couldn't be more welcome. What we're doing is not very hard—not compared to what you're going through."

"Maybe so, but not very many people are as kind as you are," Teresa said. She embraced Mary. Her eyes grew wet, and she wiped away the tears with her fingers. "I am in your debt."

"Be careful, dear. You are in our prayers." Mary returned the embrace, and Teresa and George started for her car.

"Wait," Lynn said. They stopped.

Lynn took the stuffed animal from her bag and handed it to Teresa. "One of my students gave this to me last spring. I thought you might like to give it to Rosa. Doesn't she have a birthday coming up?"

"Yes, she does. How sweet. She will love this." Teresa put her arm around her friend and kissed her cheek.

As she and George walked to the car, Lynn called after them, "I'll see you in Cloverdale!"

———

FROM THE CABIN, GEORGE CROSSED THE RIDGE ON THE Philo Greenwood Road and descended to the Anderson valley—a different world, hot and dry. They emerged from the forest and crossed the narrow Navarro River, where swimmers floated and splashed in a deep pool in the otherwise shallow stream. George pulled up at the stop sign at State Route 128.

"Turn left here," Teresa said.

"Cloverdale is the other way."

"I know, but the winery I visited with Lynn is just up the road. I need to talk to them."

George turned and crested a small rise above the river.

"There," Teresa said, "on the right."

George slowed and turned in at the split-rail fence planted with red and yellow roses and the carved sign that read Mendo Wines.

"The owner said she might have a job for me."

George parked in front of the tasting room, where the black-eyed Susans were still in bloom. "Don't you think she would have called you?"

Teresa reached for the door handle. "Maybe, but we're here. I just have to ask her. I'm sorry."

"Don't be sorry. I get it. Go ahead."

Teresa got out of the car and went in.

The same pleasant young woman greeted her. "Good morning. Would you like to taste some wines?"

"No, I'm Teresa Alvarez. I'd like to speak with Mrs. Henderson. Is she here?"

"Yes, of course. I remember. She's in the back." The woman ducked her head through a door behind the counter. "Amy, there's someone here to see you."

Amy Henderson stepped into the doorway in her blue denim overalls, her dirty-blond hair tucked beneath a red bandana. "Teresa, right?"

"Yes, ma'am. I thought you might know about the job."

"Please come on back." Amy waved her forward. "I hope you didn't drive all this way just to see me."

Teresa needn't have gone any further. "No, we were driving through."

Amy looked at Teresa with kind eyes. "Yes, I do know. I'm afraid the job didn't open up. My employee is staying. I'm sorry."

Teresa inhaled her disappointment, trying to stuff it out of mind. "That's okay. It was a long shot."

"I wish it had worked out. Kelly thinks a lot of you."

"Thank you." *That's it*, Teresa thought. She started to turn and leave, but stopped. "What about other wineries in the valley? Do you know if any of them are looking for people?"

"Not offhand, I'm afraid. But I should tell you, ICE has been creeping around. It's easy for them because the valley is so narrow. We're all cheek by jowl here. The wineries are wary of them. They want to keep their noses clean."

Teresa withered under the succession of bad news. It was all she could do to say, "Okay. Thank you."

"I wish you the best of luck," Amy said.

Teresa mustered a weak smile, turned, and left.

"You don't look too happy," George said as she slid into the passenger's seat.

"There's nothing here, and ICE is snooping around the valley, spooking the other wineries. Let's just go."

George backed out of his spot, got back on the highway, and headed southeast for Cloverdale, thirty-five miles away, beyond the far end of the valley. They drove in silence.

Teresa rode in turmoil, the bear in her lap, as the vineyards passed, with their long, green rows of grape trellises taunting her. She was sad for the loss of the perfect job, but relieved to be free of Juan Carlos and Rico. She was happy to be out from under the gaze of ICE—at least for the time being—but still nervous about them. They seemed to be everywhere. She was overjoyed at the thought of seeing Gloria and Rosa, but sad that she worried them. And she was terrified about the future. Finding safety and a good job in this part of the world was beginning to look impossible.

When they passed through Yorkville and had left the valley behind, George spoke. "I suppose I could use a good hand on the ranch. It's not vineyard work, but it's not nothin'."

Teresa looked at him and smiled. "You're sweet." She didn't know what she thought about working on a ranch—what a ranch hand did—or whether she had what it took to be one, but the gesture alone moved her. "I might have to take you up on it."

"Think about it. I mean it."

If nothing else, George had quieted the turmoil in her mind. She rode the last ten miles to Cloverdale lighter, happier for the unexpected lifeline he had thrown her.

LYNN STOOD BY THE BIG WEST-FACING WINDOW AS MARY acquainted the Garcias and Cruzes with the cabin. There was no spectacular view this morning, but the fog creeping across the coastal plain like white molasses fascinated her.

Children giggled and laughed in the loft, while Mary showed the two bedrooms to the adults—Martha and Manny, Gabriela and Jose. Lynn marveled at the shift Mary had made in her response to these people, and the kindness she showed them. Mary's genuine caring bolstered her, restoring her faith in human nature.

"You are so kind to let us stay here, Mary," Martha said when they returned to the main room. "I don't know how to thank you."

"Please don't worry about that. It's nothing. I don't have to worry about being deported."

"We are grateful. Someday we will repay you—in some small way."

"You can repay me by staying safe and being happy."

"We will try." She and the others looked worn and tired.

"Is ICE raiding the vineyards in Sonoma?" Mary asked.

"Not yet, but we heard they will."

"You don't have to worry about ICE here. You can stay here as long as it takes to find a permanent place."

The four responded in a chorus of gratitude. "Gracias, senõra. Thank you. Gracias, gracias." Their faces lightened. They smiled and laughed. Their arms hung looser. They breathed relief.

Since Karen's heart attack and Hank's injury, Lynn had resigned herself to a lonely struggle against Rico and ICE. She had found strength in that solitary role, but now, watching Mary step up to help, she felt a surge of new hope. Mary added more than another body, another pair of hands to the task. Her commitment altered the dynamic. The struggle became a communal one. It struck Lynn that—at least in this case—one and one was more than two.

"What kind of work can you do?" Mary asked.

"Pick grapes," Manny said. "Work the farm, the yard."

"I do some cooking," Jose said.

Gabriela added, "We can do housework."

"Maybe we can find work for you right here in Elk. Let me work on it."

She walked across the room and opened the refrigerator door. "There's some food in here and in the cupboard over there. I'll bring more this afternoon. Make yourselves at home, and don't worry. You're safe here."

Again the four thanked her as one.

Mary and Lynn left the house and huddled outside.

"I'll get the sanctuary team on this right away," Mary said. "I have a feeling we can do some good here."

"Thank you, Mary. I can't tell you how wonderful it is to have an ally in this work."

They climbed in their cars, and Mary led the way up the long driveway to Cameron Road and the top of the ridge.

———

TERESA'S PHONE CHIRPED WITH AN INCOMING TEXT. It was Gloria. *We're here.*

Teresa responded. *We're five minutes away.*

Hank exited the 101 at South Cloverdale Drive and pulled up behind Gloria's silver Honda CRV under the office marquee at the Super 8 Motel. It was fifteen minutes after noon, not quite two hours since they'd left the cabin.

Joy filled Teresa, displacing any disappointment she still carried from Philo. She got out of the car and hurried to the Honda.

Gloria lowered her window. "Mamá!" she said. She climbed out and embraced her mother. "It's so good to see you." She radiated youthful vigor. A white T-shirt accentuated her fawn-like skin, long black hair, and deep brown eyes.

"Look at you," Teresa said, "as beautiful as ever."

"Nana!" a toddler cried from the back seat.

Gloria lifted her daughter from the car seat, set her on the ground, and brushed cracker crumbs from her bright yellow dress.

Three-year-old Rosa ran to her grandmother and leaped into her arms.

"Rosa, Rosa." Teresa squeezed her granddaughter and kissed her on the cheek. She stroked her lustrous raven hair and rocked her from side to side.

Rosa pulled her head back and grinned into Teresa's eyes. She kissed her on the forehead and wiggled free. "Nana," she said, wrapping her arms around Teresa's legs.

Lynn arrived, and waved George from Teresa's car.

"Gloria," Teresa said, "these are my friends Lynn and George. They are my saviors."

"So glad to meet you. My mother has told me about you. Thank you so much for helping her." She turned to her mother. "It's too early to check in, and I'm hungry. Can we find a place to eat?"

Lynn googled "restaurants," and found a Mexican restaurant—El Norte—just down the street. She pulled up the menu and showed it to Gloria.

"Perfect, please join us," Gloria said.

"George?" Lynn asked.

"Why not?" he said. "We have to eat."

They moved their cars from under the marquee and walked to the restaurant. It was a plain, simple place, lacking charm and atmosphere, but that was not the point, Lynn reminded herself. It was quiet for noontime. A waiter directed them to an open booth and brought a highchair for Rosa.

They ordered familiar entrees, and the waiter brought them right away—sizzling fajitas with hot tortillas wrapped in a cloth napkin; and guacamole, Lynn's favorite; tacos stuffed with fish; a healthy portion of ceviche; enchiladas coated with melted cheese.

"What now?" Gloria asked her mother as they began to eat.

"I don't know. I want to stay here and find a job like the one I had at Valley Run, but I'm afraid of ICE." She poked at her ceviche.

"You should be. We're hearing lots of rumors in Madera."

Teresa turned to Lynn. "I stopped to see Mrs. Henderson at Mendo Wines."

"Oh."

"There's no job."

"I'm so sorry. Did she give you any leads?"

"No, she said ICE has spooked the wineries." Teresa looked at George and locked onto his eyes, acknowledging her appreciation of his offer. Yes, she could take him up on it, she thought, and maybe she would. But not now. She was tired, worn by the strain of tension and fear and hyper-alertness. Right then, sitting next to her daughter and granddaughter, all she wanted to do was rest.

"You can come home with me, Mamá. You know that," Gloria said.

Teresa didn't want to be a burden. She wanted to let her children lead their own lives. But the invitation sounded good. *It wouldn't have to be forever. Just long enough to get back on my feet.* She looked at George again—and Lynn—and said, "Okay, I think I will."

CHAPTER 18
THE IMMIGRANTS STEP UP

Lynn passed under the 101 heading east on College Avenue, the memory of Rico's pursuit, fresh and raw—the red Camaro muscling in behind her, cars swerving, tires screeching, horns blaring, pedestrians running. She pushed it all away, clenched her jaw, gripped the wheel tighter, and drove on. It was Monday morning, ten o'clock. The early morning traffic had settled down. Stores awaited their first customers.

At Santa Rosa Middle School, she turned south on Brookwood Avenue, as though headed for the hospital. But at Third Street, she turned west toward the center of town, entering a neighborhood in transition, where old cottages were either becoming offices for insurance agents and dentists or being razed for parking lots.

Lynn found a parking place in the shade of an old sycamore. Splotches of sunlight played on the hood of the car, mimicking the mottled bark of the big tree. Two-Hour Parking, the sign read. *I'm good.*

She looked in the rearview mirror, brushed a straw-colored shock of hair into place, and got out. Purse on her shoulder, she locked the car, and set off. The light was red at E Street, a major thoroughfare. She waited for it to change, crossed, and passed the county library. At D Street, she turned right, went to the end of the block, paused under the green awnings of the bookstore, and peered into the Starbucks nook. Nicki Simpson sat a table for two, one hand on a cup of coffee, the other scrolling the screen of a tablet.

Lynn pushed through the big glass door and walked in.

Nicki looked up, her face framed in shoulder-length black hair, and smiled. "Good morning, Lynn."

"Sorry I'm late. Let me get some coffee." She approached the counter, half aware of a classic Eagles song playing in the ether. A tall twenty-something with enviably smooth skin took her order—a small black coffee-of-the-day. Lynn tried not to stare at the tropical vines tattooed in red, green, and purple crawling up her arms and disappearing into the sleeves of her T-shirt. Coffee in hand, Lynn returned to the table.

Nicki closed her iPad and pushed it aside. "It's nice to see you. You've been busy, I hear."

"You got that right."

"So, you have something for me?"

"I think so. You know Rico's in jail."

"Yeah, breaking and entering. I heard you shot Sanchez. How are you doing?"

So much had happened in the previous three days, Lynn wasn't sure how she was doing. "It was surreal at the time, and it still is. And then there was the chase down Guerneville Road—something else I never imagined. I guess I'm doing okay, under the circumstances." Light from the window played on the wispy twirling steam rising from her cup. She lifted it to her mouth and held it there, savoring the aroma. *How am I doing?* For the first time since Friday night, she reflected on the cascade of events since then. She had done what she needed to do, risen to the occasion in each circumstance—rescuing Teresa from the rectory, standing her ground at the cottage, keeping her nerve on Guerneville Road, delivering Teresa to her daughter in Cloverdale. *Under the circumstances, I'd have to say I'm doing damn well.*

"And you're still at this."

"Crazy, isn't it?"

"Yeah, so what do you have?"

Lynn told her about the Cruz and Garcia families. "They're undocumented. They've worked at Valley Run, and Rico's been squeezing money out of them."

"And you think—"

"I think, what if they didn't just stumble on Rico in Santa Rosa? What if somebody at the border sent them to him? Maybe they could tell you who that somebody is. And they might tell *you* sooner than they'd tell the police." She took another sip of coffee and watched Nicki for reaction. She thought she was on to something here, and hoped Nicki agreed. From somewhere in the room, Otis Redding sang soulfully about the dock of the bay.

"You think they'd talk to me?"

"They might."

"By the way, where are you with Teresa Alvarez? Has she talked to the police?"

Lynn was still worried about Teresa and her immediate future, which was still very much up in the air. "No, not yet. ICE found her at the Catholic church in Elk. I got her out of there, but now she's gone to stay with her daughter in Madera. Maria Sandoval is threatening to subpoena her."

"What are you going to do?"

"Give it a few days and go see her." Lynn wondered if there was any point in doing that. Hadn't Karen suggested she just let Teresa get on with her life? Was Teresa still her responsibility? Maybe not, but she pushed back against the thought of her staying on the run, like Randy. And she held on to the idea of helping her find long-term safety in Sonoma, even if Teresa seemed to have given up on the idea herself. She finished her coffee and stood up. "More?" she asked.

Nicki held out her cup. "Sure. Pike Place, black."

Lynn went to the counter, paid for the refills, and returned. It was now mid-morning. The sounds of shoppers browsing in the bookstore drifted into the Starbucks nook; shoes clacking on the concrete floor, bags rustling, voices murmuring, books thumping on counters. Starbucks had quieted down, thinned out. "I'm wondering if these families are eligible for U visas. What do you think?" She was hopeful.

"They're crime victims. They qualify on that count. Would they help the police?"

"They might."

"Okay, but there's another condition—suffering substantial physical or mental abuse."

Lynn had no idea if they had. She imagined it was possible, but it seemed unlikely. They would have mentioned it. "Does extortion qualify?"

"Probably not. It sucks, but it's not like being held prisoner. There's a quota, and there are way more applications than visas. I wouldn't risk it."

Lynn studied the bubbles on the surface of her coffee, the way they clung to the inside of the cup like foam on a beach. She contemplated the injustice of a system that forced people to sneak across borders to find life-sustaining work, then left them defenseless against predators like Rico. "Well, they won't stay in the valley. They're too scared."

"And they're probably right. Places with lots of workers are easy targets for ICE."

"Maybe Mendocino is the right place." Lynn was feeling good about them being there.

"It could be. Would they talk to me? It would be on their terms—confidential—low-key."

"I'll ask them."

"Thanks. The sooner the better."

Nicki excused herself, and Lynn stayed at the table, thinking about Nicki's investigation—and the good it might do—while pedestrians passed by on the sidewalk, oblivious of her concern. She held her maple leaf pendant between her thumb and forefinger and rubbed it absentmindedly. A breaking-and-entering charge wouldn't get Rico off the street indefinitely, but a trafficking charge might—or a murder charge. *I should talk to Teresa.*

Two blocks south, Detective Sandoval entered the federal building on Sonoma Avenue from the rear parking lot. It was an hour before noon, and the pavement was already hot. She walked the long, drab hallway to the tiny office, and paused in the open doorway, waiting for the officer in the white polo shirt to notice her.

He was studying a paper on the obsolete metal desk in front of him, his head propped against the knuckles of his left hand, a yellow pencil flicking back and forth in his right hand like a metronome. The acronym ICE, embroidered in blue on his shirt, stared back at her.

How depressing. I couldn't work here. "Tom," she said.

He looked up and set the pencil down. "Maria, come in." He motioned to a chair in front of his desk. Like everything else in the room, it was worn and tired. Fluorescent lights buzzed and flickered behind translucent panels in the ceiling. The air smelled stale.

"I'm working on the Hernandez murder," she said, taking the seat. "I've got a witness who needs immunity."

He leaned back in his chair and rolled it away from the desk with a push of his feet. "That's your department, isn't it?"

"The witness is undocumented. I need to know he or she won't be deported."

Officer Swenson smiled a wry, unfriendly smile. "Don't tell me. You're talking about Teresa Alvarez."

"I am, and I need your help. I need to know she can get a U visa."

"She's a criminal, Maria. We're not about to do that."

The detective rose from her chair and placed her hands on the edge of the officer's desk. She leaned forward. "Tom, we're talking about murder here. She's the key. And we're talking about trafficking. She's a key to that, too." She slammed her hand on the desktop.

Swenson sat up. "Calm down. U visas are for law-abiding immigrants. She's a criminal. What are you going to do about the warrant for her arrest?"

Damn, he's good. "How'd you find out about that?"

"It wasn't very hard."

Maria settled back into her chair. "Look, that was a long time ago."

"Accessory is a felony—California Penal Code 32C—sixteen months to three years—and there's no statute of limitations, not anymore."

"We can get it dropped."

"But she'll have to come out in the open. Will she do that?"

Maria bit her lip and stared at Swenson. *I wonder if he gets paid by the number of immigrants he deports.* She weighed her options. They were few. This guy had it out for Teresa. She would have to get Teresa's testimony, if she could, without exposing her to ICE.

"Where is she now?" he asked.

She smirked. "You think I'm going to tell you that?"

She stood up and glared at him, sitting cross-armed in his chair, frowning back. *What a miserable little office.* At the moment, she thought as much of its occupant. "Thanks for nothing, Tom."

She turned on her heels and stepped out into the dismal corridor—a dark tunnel through the mountain of bureaucracy.

WISPS OF FOG WERE SCUDDING THROUGH THE WIND-
blown treetops when Lynn arrived at the inn late Friday morning, four
days later. The breeze carried the chill of the ocean, but to the east, the
sky was clear and bright, and the sun, now high above the ridge, had
begun to warm the village of Elk.

She found Mary Jernigan and Nicki Simpson by the side door of
the inn, chatting, Mary in a pale gray fleece with the name Blue Cove
Inn stitched above a stylistic bluff and wave logo, and Nicki, in a light
sweater. "You've met. I'm glad," Lynn said, joining them under the arbor that glowed with happy crimson roses. She took note. Roses didn't
fare nearly as well in the dry air of the ridgetop.

Mary welcomed her. "I've been telling Nicki I'd like to join you
with the Cruzes and Garcias. They trust me now."

"That's fine with me," Nicki said. "They need to know they're safe.
I'm not about to reveal their identities. I just want a picture of the
smuggling network."

"Shall we eat first?" Mary asked.

Lynn and Nicki jumped at the idea. Mary led them to the spectacular dining room at the rear of the building, with its dark, wide-planked
floors and hand-hewn ceiling beams. They took a table by the west-facing windows, where the ocean peeked through widening holes in the
veil of fog. The server brought bowls of rich, steaming Dungeness
crab bisque and a salad of local greens, and the three prepped for their
meeting in the intermingling aromas of herbed tomato broth and bal-
samic vinegar.

As she spread her napkin on her lap, Lynn addressed Mary. "Nicki
tells me it would be risky for them to apply for U visas if they haven't
suffered severe physical or mental abuse."

"You're saying they might have to stay underground?"

"Unfortunately, but people do it for years. Look at Teresa."

"Then maybe Elk is the best place for them."

"That's what we've been thinking."

As they ate, Mary explained that Jose had started to work in the kitchen at the inn, and Martha was doing housework for several members of the church sanctuary committee. And both families were considering sending the kids to the local elementary school, a tiny K-through-Three school ten miles north in Albion, halfway to the town of Mendocino.

"Maybe we should leave well enough alone," Lynn said, scraping the bottom of her bowl. "The bisque is wonderful, Mary."

"Thank you. It's the local ingredients—crabs, tomatoes, milk—and the tarragon. Coffee? We serve only the best."

The server cleared the table and brought three heavy mugs decorated with the Blue Cove Inn logo, filled with coffee the hue of ebony and the fragrance of African highlands.

Mary asked Nicki about the purpose of her newspaper story.

"It's not so much about breaking up a smuggling ring, as shining a light on the abuse of undocumented immigrants. People are going to keep coming here for a better life. There's no stopping that, and unscrupulous people are going to keep abusing them. So I feel I have an obligation to describe a system that needs fixing."

"Good for you." Mary rose and pushed her chair in. "Shall we go?"

She retrieved Jose from the kitchen, and drove the four of them the five miles up the Philo-Greenwood Road to the cabin.

When they arrived, Martha and Gabriela shooed the children outside, and the adults—Manny, Martha, Gabriela, and Jose—stiff and pensive, gathered around the big table by the picture window. Mary, Nicki, and Lynn joined them. The room was surprisingly dark. The sun was past its zenith, but it hadn't moved far enough to the west to brighten the cabin much. The sink was piled high with dishes, and the smell of sautéing filled the place—onions, chicken, peppers.

"This is Nicki Simpson, the woman I told you about," Mary said. "She's a reporter in Santa Rosa."

All eyes turned to her. Lynn wondered how she would coax these frightened refugees into revealing what they knew about the smuggling pipeline.

"You know Rico Guerrero," Nicki began.

"Sí," Martha said.

All four of the refugees nodded.

"Do you know he's in jail?"

All four stirred in their seats, alert. They looked at each other, and back at Nicki.

"No, we didn't," Martha said.

"He was arrested chasing Lynn in his car."

They turned to Lynn with more surprise and alarm.

"I'm okay," she said.

Nicki went on. "Lynn told me Rico has been taking money from you—for protection."

They nodded. The only sounds were the muffled voices of children playing outside.

"When you came to Sonoma, did you know you would have to pay him like that?"

"No, senõra. We did not," Martha said.

"How did you meet him?"

Lynn watched this drama with fascination, for this was exactly what she had hoped to learn here. Martha's answer could be the key to Rico's trafficking network. The four immigrants glanced at each other, as though searching for direction or confirmation, or both.

"We would like to talk privately," Martha said.

"You mean among yourselves—without us three?" Nicki asked.

"Sí, senõra," Martha said.

"That's fine," Nicki said. She, Lynn, and Mary stepped out the back door to the driveway, where the children had taken up a game of hide-and-seek. Margarita stood at the back corner of the house, alternately venturing away to search behind a bush or a tree, and dashing back to protect her base, screeching with excitement at the sight of a hiding playmate.

"That's the crux of it," Nicki said, leaning against the stair railing. "Someone sent them to him. I'd love to know who."

"What do they have to lose?" Mary asked.

"A lot, if they go back to Santa Rosa. Nothing, if they start a new life here."

"They already have," Mary said. "Maybe you'll get lucky."

The door opened, and Manny waved them back in.

"We will tell you," Martha said when they sat back down at the table. "A pollero [smuggler] in San Diego sent us to him ten years ago." She explained the whole process; engaging an American smuggler—the *pollero*—in Tijuana, who took them across the border to San Diego with false documents; waiting in a safe house somewhere north of the city; paying the pollero through an intermediary; and making a long, ten-hour trip in the back of a delivery van to Roseland, where they were delivered to Rico.

"And what did Rico do for you?"

"He introduced us to Juan Carlos Hernandez, who got us work," Martha said, long-faced.

"Did he explain the payment system?"

"No, Juan Carlos did, after we began to work."

"Did they abuse you?"

"No, because we paid them."

Because we paid them, Lynn thought. *Those bastards.* She looked at the four—Martha, Manny, Gabriela, and Jose—brave, hard-working, earnest—and she recoiled at the irony and injustice of their situation—having to pay a thug for safety here in the land of opportunity and justice.

"I'm sorry you had to do that," Nicki said. "That's the story I want to write. I promise I won't use your names or identify you in any way. But I want to expose this system so others won't suffer—and so our laws might change. Can you give me names?"

The four eyed each other again, and assented with faint nods.

"Sí, we can," Manny said.

WHILE NICKI RETURNED TO SANTA ROSA THROUGH THE Anderson Valley, the route George and Teresa had taken earlier in the week, Lynn drove south on the Coast Highway. At Sentinel Rock State Park, she turned left on Simpson Ranch Road, the steep, narrow dirt track that led through the rhododendron reserve to the Buddhist retreat center at the top of the ridge. She felt better about the Cruzes and Garcias—about their being in Elk with Mary and Ted and their friends, who, after only a week, were helping them build new lives.

Her thoughts shifted to Teresa as she wound up through the dense forest. Would Teresa stay in Madera with her daughter? Would she give up on a life in Sonoma that had offered her some degree of fulfillment?

At the tin barn, she turned right on Mountaintop Road. To the left, a pasture stretched up and over the ridgetop. Above it, two vultures floated motionless on the warm air. A white cistern on a low wooden platform promised water for the languid Black Angus cows that watched her over a weathered split-rail fence.

To the right behind a wire-mesh fence, an old pasture sprouted rows of trellises that ran down the slope toward a wooded ravine. New grape vines rose from white plastic tubes—mouse protection—and wound from post to post, a foot off the ground, on galvanized wires.

Lynn pulled over on the shoulder and got out. Purple asters with bright yellow centers and flaming-orange poppies dotted the dry grass. She bent down, picked an aster, and twirling it between her fingers, walked to the fence. She studied the vineyard; hundreds, no, thousands of new vines in an old pasture—a new use for an old place.

Her eyes swung across the road, where the cows still watched her. She took out her phone and called Teresa.

"Lynn?"

"Yes. Teresa, how are you?"

"Feeling better. This has been good for me."

How good? Lynn wondered where to go next. She couldn't pretend to know what was best for her friend. In the end, it was Teresa's life to live. But now more than ever, she believed Teresa could find a safe, rewarding life in Sonoma, and Lynn felt an obligation to hold out that possibility.

Teresa's life was at a crossroad. She had started down one road—to Madera. Lynn debated whether she should pull her back to consider another. *We've been through too much. I have to.* "Do you think you'll stay in Madera?"

"I don't know, Lynn. I'm not thinking about that right now. I'm just trying to decompress."

"I get it. Would you come back to Sonoma if you thought you could be safe here?" Lynn knew Teresa was all too aware she could never be completely safe anywhere in the country.

"If I could find a good job, maybe. But I'm not ready. I need time."

"I understand. It's not my place to convince you. But I know you've wanted to stay here."

"I have."

Lynn hesitated. She didn't want to be pushy, but she had to mention the police. The last thing she wanted was Detective Sandoval blindsiding her friend. "You know Rico's in jail."

"Yes, you told me."

"Well, the police found the knife you described to me."

"Really? Where?"

"In the river. They need you to identify it—and tell them about the connection between Juan Carlos and Rico." Lynn understood Teresa's fear of the police. It made perfect sense; it had been a survival mechanism. But somehow she had to break through that barrier. It couldn't be with the threat of subpoena, as Detective Sandoval had suggested. She had to convince Teresa that Maria was on her side.

"I want Rico in jail, too, Lynn, but I can't risk that."

How do I convince her Maria is on her side? "The detective on the case is Maria Sandoval. She's a good person—fair. She can offer you immunity and shield your identity—and protect you from ICE."

"How can I trust her?"

"I trust her. You'll have to trust me." She resisted the impulse to mention the subpoena. "Maybe you could just call her. What harm could that do?"

"I'll think about it."

Lynn took that answer as progress. She hadn't expected more. Teresa needed time to recuperate and to adjust to the idea the police might actually be on her side. Lynn would give her that time and hope to convince Maria to do likewise.

———

IT HADN'T BEEN TOO MANY YEARS SINCE SHE'D LEFT THE San Joaquin Valley for Sonoma, but Teresa was struck again by its flatness—flat as a table in every direction. One crop followed another across this agricultural wonderland—walnut and almond groves, oranges, peaches, tomatoes, table grapes, mile after mile of table grape trellises. It was Monday morning, and she was northbound on the 92, the backbone of the valley. The air was hot and still.

At Chowhilla she turned west on the 152—across the valley—and fell in behind a dusty pickup and a grain truck. Ranks of grain elevators guarded the road like medieval fortresses. Small armies of workers moved through fields of ripe tomatoes and peppers, picking with practiced grace, bending and reaching and plucking, breaking the motion only to wipe the sweat off their brows, leaving behind plastic bins piled high with produce red and yellow and green. And from atop a telephone pole, a chestnut-breasted Swainson's hawk scanned the shoulder of the highway for careless mice.

Teresa had called Maria Sandoval on Friday.

"I'm on your side," the detective had said. "I'm interested in justice, not deportation."

"How can I know that?" Teresa had asked.

"My parents are undocumented, that's how. I wouldn't betray them. I wouldn't betray you. Trust is everything to me."

Teresa had asked Maria for some time. She took Rosa to the park, pushed her on the swings. She shopped. She cooked. She relaxed with Gloria and her husband, Ramon, in the evenings, pretended to be interested in the Oakland A's. And the trauma began to fade.

In quiet moments—washing vegetables at the sink, folding laundry—she tried to imagine a life in Madera—a life with her family—and she weighed that imagined life against the one she had left in Sonoma. All along she had wanted to stay in Sonoma—to stay in la uva. What had changed? Nothing, she decided. If anything, the risk to her had lessened. And there was George's offer. She wouldn't have to be a ranch hand forever, if she didn't like it, but it was a good offer, and he was a good man.

Finally, Teresa had decided on gratitude, loyalty, and trust. Where would she be if Lynn hadn't taken her in and shielded her from Juan Carlos and ICE and Rico? Lynn had put herself in harm's way. The least she could do to repay her kindness and courage was to be brave herself.

If she could help Maria put Rico away, she might be doing for other campesinas what Lynn had done for her. And if she could help Maria put Rico away, maybe Maria could help her. So she had called her again. "I'm coming back," she had said. "What do you want me to do?"

"Come to the station on Sonoma Avenue, and we'll record your testimony. We'll disguise your voice. There's nothing to worry about."

Five miles beyond Los Banos, Teresa turned north on the 5, three hours from Santa Rosa. She would try not to worry.

CHAPTER 19

TERESA TALKS

"That's five acres, right there," George said. He and Lynn surveyed the steep pasture below the barn, shielding their eyes from the rising sun. It was another clear late-summer day, and the air on the ridgetop was filled with the herbal scent of dried grass. The flute-like trill of a hermit thrush sounded from the dark forest beyond. "I wouldn't want to plant any more than that, not for starters."

It was early Monday morning—eight o'clock—and Lynn had come to share her idea with him. It had been all she could do to contain her enthusiasm over the weekend and resist the temptation to dash down the road from Bella Vista.

Hank had counseled patience. "Do some research," he'd said. "They talk about the microclimates. Does George have the right microclimate? What about soil?"

So Lynn had spent the weekend at her kitchen table, leaning over her laptop, learning about the grape-growing and winemaking going on all around Bella Vista, a movement that had begun in the early 1970s with back-to-the-land wine pioneers turning ridgetop ranch land into vineyards. The vineyard by the tin barn was just one of the newest.

She learned that the ranches on Mountaintop Road were in the Fort Ross/Seaview American Viticultural Area, a winegrowing region known for premium pinot noir and chardonnay. And she learned that the San Andreas Fault and the Pacific Ocean, each just a few miles to the west, were responsible for the soil and climate conditions that favored those varieties. The ridgetops were above the fog line—a good thing for grape-growing—but they were close enough to the coast to benefit from the winter storms that blew in off the ocean, bringing the bulk of the region's eighty inches of annual rainfall. Until she began this research, she had not known she was living in a coastal rainforest.

The websites of wineries near Bella Vista fascinated her with their details of soils and rootstocks and climate and vineyard design. She googled grapevine life cycles, trellising systems, vine pruning, more. She learned that a vine did not produce harvestable grapes until it was three years old, that rootstocks were selected for their compatibility with soil type and drainage, that the rootstocks used in California vineyards were those native to North America, whereas the vines grafted to them were European varieties of the *Vitis vinifera* grape, that trellising systems, like Vertical Shoot Positioning, were chosen for the conditions of sunlight, humidity, and wind in a given microclimate.

It was a crazy idea, but she couldn't shake it. George could plant a vineyard, or someone could plant it for him. *I could. I'd love to do that. And so would Teresa. We could do it together, with Hank's help.* That's what she told him Monday morning, standing beside him behind his barn, looking at a five-acre pasture. "What do you think, George? Would you do that?"

"I might. I'll have to think about it."

"You can think about it on the way to Santa Rosa. Let's go."

THE SANTA ROSA POLICE STATION LAY BEHIND A GRASSY berm on Sonoma Avenue like a long, low bunker, its south-facing façade shielded from the sun by a steep rust-colored metal roof that reduced its windows to narrow black slits. Teresa sat at the Brookwood Avenue intersection, waiting for the light to change. It was a few minutes after eleven.

She glanced across the street, and her pulse leaped. In front of the station sat an unmarked black SUV, windows darkened, menacing. *ICE. Damn it.*

An ambulance raced by, siren wailing, horn blaring, red lights flashing. The traffic on Sonoma Avenue stopped to let it through. The ambulance passed and traffic resumed.

The light turned green. She swung left and drove past the station, averting her eyes from the building and the vehicle in front of it. She put her foot down, and the engine responded with a high-pitched, complaining whine.

What now? Madera? I should have stayed there. What was I thinking? A few weeks earlier she might have driven straight to the 101 and headed south the 130 miles to Madera. But this morning she didn't. ICE had stalked her, and she had evaded them. She had accepted them as a threat in her life, and in a strange way, she had become stronger for it. No, she would stay in Sonoma and see this through, if there was a way.

Twenty-five years earlier, drug traffickers had taken over her family's village in Michoacán, threatening her parents, killing their animals in demonstration of power and ruthlessness, spreading fear. Two of her cousins had disappeared.

With her parents' blessing she had escaped that place. Now another gang—Rico's—threatened her, in another land, with the same kind of intimidation. She could shrink from it or fight it, with the only weapon she had: her voice. For her parents—and for all her people living in fear—she chose to fight.

At the next light, E Street, she turned right, then right again at Second Street. Halfway around the block from the station, she pulled over and parked. The leafy residential street was quiet. It calmed her nerves. But the air was hot, and the pavement, hotter. She lowered her window and called Detective Sandoval.

"Teresa? Are you on the way?" Maria's voice, too, was calm, soothing.

"I was, until I saw ICE sitting outside your front door."

"Where are you now?"

"On the next block." Teresa still wanted to talk with Maria. She had come around to the idea. ICE's presence at the police station had scared her, but it had also bolstered her determination to fight back against Rico, steeling her resolve. But she wasn't about to walk in that front door. "I can't see how this is going to work."

"I think there's a way," Maria said. "I can pick you up and bring you in the back door."

That seemed risky—more risk than Teresa wanted to take. "How do you know ICE won't see me?"

"They don't go back there."

It still seemed too risky. *I've gotten this far without being caught. I'm sure as hell not going to get caught now.* "What if they see me in your car before we get there?"

"They won't. You can lie down on the back seat if you want, but they're not going to see you. We won't be driving by them."

In the end, Maria's tone convinced Teresa to go along with the plan. Teresa described her car and her location, and waited for the detective to arrive.

Five minutes later, a black squad car with "Santa Rosa Police" emblazoned on its white doors pulled into the space ahead of Teresa. The throaty V8 growled through its tailpipes. Maria turned the engine off, stepped out of the car, and walked back to the Camry. She was dressed as she'd been the day Lynn met her in Hank's hospital room—long-sleeved khaki shirt, jeans, and her neon-green sneakers.

Teresa tensed. The approach of an officer—those measured, authoritative footsteps— had always meant trouble.

"Teresa?" the detective asked, leaning toward the open window. She smiled.

With that simple gesture, Teresa relaxed. "Yes."

"I'm Maria Sandoval. Are you ready?"

"I think so. What about Lynn and George Nicholson?"

"They're on the way."

"Okay." Teresa raised her window and climbed out of the car.

Maria opened the street-side passenger door.

Teresa stepped toward it, but flinched and froze at the piercing whine of an engine. A souped-up Honda Civic, low to the ground, roared past. She exhaled and tucked herself into the back seat. "Gracias." She slid down until she was just able to see out the window.

"It's going to be okay, believe me," Maria said.

"I'm trying." She closed her eyes. *God, help me. God, help me. God, help me.*

Maria swung around the corner onto Brookwood Avenue, and then through the high, black metal gate that guarded the back lot of the police station. The trip had taken all of thirty seconds.

Teresa peeked out, checking for vehicles like the one she'd seen in front of the building.

Maria pulled up to the rear entrance. Two blue-uniformed officers walked by toward an identical black and white police car. "The coast is clear, Teresa. Shall we go?"

"I guess so." As committed as she was to Lynn and this mission, Teresa struggled. To her, police stations were forbidding, threatening places. She had avoided them. Now she had to force herself to enter one.

"It will be fine. Trust me." Maria got out and opened the rear door.

Teresa climbed out, scanning her surroundings for threat, and hugged close to Maria as they walked toward the station.

Inside she waited while Maria checked in with one of several officers behind a wooden counter. Policemen passed through the lobby. Citizens waited in chairs—*For God knows what*, she wondered—their muffled voices unintelligible. The mysterious workings of the place bewildered her. It looked and smelled impersonal, antiseptic.

Maria led her down a narrow corridor lined with plain, numbered doors. She opened the one labeled room three, and held it for her. "Here we are. This is where I'll take your statement. Don't worry. It will be painless."

The room was gray and windowless, unadorned, unfriendly—cell-like. In the middle, sat a black metal table with two matching chairs on each side. On one side, behind the chairs stood a camera mounted on a tripod, pointing across the table. Bright LED spots in ceiling cans filled the room with light.

"You can sit here," Maria said, her hand on the back of a chair facing the camera. "And I'll sit there." She pulled out a chair on the opposite side.

Teresa was rigid with fear, associating this sterile, forbidding place with torture and harassment—nothing good. "I don't know, Maria. I'm scared."

"I know. But it's easy. I'll ask you a few questions. You just tell me what you know."

The thought of going on record as an undocumented immigrant seemed suicidal. "You said you would disguise my voice and face."

"Yes, we'll do that. Don't worry."

She worried. "What about Lynn and George?" Teresa had talked to both of them, and, with Maria, they had crafted a plan to address her safety concerns. Lynn and George would come to the police station, and the four of them would return to Cazadero, rendezvousing at George's place for protection—Lynn in Hank's VW, George in Teresa's Toyota, and Teresa with Maria in the squad car. It seemed only prudent for Maria to escort Teresa out of harm's way, given the zeal with which ICE had pursued her.

"Let's think about that," Maria said. "With ICE out there, maybe they shouldn't come to the station."

Teresa was disappointed. It would have been comforting to have Lynn and George by her side, but it made sense. ICE knew Lynn. It wouldn't help for her to attract their attention.

"I'll call them," Maria said. Her call was none too soon. Lynn and George had reached Santa Rosa. Maria directed them to Teresa's car on Second Street. She and Teresa would join them there when they were through.

"Are you ready?" Maria asked.

"I think so." Teresa felt far from ready, but she never would be.

Maria turned on the camera. A red light blinked, and she began to speak. "This is Monday, September 19, 2016, 11:32 a.m. Detective Maria Sandoval taking the testimony of Teresa Alvarez in the case of the murder of Juan Carlos Hernandez."

She pulled on a pair of blue latex gloves and removed an object from a plastic bag lying in the middle of the table. "Ms. Alvarez, do you recognize this knife?" It was a hunting knife with a long, imposing blade. Its keen edge glinted in the light.

"Yes, ma'am. That's the knife I saw Rico Guerrero waving at Juan Carlos." She imagined it slicing through Juan Carlos's neck, dripping with blood.

"And how do you know that?"

"By the carving on the handle—the mountain lion. Rico pointed to it and told Juan Carlos he would carve him up like a mountain lion if he didn't collect the protection money."

"And where did that happen?"

"At Rico's house in Roseland."

"Thank you, Ms. Alvarez. Can you tell me about the relationship between Mr. Hernandez and Mr. Guerrero?"

Anger rose in Teresa as she thought about the two men who had poisoned her life in Sonoma. "Juan Carlos—Mr. Hernandez——was working for Rico, Mr. Guerrero. His job was to collect the money every month from the undocumented workers in the vineyards. But he forced *me* do the collecting. Then *he* took it to Juan Carlos."

"How did he force you?"

Her jaw tightened. "He threatened to turn me in to ICE."

"How much money did you collect?"

"One hundred dollars a month from each one. Juan Carlos also stole wine every week from the tasting room at the winery where we worked—Valley Run—and sold it to Rico."

"Did you see him do that?"

"Yes, I did."

"Is there anything else you want to tell me about Mr. Hernandez or Mr. Guerrero?"

The ugly memory of that night in the vineyard resurfaced. Teresa would rather have pushed it back out of mind. But here was a chance to report it. She looked at the camera and back at Maria. "Juan Carlos Hernandez raped me in the vineyard—three weeks ago, a little more. It was a Friday night."

"I have to ask this, Ms. Alvarez. I'm sorry. Do you have proof of the rape?"

Maria's question brought back Karen's kindness. "Yes, I do. A nurse met me at the Guerneville Clinic. She used a rape kit."

"But you didn't report it then."

"No, I was afraid if I did, Juan Carlos would turn me in to ICE."

"But he turned you in anyway."

"Yes."

"Who was the nurse?"

"Her name is Karen Boyd."

"Is that all you want to tell us?"

"I think so." She knew so. Maria's questions had all been fair and straightforward, but each had dragged Teresa back to a place she would rather not have revisited. She was ready for the interrogation to be over.

"Thank you for coming forward, Ms. Alvarez."

Maria turned off the camera. The red light disappeared. "That wasn't so bad, was it?"

"No, I guess not." Teresa breathed, relieved. It hadn't been fun, but she'd gotten through it. For the first time since she'd entered the room, her senses reached beyond that oppressive space. She heard the voices of people walking by in the hall, the slamming of a door.

"I told Lynn you might be eligible for a U visa."

"Yes, we talked about that."

"If there wasn't a warrant for your arrest."

"You know about that? Did Lynn tell you?"

"No, she didn't. But it wasn't hard to find. I'm a detective. Can you tell me what happened?"

Teresa explained the incident as she had for Lynn: Twenty-five years earlier, her boyfriend's gang got in a shoot-out with a rival gang in San Diego; he killed one of the rival gang members; she escaped, left her boyfriend, and came north. What she hadn't told Lynn was that the gang had threatened to kill her if she talked to the police.

"That's reason enough for dropping the charge. I can look into it."

"That would be wonderful, but I don't want to risk getting caught."

"Let's do this. I'll look into it, but I won't do anything to get you in trouble. Is that okay?"

"Yes, it is, but I still might not go for the visa. What happens if I go out in the open and don't get the visa? ICE knows where I am. I've turned myself in."

"I understand. Now, let's get you to Cazadero."

WHEN THE CARAVAN REACHED CAZADERO, LYNN TURNED into Karen's driveway, letting the others go ahead to George's place. It had been over a week since she'd seen Karen, and she was feeling the need to touch base.

Summer was hanging on in the valley. The air was hot and still, but comfortable in the deep shade. Lynn found Karen on her back porch, facing the creek, a glass of iced tea sweating on the arm of her chair. She climbed the steps to the porch, flushing a pair of mountain chickadees from a feeder on the railing.

"Hello, stranger," Karen said, putting her book down. She started to rise.

"Don't get up. You look way too comfortable." Lynn plopped down in a chair beside Karen and sighed.

"What was that for, dear?"

"It's just been a long slog."

"I know—no thanks to me. What's the latest? Bring me up to speed."

Lynn played Karen's words back. *Up to speed.* In the tranquility of the porch setting—towering redwoods, a sparkling creek; the only sounds, those of chirping birds and the occasional distant car—it dawned on her that her world had changed. It was as though she had passed through a veil into a different land—quiet, serene—like the one she now shared with her friend. The need for speed was gone, the furious, driving pace of her harrowing ordeal behind her. "It's over, Karen. It's over. I'm almost afraid to say it, but I think it's over."

"Tell me about it."

"The Cruzes and Garcias are in good hands in Elk. Teresa just gave a deposition to the Santa Rosa police, and the detective drove her to George's place. He's offered her a job and a place to stay."

"Is there something else going on there?"

Lynn had wondered that herself. "I don't know. I suppose it's possible. But if there is, wouldn't that be wonderful?"

"Of course, storybook stuff."

A sharp crack like a rifle shot broke the quiet of the vale. Something hard had fallen on Karen's roof. It rolled off and fell on the porch between them, green and small, no larger than an acorn. Lynn picked it up and held it in the palm of her open hand. It was something new to her.

"That's a redwood cone," Karen said. "This time of year they wake me up at all hours of the night."

"It's so cute. You would think a giant tree would have a giant cone."

"Just as you would think a giant spirit would have a giant body."

Lynn looked at Karen, trying to unravel her meaning.

"I'm talking about you, honey. You're a giant in my eyes. I wanted you to know that, and that seemed like a good way to say it."

"Thank you. I'm flattered." Feeling self-conscious, Lynn looked down at her nails.

"Would you like some tea? I'm going in for more."

"Sure. That would be nice."

They chatted for an hour, until Lynn rose to leave. "I should get back up on the ridge to check on Teresa—not that she can't take care of herself. It just feels like I need to release her formally to her own devices."

"Good idea. You know I'm one for ceremony. And oh, what are you going to do next?"

"I don't know. It's all up in the air. We probably shouldn't make any drastic moves until Hank's leg heals."

"You can stay here, if you want. I'll be going back to the reservation in South Dakota for a month or so. You could be my caretakers."

"That would be nice. We just might take you up on that."

Lynn reached down and pulled Karen from her chair. She put her arms around her and held her in a warm embrace, acknowledging both the friendship that was, and the friendship that would be, regardless of where life took them.

———————

THE RIDGE, TOO, WAS IN ITS FULL GLORY WHEN LYNN eased down George's long drive. She stepped from her car and stretched, floating in a growing sense of calm relief. Not a single cloud broke the deep cerulean blue of the sky. Summer remained a bulwark of dry warmth against the rain and cold of winter. Cicadas buzzed. High above her, a raven croaked, soaring like a hawk on a rising thermal. A light breeze from the east carried the rich, resinous fragrance of evergreens and the pungent smell of dried grasses over the dusty barnyard.

She knocked on George's back door. When no one answered she opened it and called, "Hello, anyone home?" Again, there was no answer.

She closed the door, turned toward the barn, and saw George and Teresa walking along the treeline on the far side of the five-acre pasture. She hollered and waved.

They waved back.

She hurried toward them, flushing tawny grasshoppers as she waded through the ankle-deep meadow. She reached them and took Teresa's hand. "How did it go?"

"It wasn't a lot of fun. I felt exposed—like someone was about to arrest me any minute and haul me away."

"That wasn't Maria's doing, was it?"

"No, it was just the place. She said she would try to get the accessory charge dropped."

"Good. So, it's over."

"Yes, at least for now."

"I'll leave you two. I need to check on Hank." She hugged Teresa. "I feel so good for you now. I hope you feel the same way."

"I do. Thank you for everything."

Lynn smiled and walked back up through the pasture to her car. Her sense of relief grew richer, blossoming into joy, pride, satisfaction that she could not have anticipated in the midst of the struggle.

She lowered the windows and let the fresh air of the ridgetop sweep through the car as she drove the last mile to Bella Vista. She pulled up in the shade of the big live oak and studied the simple little cottage. For the first time in weeks, it felt like home. A mild melancholy dampened her joy. She had loved the place. Her time there with Hank would never have been permanent, but she had imagined it as years—not months. She was not ready to go.

A visitor greeted her in the kitchen: Becky Tillson, sitting at the table with Hank, dressed more for ranch life than the last time Lynn had seen her, in faded jeans and scuffed boots, smudges of dirt—evidence of yard work—showing on her white Cazadero General Store T-shirt. "Hank's been bringing me up to speed. He says you're a miracle worker."

"I wouldn't say that. I've had a lot of help."

"No, I think he's right. What's next, now that your charges are safe and sound? More sanctuary work?"

The breakfast dishes were still in the sink. Lynn wished she'd washed them.

Her eyes were drawn to the sunlight gleaming on the stainless-steel faucet. The kitchen was warm, but not oppressively so. The doors were open, allowing air to move through the house. It had not yet taken on the heat of the day. She pulled out a chair and joined Becky and Hank at the table.

She hadn't thought of herself as a sanctuary worker. Karen and Teresa had awakened a long-repressed ghost, and she had simply decided to face it, acting for herself as much as for Teresa and the others. *Would I do more sanctuary work? Is that my future?* "I don't know."

She looked at Hank.

He offered a faint, knowing smile, but stayed silent, letting her continue.

"I don't think I'll go looking for it," she said. "But if it comes to me again, I'll know what to do, where to send people. We've built a little network, I guess."

"So, you're not tied up with it now."

"No."

"Then you might have time to plant some grapevines."

She straightened up in surprise. "What?"

Becky's eyes sparkled. A broad grin spread across her face. She leaned back in her chair, arms folded across her chest. "Hank told me about your idea for George's place. I don't know if it makes sense for him, but it might for me."

"Really?" Lynn asked. She had thought of Becky as a rancher, content with the status quo, with the easy life of letting George care for her herd—not as a risk-taker, an adventurer.

"I like wine. It's a good use for the land—maybe better than ranching. And it might be fun."

"I think so, too. I'd like to see you do it." It saddened Lynn to think Becky might act on her idea just as she was leaving the ranch.

"I might," Becky repeated. "But whether or not I do, with the way things have worked out, you're welcome to stay here."

Lynn's gaze moved around the kitchen and beyond, to the front room. The soft bleating of the goat carried through the back door from the near pasture. She felt the slow beating of her heart. She listened to her breathing. She felt good. She smiled.

CHAPTER 20

WORKING THE GRAPEVINE

LYNN PULLED THE COVERS CLOSER, NOT FULLY AWAKE, but aware of rain prancing on the metal roof like gods at an all-night ball. It was mid-November. A week ago, the winter rains had come; heavy, windblown rain that saturated the parched soil. The ridgetop had seen only a few drops since April, a month before Lynn and Hank arrived. Lynn had never seen it rain so hard for so long. She wondered how much water the sky could hold.

In the cold steel-gray darkness, her bed felt as warm and cozy as a womb. She rolled over and tucked her head into her pillow, pushing toward Hank and his warmth. But there was nothing to push against; he wasn't there. Disappointed, she slid out of bed, dressed quickly in old jeans and her chamois shirt, and stepped out into the kitchen.

Hank was at the table, staring at his laptop. "Good morning, honey. Coffee's ready."

She shivered. "Hank, it's freezing in here. Have you lit the fire?"

"No, I'm sorry. I got distracted."

She went into the front room and opened the door of the wood stove set into the fireplace. Inside, the coals were still warm.

"Take a look at this caretaking gig!" he called. "A vacation home in Hawaii—on the Big Island. How'd you like to live there for a while?"

She wasn't interested, but she would humor him. "Just a minute." She laid in a few sheets of wadded-up newspaper, a handful of cedar kindling, two hefty billets of oak, and blew. The paper smoldered. She blew again, and it burst into flame. The cedar snapped and crackled. Smoke billowed up the flue. She closed the door and stood by the stove to let its new heat seep into her bones.

"Take a look at this, honey. Wouldn't you love not to worry about the weather—never too hot, never too cold?"

"Okay, just a minute." Hank had gotten itchy for change. She wasn't sure why. Maybe it was the accident, being laid up for so long. Without an active role here, maybe he had lost his tie to the place. The thought gave her an uneasy feeling.

She poured a cup of coffee into her favorite hand-turned mug and looked over his shoulder at the screen. The house was beautiful— modern, with big windows facing the ocean, walkways leading down through terraced gardens to the water; a resplendent tropical paradise. "It's gorgeous, Hank."

"So?"

"So, I need to think about it."

Lynn finished her coffee and put her mug in the sink. In the hall she pulled on her rubber-bottomed Bean boots and yellow slicker, and opened the back door. Water cascaded from the valleys of the metal roof panels. The sky had lightened enough to reveal the dark line of trees behind the barn, their tops bending in the wind.

She tightened up her slicker and stepped out into the rain driving from the west. Head down, she crossed the yard to the little wooden barn, stopping at the door to listen for the animals—a daily ritual.

As always, they heard her coming and began their bleating and clucking before she walked through the door. And as always, it warmed her spirit.

She flipped on the lights and flipped down her hood. The barn was chilly, but its wooden skin and skeleton, wearing the hue and scent of its long history, imparted an emotional warmth, stored in fibers once those of a living, breathing redwood giant. She inhaled the muskiness of hay and animals that never got old for her and opened the goat stall.

She pulled up the stool and began the rhythmic milking, squeezing the little teats—left, right, left, right—and milk streamed into the pail, first with a metallic ping, then, as it filled, with a liquid swoosh. Finished, she filled the manger with fresh hay and stroked the goat's silky white back as it chewed.

In the coop, the chickens swarmed around her feet and clucked with happiness when she scattered grain. *What does it mean that I take so much joy, still, from these silly creatures?*

She sat on the stairs to the hayloft and listened to the rain pelting the roof. For weeks after Juan Carlos's attack, she had not wanted to be in this place. It had evoked only fear and dread. But its association with him had faded, not because of the passage of time; it hadn't been that long. Rather, because of the ascendancy of her own strength and courage—repelling Jorge, leading Rico into the police trap, rescuing Teresa from the rectory. As her fear subsided, the barn became once again a place that welcomed and warmed her.

She wrestled with Hank's need to move on, to find a new Shangri-La. She had come to Bella Vista for tranquility, and found it. Oddly the ensuing dramas and their challenges had nourished her in deeper ways. Far from crushing her, they had drawn out her best self, offered her friendship and purpose she was not eager to abandon.

The door creaked and swung open. Cold rain blew in, soaking the barn floor. The goat bleated her complaint. Hank stepped into the barn, water dripping from his broad-brimmed Stetson. He leaned against the door and pushed it shut against the driving wind.

"More coffee?" He held two mugs and a thermos bottle.

"That's sweet of you, honey. Thanks." Lynn climbed down from the stairs and kissed him.

Hank set the mugs on the bench by the goat stall and poured. Steam rose, swirling from the mugs. He handed her one. She held it in both hands, soaking up its warmth, raised it to her mouth, and breathed in its dark, chocolatey earthiness. "Mmm, perfect. So what's up?"

"You weren't thrilled with my idea about moving to Hawaii—or anywhere. Figured we'd better talk about it."

"You didn't need to come out. It could have waited." She smiled, pleased with his thoughtfulness.

"I know, but it was on my mind." He shook the water off his hat and hung it on a wooden peg protruding from a beam. He picked up his mug, sat on the bench, and leaned back against the wall.

Lynn was glad she'd thought about his suggestion. She sat down beside him. "Maybe if you'd suggested it back in August, but this place means more to me now."

"How so?" He took a long sip of coffee.

"I'm engaged here—in the life of this place. I have friends. I'm doing interesting things. I'm making a difference. I may never take another un-documented immigrant to Father Angelo—or Mary and Ted—but they mean a lot to me. And it's not just them. It's George and Teresa and Karen, and now, Becky. It's a community—a kind of community I've never experienced—people living and working together in this way. And I like it."

Hank said nothing. He looked into her eyes, straining to understand. Then he looked away.

Wind buffeted the old building. Beams creaked. In the thundering music of the rain, individual beats merged into one long, continuous roar. They both listened to the storm.

"And now there's the vineyard, Hank."

Becky had been serious about the idea, and invited Lynn to learn and plan with her for what she hoped one day would be Bella Vista Vineyards. They had visited winemaking neighbors—friends of Becky's—who encouraged her and offered advice. They had identified the several soil and subsoil types on the four-acre pasture they would plant first: a gravelly loam, for Chardonnay, and a clay loam, for Pinot Noir. With help from their neighbors, they planned the orientation of rows and the spacing between them. And they learned how to build grape trellises. All this, in a busy two months.

"It's exciting, don't you think? Who would have thought we'd have a chance to help create a vineyard?" With Hank on the mend, walking without crutches, Lynn had imagined them doing it together.

A deer mouse stirred on the far side of the barn and froze when Lynn caught its eye. She turned her head, and it scurried along the wall toward the chicken coop.

"It looks like a lot of work," Hank replied. "How many wooden posts are there in a four-acre plot? Hundreds? Probably thousands. That's a lot of hole-digging and wire-stringing. Aren't you ready for a rest? Under a palm tree in Hawaii?" He laughed.

She swatted his shoulder. "I was when I finished teaching, but not anymore. I'm not ready to put my feet up. I'd rather be digging a hole than sitting back in a lawn chair. Does that make sense?"

"I guess, but you have to remember I've been a bystander for the past couple of months, watching you build a life in the community, as you say. I've got some catching up to do."

"Fair enough, I'll let you do that, if we can put off the moving idea. Can we?"

"Let me think about it."

Lynn stretched her arm around his shoulders and pulled him close. She kissed him and whispered, "Thanks."

For the next six weeks, Lynn and Hank worked in the vineyard, with occasional help from Becky, Teresa, and George, laying out trellis lines and digging post holes. Lynn was grateful Hank had come around to her perspective on Bella Vista and Sonoma. She had worried about the course their life might take if he insisted on leaving. But it never came to that, and Hank grew as engaged in the new work as Lynn.

Two days before Christmas, at the end of a long work day, Lynn was driving the tractor toward the big metal equipment barn, bobbing on the seat in a gentle carousel-like rhythm, nodding to the satisfying drone of the engine. The winter rains had renewed the pastures. They glowed as green as an Irish meadow in the glorious late-afternoon light. Gone was the sharp scent of hay. The subtle perfume of tender, new growth filled the air. A light westerly breeze brought a hint of salt. And below it all were the earthy aromas of the old leather seat and axle grease. She took it all in—the lush new grass, the brilliant light, the long shadows of trees and fence posts. She was tired, but happy.

Lynn and Hank were returning from the new vineyard, the weather having given them a break from the rain. They had spent the day digging post holes with the power take-off attachment of the ranch's smaller tractor. Hank followed on foot, examining their work. If the forecast held and the next day was dry, they would set posts in the new holes.

George was climbing into his truck when she pulled up beside him in the barnyard. "How'd it go out there?" he asked through his open window.

"We dug close to a hundred holes—six rows." Beneath her fatigue, pride flickered like fiery coals in a stove.

"Not bad. You running that rig now?"

"I am."

"Good for you. And Hank?"

"He's marking the spots for the posts and dropping them in the holes I've dug."

"Gonna set 'em tomorrow?"

"Hope so."

"I'll drop some bags of Quikrete out there for ya in the morning."

"Thanks, George. That would be a big help." The words were barely out of her mouth when a strange car—a gunmetal-gray, late-model Honda CR-V—slowed at the big oak and turned into the drive. It crept up to the house and stopped.

"You recognize that car, George?"

"Can't say as I do."

Lynn climbed off the tractor, brushed her jeans, and approached the car.

A short, slim young man, Latino, stepped out, neat and trim—even stylish—in his black Nike baseball cap with its white Swoosh, blue insulated jacket, bright orange running shoes. "Are you Lynn?"

"I am."

"Kelly Ahearn told me you could help us."

"Us?"

A woman emerged from the passenger seat—no older than thirty, Lynn guessed—with a blonde ponytail and blue eyes, wearing an oversized gray sweatshirt with "Cal" scrawled across it in familiar blue script. Her face was drawn, sad. She looked exhausted. She opened the back door and pulled a sleeping baby from a car seat, elf-like in a tiny, green hooded jacket. It fussed at the disturbance, wiggling and murmuring. The mother nestled it in her arms and rocked gently from side to side.

"Us," he said.

"I see." Behind the three, the sky flamed red and orange, auguring a clear day to come. It was a brilliant backdrop for a tableau she had not expected. When the last crises had ended back in September, she had filed away the possibility of another dramatic rescue and moved on to her new life at the ranch.

"I'm undocumented, and ICE is looking for me." The young man put his hands in his pockets and looked down, as if to hide his shame. "I'm Roberto, and this is my wife Cindy, and our daughter, Mayela."

Their plight was clear. Yet again Lynn ached for terrified people fleeing a system that would not recognize their need, their goodness, or their humanity. "Come on in." She led them onto the porch and through the front door. With the sun down, the house was dark. She turned on the floor lamps in the front room and the light over the sink in the kitchen. "Let me get you something. Beer? Tea? I can brew a pot."

"Tea would be nice," Cindy said. "Thank you."

Lynn was struck with her simple beauty, smooth radiant skin, a long ribbon in her lustrous hair streaked with hues of red and yellow, the colors of the sunset, polished red nails matching the ribbon. "Please sit down." Lynn filled the kettle and put it on the stove. She snuck a peek at her own nails. *It's no use. That's what I get for digging in the dirt.*

She took three mugs from a shelf beside the sink, the ones with the turquoise glaze thrown by a potter in the village. From the cupboard, she took a box of tea. "A friend brought this from the Khasi Hills of India. I think you'll like it," she said.

Cindy mustered a smile and nodded.

Lynn filled a tea ball and dropped it in the pot, draping its chain over the lip.

The hinges on the back door squeaked, and Hank came through, scraping his boots on the mat. He hung his jacket on a hook in the hallway. "Who do we have here?"

Roberto stood and introduced his family, leaning forward just enough to suggest a bow.

"And I'm Hank, Lynn's husband." He extended his hand, first to Roberto, then to Cindy, and pulled up a chair.

The kettle whistled, arousing the baby. While Cindy tried to whisper the little girl back to comfort, Hank took a red bandana from his pocket, wrapped it around his fingers, and wiggled it like a puppet.

Mayela giggled, and so did her mother.

Lynn filled the teapot and returned to the table. The little family in front of her looked like any other healthy, prosperous young family but for the desperation in their eyes. She responded instinctively. "Tell me what you need."

Roberto and Cindy had met in college at UC Davis, where he majored in viticulture and enology—winemaking. A few months earlier he had taken a job at Valley Run Winery, as an assistant to Kelly Ahearn. "ICE came looking for me this morning. First they went to Valley Run. Kelly told them a story, said she'd given me the day off to do some Christmas shopping. Actually, I was running an errand for her in Santa Rosa. She called to warn me and gave me your name. Then they went to our apartment in Guerneville. Cindy told them she didn't know where I was. She met up with me, and we came here."

Roberto fidgeted, shaking a leg with nervous regularity, crossing and uncrossing his arms, as though they were strange, unfamiliar objects.

"And you're undocumented."

"Yeah. I'm a Dreamer. Came to the US with my parents, lived my life like an ordinary American, went to college, graduated, got a job. And nobody hassled me until now, this goddamned ICE."

Outside, twilight had descended. A breeze brushed finger-like limbs of the big oak against the house. Lynn got up to serve the tea. The little kitchen felt warm to her with the table full, despite the circumstances. She put the teapot on a wooden tray with the mugs and matching sugar bowl and milk pitcher. "I have some wonderful local wildflower honey, if you like it in your tea. My neighbor is a beekeeper."

"I'll try some," Cindy said.

Lynn unscrewed the cap of the jar and set it in front of Cindy. She poured the tea and handed the mugs to her guests.

Cindy set Mayela on her lap and held her with one arm while she scooped a spoonful of honey from the jar. She waved it by her nose, exclaiming it "lovely." As she stirred it in, Mayela wiggled. Cindy pulled cheerios from a colorful Guatemalan bag draped over her shoulder, and spread them on the table in front of her.

Mayela reached for them and quieted as she ate.

Tears formed in the corners of Cindy's eyes. They pooled and ran down her cheeks. She wiped them away with her fingers and stifled a cry that shook her shoulders.

Lynn fetched a napkin from a drawer beneath the counter and offered it to her.

"Thank you. I'm sorry."

"Don't be. You have every right."

Cindy reached out to Roberto, taking his hand. "Where will he go if they deport him? He doesn't remember Mexico. What will I do? He has a good job. He's contributing to society. I'm in school, becoming a social worker. They're trashing our lives—good lives."

"I know. It's inhuman," Lynn said. "Don't you have any protections, Roberto? What about DACA—deferred action?"

"DACA was a good idea," Roberto said, "but I didn't trust it, never applied—didn't want to take a chance. What if a wall-builder became president?" His hands shook. He cradled his mug with both hands to steady it.

Cindy sniffled and wiped her eyes again.

Mayela busied herself with the curious little circles of oats.

What if? Lynn thought. Her mind raced through the implications of their being at Bella Vista. ICE had been to Valley Run. Knowing her connection—through Teresa and Juan Carlos—they would surely come to the ranch. They'd come a couple of times in the past few months, looking for immigrants on the run. She could help these people, get them to Ted and Mary; the network was well established. But she would have to act quickly.

"May I?" Hank asked. "I'd like to talk outside." He led Lynn out through the back door and closed it.

Lynn noticed the new trim and doorstop that still needed paint. "What is it?"

He leaned toward her, his face taught and strained. "You're not really thinking of getting involved in this stuff again, are you? I'm all in with the vineyard, but I don't know about this."

She understood his concern. Helping Teresa had been traumatic—the attack by Juan Carlos, the car accident, the near-arrest by ICE, the late-night escape from the rectory, the shooting, the car chase. She weighed all these things, but said only, "I can't turn them away, Hank. Look at them. They're desperate."

He brought up her childhood friend Ellie and Ellie's boyfriend, Randy, sent back to Vietnam, to his death, when Lynn failed to protect him. "Didn't you exorcise those ghosts months ago?"

The question jolted her. She heard Ellie wailing, felt her fists pounding on her chest, but she also saw Roberto and Cindy and Mayela—in pain. "Yes, I did, thank God. But that's not what this is about. It's about justice and doing the right thing. Somebody has to do the right thing."

"But you can't save the whole world."

"No, I can't. But I can save one person at a time, when they come to me."

The sky had darkened, reminding Lynn that precious time was passing. Her phone rang. It was Karen.

"Lynn, honey, is there something going on up there? I'm at the general store, and ICE just roared by, heading your way."

Lynn felt the familiar surge of adrenalin, the call both to flight and fight, pulling her into action. "Yes, there is. Better go, Karen. You're a lifesaver."

"What's that?" Hank asked with escalating concern.

"ICE. They're on the way, Hank. We gotta get out of here." She pocketed her phone and raced back inside.

Hank followed.

Roberto and Cindy had not heard the words, but they understood the tone. It shone on their faces as fear and anxiety. "What is it?" Roberto asked. "Is it ICE?" He pushed his chair back and stood up.

Cindy stood, too, with Mayela wrapped in both arms, her cheeks marked by the tracks of dried tears.

"Yes, it is. We have to move—now. They're on the way. I'll drive your car, Roberto, if you don't mind. Hank, thanks, honey. Come and get me tomorrow at the inn."

"Where are we going?" Roberto asked.

"I'll explain on the way. You'll be safe, if we hustle. Let's go."

They hurried into the CR-V, and Lynn pulled out to the road.

She looked back. Hank stood under the light on the front porch, waving and smiling.

She turned north and sped toward Mendocino—and safety.

THAT WOMAN IS UNSTOPPABLE. SHE'S A FORCE OF NATURE.